Praise for the Wind Dragons Motorcycle Club series

DRAGON'S LAIR

"*Dragon's Lair* proves a badass chick can tame even the wildest of men. . . . Not to be missed. A biker book unlike any other . . . [with] a heroine for strong-willed women and an MC of hot bikers. Chantal Fernando knows how to draw you in and keep you hooked."

—Angela Graham, *New York Times* and *USA Today* bestselling author

"*Dragon's Lair* was witty and fast-paced. A delicious combination of badass biker men and laugh-out-loud humor."

—Bookgossip.net

ARROW'S HELL

"Cheek-heating, gut-wrenching, and beautifully delivered! *Arrow's Hell* took me on the ride of my life!"

—Bella Jewel, *USA Today* bestselling author

TRACKER'S END

"Fernando's vivid characters burst onto the page . . . pulling readers into their world immediately and completely. This tightly told tale will leave readers eagerly waiting for the next installment."

—*Publishers Weekly*

"The charismatic characters have captured my heart. . . . *Tracker's End* is my favorite book in this series."

—*Smut Book Junkie*

"Don't miss out on the Wind Dragons MC series. . . . Chantal can really pull off the sexy times and give you some new BBFs to add to your list!"

—*The Literary Gossip*

The Wind Dragons Motorcycle Club Series

Dragon's Lair

Arrow's Hell

Tracker's End

RAKE'S REDEMPTION

Chantal Fernando

Gallery Books

New York London Toronto Sydney New Delhi

G

Gallery Books
An Imprint of Simon & Schuster, Inc.
1230 Avenue of the Americas
New York, NY 10020

First Gallery Books trade paperback edition June 2016
GALLERY BOOKS and colophon are registered trademarks of Simon & Schuster, Inc.

For information about special discounts for bulk purchases, please contact Simon & Schuster Special Sales at 1-866-506-1949 or business@simonandschuster.com.

The Simon & Schuster Speakers Bureau can bring authors to your live event. For more information or to book an event contact the Simon & Schuster Speakers Bureau at 1-866-248-3049 or visit our website at www.simonspeakers.com.

Interior design by Devan Norman

Manufactured in the United States of America

10 9 8 7 6 5 4 3 2 1

Library of Congress Cataloging-in-Publication Data is available.

ISBN 978-1-5011-3955-0
ISBN 978-1-5011-3956-7 (ebook)

For Tenielle "Nush Nush" and Sasha Alexis.
I just want you both to know that I love you,
And I'm proud of you,
And there's nothing I wouldn't do for each of you.
I'll always be there for you, your safety net, catching you when you fall.
For that's what big sisters are for.

ACKNOWLEDGMENTS

FIRST of all, I'd like to thank all my readers for wanting more from the WDMC, and for Gallery books and Abby Zidle for making it a reality.

To my agent, Kimberly Brower, I'm so lucky to have you! Thank you for everything you do, as always, I know I can always count on you, and I'm so grateful.

A big thank-you to all my beta readers, the women who are always there for me on a daily basis.

Mallory Green, Kara Brown, Stephanie Knowles, Rachel Brookes, Rose Tawil, Eileen Robinson, and Melanie Williams, I don't know what I'd do without you!

Arijana Karcic thank you for all you do for me. You're seriously the best and deserve the world.

Natalie Ram I'm so glad you came back into my life. I don't know what I'd do without you, but I won't have to find out because I'm never letting you go. Like ever.

Thank you to my parents for helping out whenever I need more writing time, I appreciate everything you do for me, and to my three sons for being patient when they know their mama has to work. I love you all so much.

FMR Book Grind, thank you for everything, I appreciate all the hard work you all do for me!

Emily & Sarah Channing I love you both, thanks for always being there for me.

Last but not least, a shout-out to all the OGs. May you forever inspire my hilarious and sexy characters.

If two people love each other
there can be no happy end to it.

Ernest Hemingway

RAKE'S REDEMPTION

PART 9 REDEMPTION

PROLOGUE

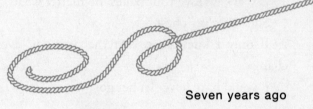

Rake

DON'T want to go home," she says, her face buried in my neck.

"Just stay, they won't notice," I tell her, rolling her over onto her back and bracing myself on top of her. "You can borrow some of Anna's clothes and just come to school with us."

"Maybe," she replies, flashing me a cheeky smile.

My mom is hardly ever home, and we have no contact with our so-called father, so it is just Anna and me here anyway. We don't have much, but Bailey doesn't seem to mind. That is only one of the reasons I love her so much. I kiss her forehead, closing my eyes, wondering what I'd do without this girl. As I draw back, she kisses my lips, a soft, sweet kiss.

"I love you," I whisper against her lips.

"I love you too, Adam," she says, smiling. "You don't have to tell me that to get me to stay though."

I chuckle and kiss her again.

She wraps her arms around me and sighs in contentment. We may not have much, but we have each other, and I wouldn't change that for the world.

"Wherever you are is my home," she says, rolling me over so she's on top now. She lays her head on my chest and closes her eyes. I cup the back of her head, my other hand on her back, just holding her.

"I'll always love you, Bailey, no matter what."

She kisses my chest.

If only I knew then that the next day, everything would change.

I would have never let her go.

ONE

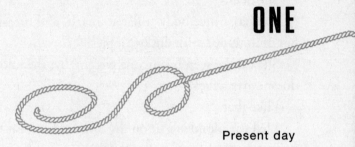

Rake

THE redhead sucks my cock deep into her throat. She's good, but I've had better head. I watch her try to take every inch of me in her mouth. She starts to gag, then pulls away, sucking on the head.

I look around the clubhouse, already feeling bored. Sometimes I get this feeling like something is missing. I can't pinpoint it exactly, but it's almost like I'm looking for something I know I'll never find. Like there's a hole inside me that nothing will ever fill. Emptiness mixed with a feeling of longing. For what? I don't exactly know. All I know is that I need a fuckin' distraction, constantly.

And nothing is working these days.

I call over a cute blonde walking past, and she comes to me instantly.

I like that she doesn't bother to play hard to get, when we both know she isn't.

I push the redhead away gently, then lie back on the couch. I hand her a condom. "Put it on me."

She nods her head and gets to work.

I watch her to make sure she's doing it properly, then look at the blonde and tell her to undress.

She does.

She has a nice body, a flat stomach, and breasts the perfect handful, tipped with dusky nipples.

She can be seen by anyone passing by; she knows it, yet she doesn't give a fuck.

I like that.

I tell the blonde to sit on my face, so I can eat her out while the redhead rides my cock.

After we all come, I'll take them into my room, tie them up, and do with them as I please.

And they will love every second of it.

Bailey

I've never been to Rift before, but the club seems pretty cool. I feel out of place, even though I'm dressed like the other women around me. Maybe my black skirt isn't as short, but it's tight and figure-hugging. The black off-the-shoulder top I've matched it with clings tight around my boobs, then flares out to hide my stomach. My stomach never completely went flat again after giving birth, no matter how many sit-ups I've done, so tops like this are a godsend. Still, I feel like an imposter. It's been *that* long since I've been to a club. I've had only one drink, and I've already lost Amethyst, the girl I came here with, to some hot biker. The two of them are dancing in the corner.

I met Amethyst at the school where we work; she was the

receptionist there until recently, when she left to take a better-paying job elsewhere. She definitely isn't the type of girl I'd usually be friends with, but when she invited me out I decided to accept, for a change. I had no idea, however, that I'd be ditched for the first guy who approached her.

Great.

I knew I shouldn't have come out, but I wanted to do something different for a change, to push myself out of my comfort zone. Act my age. Enjoy being out. Try to have a carefree night. When I hear Chris Brown's "Zero," I head to the packed dance floor. Alone or not, I'm not going to miss out on dancing to this song. With my eyes closed, my hips move on their own accord, swaying in time to the music. I open my eyes just in time to see two beautiful women rush at me. It takes me a second to realize that I know them.

Holy shit.

I haven't seen Anna and Lana since high school. I was a year older than them but still saw the two of them daily because of Adam. My chest suddenly hurts. Adam usually wasn't too far away from Anna, but surely that had changed with time?

"Hello, stranger!" Anna says, smiling widely.

I shake my head in surprise, beaming at the two of them.

"Anna Ward? Oh my god!" I say, my eyes on her face. I then turn to Lana. "Lana Brown! I should have known the two of you would still be friends. Do you want to go outside so we don't have to talk over the music?"

They've been best friends ever since I can remember. I feel a pang of jealousy at everything I must have missed out on over the years, but I push it aside. Anna moved away the year Adam and I broke up, but I have no idea what's happened since then.

I've been completely out of the loop. My relationship with these two was lost along with Adam.

Anna nods, smiling again, and we all walk out the front. The bouncer eyes us warily until Anna says, "We won't leave this spot," which has me confused.

"How have you been?" Lana asks me, bringing my attention to her.

"Good," I tell them. "Just got out of a relationship, getting back into the dating scene."

If you can call what Trevor and I had a relationship.

"How's that going for you?" Anna asks me with that cheeky grin of hers.

I wince. Not so well. "I feel like I've been thrown back into the dating pool with no floaties."

Trevor ended up being a train wreck, so who knows what else is waiting for me out there. We dated for only a month, after meeting at a museum. I'd taken my class there for an excursion, and he'd been the tour guide for the day. He'd slipped me his number as we left, and after two days I'd finally called him. He was good-looking and I hadn't been on a date in so long, so I'd accepted. He started to get really clingy after the first two weeks, wanting to see me every night and blowing up my phone asking where I was. I didn't want him to meet Cara, and I wasn't exactly flexible to meet him whenever he wanted, which was way too regular for my liking. When he told me about his foot fetish, yeah, I was done.

We all giggle.

"I can be your float," Anna jokes.

"You're not single," Lana reminds her best friend.

"Oh," she replies, squinting her eyes. "Is that a rule? Do I have to be single to guide her in the right direction?"

I need more than a guide: I need a miracle.

And I need to stop wishing she would tell me about Adam. Is he married? Does he have children? How would I even feel about that? I hate the man, but I also love him. I always will. It is complicated. Do I want to see him? No. But knowing how he is doing wouldn't hurt my soul.

Lana giggles. "No, but you have to know what you're talking about."

Anna scowls, while Lana and I share a laugh at that.

"I got Arrow, didn't I?" Anna says, on the defense, her hands on her hips. "And trust me, it wasn't easy."

"You're with someone?" I ask, interested to hear about the man who stole Anna's heart.

Her face lights up. "Yeah. His name is Arrow. He's . . . amazing."

Lana and I share an amused look as a dreamy expression plays on Anna's face.

"How did you meet him?" I ask.

She suddenly looks a little unsure. "Through my brother, actually."

"Oh," I say, keeping my expression neutral. "Well, I'm glad you found someone, Anna. And I hope your brother didn't give him too much of a hard time. He always used to tell me that he thought you were too good for any man."

Anna makes a face. "He still thinks that. So, tell me everything. Where have you been all these years?"

"I've been here," I tell her. "I never left the city. I went to college and got a degree in early-childhood education."

That is the truth, sort of.

Really I'd gotten pregnant and had my daughter, Cara, when

I was twenty. Being a single mother, I struggled. Cara's father didn't want anything to do with her, and so I never asked him for anything. I worked and put myself through college, barely having enough money to eat most days but making sure my daughter had everything she needed. They were rough times, but I knew they'd pay off in the long run, and they did.

"You're a teacher? That's awesome!" Lana says, smiling widely.

"You'd make a good teacher, I think," Anna inserts, laying a hand on my arm. "It's really good to see you, Bailey."

We stare into each other's eyes.

"You too," I say, suddenly feeling emotional. I knew this girl. We practically grew up together: I was fourteen when I came into her life. I thought that one day she'd be my sister-in-law, but I was wrong. So wrong. Embarrassingly so.

She's about to say something when a man storms out of the club, coming to a halt when he sees us standing there, his eyes on Lana and Lana alone. He's handsome. Okay, he's more than handsome—he's magnetic. Tall, with blond hair and a body worth sinning for. Is this Lana's man?

Yeah, I need to start hanging out with these girls again.

"Christ, Lana. Pretty sure I told you to stay where you were," the man growls. He looks at Anna, then at me, his eyes narrowing. "Who are you?"

Lana answers him, which I'm thankful for because I'm still surrendered speechless. "Tracker, this is Bailey, an old friend of ours. Bailey, this is Tracker."

He smiles, exuding sex appeal. A man who knows exactly who he is and the effect he has on women. A confident man. "Nice to meet you."

"You too," I squeak, then glance at Lana with wide eyes.

Arrow? Tracker?

They're weird nicknames, and it's now obvious they're bikers: the leather vest Tracker is wearing gives it away. Adam is letting his sister date a biker? I don't know what to think, but if these two are with them, I'm sure they're good men. Although I have to admit, Lana is the last girl I ever thought I'd see with a biker.

"We came out here to catch up," Lana tells him.

"I can see that," he murmurs. "Do you guys want to go into the VIP room? It's much quieter and safer than standing out here where any man who drives past can see you. Rake's in there, but you can just ignore him."

Anna and Lana share a glance that I don't miss. What are those two up to?

"Can you give us a second?" Lana asks Tracker, eyes pleading with his.

Tracker nods at Lana, his expression gentling. He says something to the bouncer, then heads back inside Rift.

"You're dating a biker?" I ask, watching Tracker disappear.

"I am," Lana replies slowly, as if unsure of what I'm thinking. "So is Anna."

The two of them never did anything without each other, so I'm not surprised.

I grin at Anna. "No shit? What does your brother think of that?"

Anna mock-winces, her expression changing to amusement. "He didn't like it at first, but now he's okay with it."

I want to ask more, but I don't. I know there's more to this story, but it isn't really any of my business. Adam isn't my business, hasn't been for years, and will never be again. It's a new chapter for me. I don't need to be thinking of my first heartbreak.

"Let's go check out this VIP room," I say, trying to sound excited. I lead the way, guessing the direction, with Anna and Lana close behind.

"It's this way," Anna says, threading her arm through mine. "Can I ask you something?"

"Sure," I tell her. We stop in front of the VIP area, and I turn to face her. "What is it?"

"Why did you never keep in contact with me when I left town? You said you would."

I look into her familiar green eyes, and my chest suddenly hurts. "Didn't Adam tell you what happened? I didn't think you'd want to talk to me after that."

She shakes her head. "He just said the two of you broke up. That was it. End of discussion."

I cross my arms over my chest, suddenly feeling extremely exposed. "It's a long story, Anna. And it's in the past. I never stopped caring about you. I guess I left Adam behind, and you were a part of him."

She tilts her head to the side and nods. I smile at Lana as she catches up to us.

When I look back at Anna, I see her eyes widen. Then she visibly cringes. She's not looking in Lana's direction but behind me. Almost afraid to look, I turn and see the man I loved more than anything in my life, the man I thought I never wanted to see again.

"Adam?" I gasp, wishing like hell I was anywhere except here right now.

This is the first time I've said his name out loud since high school.

Even saying it breaks my heart a little.

"Bailey?" he whispers, looking at me like he is seeing a ghost. His green eyes widen and his jaw goes slack.

Only a few seconds pass, but it feels like years as we both take each other in.

He looks as happy to see me as I am him.

Which is a big fat not at all.

I don't think his scowl can get any deeper, and his eyes are narrowed to slits. He looks like he hates me.

I don't want to face him. I'm not ready; I don't think I'll ever be ready. I need a do-over for tonight. One where I never come out at all.

He's the same . . . but completely different.

I don't know how to explain my emotions right now, because they're all rushing at me, pulling me in different directions.

Over the years, I'd planned out what I wanted to say to him if I ever saw him again, but now that I'm here, I have nothing. I want to yell; I want to rage; I want to cry. I want to ask him if he's happy.

He's even more beautiful than I remember, but now it's in a deadly way.

Just looking into his eyes, I can tell he lives his life in murky shades of gray.

I notice a piercing in his lip that wasn't there before, another in his eyebrow. They both suit him. I also see tattoos peeking out from under his vest. When he was mine, his skin was ink-free.

"I'm going to get your name, right here," he says, pointing to his heart. "I'll get it done when we're married."

I place my hand where the future tattoo will go. "I like that, Adam. Maybe I'll get your name written on my ring finger, because, unlike a ring, that can never come off."

I close my eyes and bring myself back to the present. I never expected or wanted to see Adam again, and now that I have, I need to try to calm my emotions, keep them locked away. The past has no place in the present, or in my future. Adam and I need to stay in the past, but I know it's not as simple as that. He was my first and only love, and that's not something one forgets. He also hurt me more than any other person has, more than any person could. I don't know what to say right now. I want to cry. I want to scream. I want him to hold me.

Not surprisingly, I look down to see him zipping up his jeans, and a beautiful woman curling into his side.

Women always flocked to Adam. But once upon a time, this man was mine.

My everything.

And now? Now he's just a stranger.

I look at the woman by his side, my emotions all over the place. "I see some things don't change."

The air thickens, uncomfortably so, but the two of us are locked in a silent battle, having conversations with our eyes.

"Should we go into—" Lana tries to defuse the tension, but Adam cuts her off.

"Anna, you and Lana go inside. Bailey and I need to talk."

So much has already been said between us with no words used, I wonder what he could want to actually talk about. "What about me?" his woman snaps. "I just had your dick in my mouth and now you want to talk to this bitch?"

Bitch? *I* was the first woman to have Adam's cock in her mouth! I cringe at my own thoughts. I'm seriously glad no one else can hear them.

Anna grabs Lana by her arm. "Let's give them some privacy."

I silently plead with them to stay, but they won't even look in my direction. Yeah, no help there. I watch them disappear into the VIP room, then send my dirtiest look in Adam's direction, but he's not even looking at me. He's trying to get rid of the woman who is still pasted against him.

"Go," he demands, tone cold. "Don't make me have to tell you again, because I won't be so nice the next time."

She storms away, shaking her ass so much I'm surprised her hips don't dislocate. She *does* have a nice ass though.

Bitch.

He turns to me and we continue our silent conversation. His eyes say, *I can fuck whoever I want.* While mine say, *Perhaps you should grow some fucking standards.*

Now that Adam and I are finally alone, I kind of wish she would come back.

Desperate times, apparently.

"Now, what the fuck are you doing in my club?" he growls, stepping closer to me.

His club?

Shit.

"You own this club?" I ask, eyebrows rising.

How fucking unlucky am I? Is this the *only* club he owns? Because that would be pretty damn unlucky. Then again, good luck and I have never really mixed. "Heartbeat" by Childish Gambino starts to play, but I can't even enjoy the song under Adam's intense stare.

"I do," he replies slowly, taking me in from head to toe in a painfully slow inspection that has me feeling a little self-conscious.

"Okay," I say, looking around. To the left, to the right. Behind him. Anywhere but into his eyes. I don't know the man standing before me, and while a small part of me wants to run into his arms, the rest of me wants to slap him across the face.

"Who are you here with?" he asks, making my gaze reluctantly meet his once more.

"A friend," I say.

"Where is this *friend*?" he asks, crossing his arms over his chest.

I shrug, feeling a little sheepish. "Around here somewhere."

I said I was with a friend, not a good friend. Trust me, there's a difference.

He nods his head, his lips as tight as I've ever seen them. "You gonna come back here?"

I shake my head. "Definitely not."

He scrubs a hand down his face. "Good. Unless you want to fuck, you know, for old times' sake?"

Is he serious right now? Did I want to fuck *for old times' sake*?

I grit my teeth and count to ten in my head. If he wants to unsettle me, he's sure doing a good job of it.

I actually contemplate slapping him, but no, that won't help the situation. Best not to let him know how much his words affect me. I won't give him the satisfaction of knowing how just seeing him again makes my soul whimper in pain.

I force out a humorless laugh. "I do want to fuck," I say, licking my lips. His eyes widen, surprised at my words. I take a step closer. "Anyone except you, Adam."

"It's Rake," he says, expression now blank. "No one calls me Adam anymore. And to tell you the truth, my name on your lips is just pissing me the fuck off."

"Right," I mutter, looking at my feet before back up at him. "Well, Rake. Please tell Anna and Lana I said 'bye."

He scowls. "Stay away from them, Bailey. I don't want you to have anything to do with me or anyone I care about. You're nothing to me anymore. You haven't been for a long-ass time. Now get the fuck out of my club."

The last line of the song plays, the words lingering between us.

They hurt.

The past hurts.

Everything fucking hurts.

The last thing I need is to open those old wounds. I worked so hard at burying everything, at moving on. Apparently all it takes is one look at his face to bring every pain back.

So I turn and leave.

He isn't worth it.

Rake

I watch her walk away from me, my chest feeling constricted— so tight it hurts to breathe. Seeing her again here, of all places, really has me feeling off-fuckin'-kilter. I rub the back of my neck, staring at the spot where she was just standing.

Fuck.

I'm not him. I'm not the boy whose heart she broke, not anymore. I shouldn't be feeling anything when I see her. It's been years, but it feels like Bailey is still mine. She still looks good—I'll give her that. Her brown hair still looks fuckin' soft and I know it would have smelled good too. Her brown eyes can still peer into my fuckin' soul.

I can't see her again.

She's nothing to me. I must be feeling like this because of the surprise of seeing her again. That's all. Yeah, she has no hold over me.

None.

Fuck, I need a smoke, even though I quit.

"She's pretty," I hear Tracker say from behind, placing his hand on my shoulder for a second before removing it. "Lana seems fond of her. We gonna have any trouble with her?"

"No," I growl instantly. "No trouble." I turn to look at my brother. "And only I deal with her, all right? No one else goes near her."

She's my burden to bear. The walking example of what happens when you let a woman get close to you. My own personal walking lesson.

"You want me to call Kira back?"

"Who?" I ask Tracker distractedly.

He barks out a laugh and shakes his head. "Never mind."

Bailey is back.

And my guard is up higher than motherfuckin' ever.

TWO

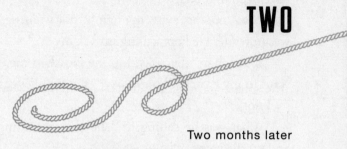

Two months later

Bailey

H E said what?" Tia gasps, then giggles.

I take a small sip of my coffee and hesitantly repeat, "He said that one of my boobs was the size of his head."

She laughs harder, clutching her chest, her blond hair framing her oval face like a curtain. "Men these days. How hilarious are they? And by *hilarious* I mean *stupid*."

I giggle at that. "Right? I think I've had enough dating to last me a lifetime."

"You went on two dates after the whole Trevor fiasco," Tia points out with a smirk. "And one ended between the sheets."

I groan and put my coffee down on the table. "Please, don't remind me." I pause. "At least none of them had a foot fetish."

"I don't think he meant the boob thing as an insult," she continues, blue eyes wide on me. "It would have been a compliment. He was merely making an observation. You do have huge boobs."

I look down at the boobs in question. "Yeah, but he should enjoy them, not compare the size to his head! Maybe his head is just really small."

Tia's shoulders shake, and she wipes her eyes, which are starting to water. She always cries when she laughs. "The sex couldn't have been that bad!"

I cover my face with my hands, not wanting to relive it. "It was horrible. He kept calling my . . . my . . ."

"Your what?" Tia asks, leaning closer to me. I point downward to my crotch. "Your pussy?" she supplies casually.

I nod.

"What was he calling it?" she asks, sounding both curious and on the verge of laughter.

I groan, yeah I'm not going to say that word out loud. "The c-word."

Tia grins, slamming her hand down on my dining table. "A cu—"

"Yes," I say, cutting her off. "That."

"A little dirty talk never hurt anyone," she huffs, lifting her mug to her lips, hiding her smirk.

"There is something seriously wrong with you," I tell my neighbor. I moved next door to Tia over a year ago. We became fast friends, and so did our children. My daughter, Cara, and her son, Rhett, are almost the same age and spend a fair bit of time together; we take turns having each other over for meals and company. We became family in such a short time, and I love them both to death.

"I'm all for the dirty talk," I agree. "But that word? Yeah, no. Why can't he just say *pussy* like a normal dirty-talking man?" Even the word *pussy* sounds foreign on my tongue. Before I became friends with Tia, I never really spoke about my sex life.

When he told me he loved fucking my c-word, I kind of wished I was anywhere except under him.

"Did he make you come, at least?" she asks, not shy at all.

"When did the two of us lose our boundaries?" I ask myself, staring at the ceiling for a second.

"Probably when you walked in on me having sex with—"

"Oh god, don't make me relive it!" I shriek, cutting off the rest of her sentence. I'd once come over to her house to find the door unlocked. Panicked, thinking someone had broken in, or something was wrong, I ran into the house while dialing the police, only to find her riding some guy. It was awkward. She didn't think so, but I did and still do.

"Bailey," she says in a serious tone. "You're a catch. A great woman. The best. And a fucking babe. If you can't find a good man, what chance do the rest of us have?"

I smile sadly. "Maybe not all of us are meant to be with someone. I have a house. A job. A beautiful, healthy daughter. If that's all I get in life, I'll be happy with it."

"Bullshit," Tia says, narrowing her blue eyes. "You'll find someone, when the time is right. Someone who isn't a creep like Trevor."

Yeah, I sure know how to pick them. Tia knows a few things about Adam, but not the whole story. No one knows the whole story except me.

I push my dark hair back behind my ear and mutter, "I won't hold my breath."

Cara and Rhett run into the kitchen, saving me from Tia's attempt at a motivational speech.

"You two finished playing games?" I ask my daughter, hugging her as she runs into my arms, her brown hair flailing around.

"Yeah," she says, her big brown eyes glancing up at me. "Can we go play outside now?"

I nod. "Yeah, okay. How about a snack first?"

"Yes, please!" Rhett calls out, always hungry. His blond hair falls over his forehead, his blue eyes identical to Tia's peer up at me in excitement.

"Okay," I tell him. "Wash your hands while I fix you both something."

They wash their hands and wait patiently at the table while I make them some fruit salad, and pull out some Jell-O from the fridge to go with it.

"Thanks, Mom!" Cara says, picking up her fork and stabbing a piece of watermelon.

"Thanks, Aunt Bailey," Rhett says, doing the same. I always get a little emotional when he calls me Aunt, even though we aren't blood related. Tia says I'm more family to them than their own family, and that I've done more for Rhett than his real aunts, so I've earned the title.

I share a glance with her. Here we are, both single mothers, doing the best we can, but even I have to admit we both have great children.

Tia smiles, reading my thoughts. "We've done well, haven't we?"

Cara looks up at me and grins before returning her concentration to the food.

"Yeah, we did."

The last place I ever thought I'd see Lana and Anna again is the school I teach at, so when I hear them both calling my name, I turn around with my mouth open in shock.

"What are the two of you doing here?" I ask, hugging Anna, then Lana.

"We're here for Clover," Lana replies, then points to a cute dark-haired girl in the crowd.

"She's gorgeous. Neither of you mentioned having a child!"

But then again, neither had I.

Anna's green eyes widen. "Oh, she isn't ours. She's Sin and Faye's daughter. Friends of ours."

"Oh," I say, putting the pieces together. "You're here to watch her race?"

Today was Field Day, and other schools were here to compete. The younger children came to play team games and have a friendly race or two.

Anna nods. "Yeah, we all came out to cheer for her. It's her first race. She's so excited, you should see her."

Lana looks down at her shoes and shuffles them in the grass. "Why didn't you call us after we saw you at Rift? We thought we'd all have caught up by now."

My mind races with how to handle this. I don't want to tell them the truth, but I don't want them to think I don't want to see them either. "I didn't have your number."

With social media, it was a lame excuse at best, but Anna's eyes narrow. "Rake said he gave you my number."

Well, fuck.

That bastard!

"Well, he didn't," I tell her. "Look, girls, the truth is, I'd love to hang out with you both, but I don't want to see Adam. There's too much history there, and to be honest, I don't even want to be around him. Trust me when I say the feeling is mutual."

Anna crosses her arms over her chest. "Who says Rake has to be there? We can have ladies' nights; he can do his own thing. It's not like he told us to stay away from you."

Now it's my turn to look down at my feet, as though they suddenly became interesting.

"What the fuck?" Anna growls, her hands falling loose and clenching. "He didn't?!"

Even Lana looks surprised. "He doesn't want you around that badly? Damn. That doesn't sound like Rake at all. He's normally pretty easygoing."

"Not around me," I grumble. "He told me he didn't want me around the two of you. You're his sister, Anna—unfortunately he got you in the breakup. I can't go against his wishes, because if he finds out, he's going to be in my face and that's the last thing I want. I never want to see him again if I can manage it."

Lana and Anna share a speculative glance.

"What?" I ask, dragging out the word.

Anna grins, her eyes lighting up. "Rake's going on a run next weekend. He'll be gone for a few days. We can catch up for a drink or two. He won't find out; it'll be fine."

"Famous last words," I say with an exaggerated sigh, even though all three of us knew damn well I was going to go out with them. "Is he here to watch Clover?"

They both shake their heads, but Anna answers. "Nah, Sin and Tracker are here. The rest of the men had shit to do."

I look behind the girls and see Tracker sitting on the hood of a black four-wheel drive. Next to him is a man with dark hair. His arm is around a woman who is waving her hands in the air in Clover's direction. The two men are wearing the vest things I've seen bikers wear, and both look extremely imposing.

In fact, all the other parents have given them a wide berth.

Lana pulls out her phone and hands it to me. "Give us your number."

I put my number in and save it. "I guess he's going to find out you two saw me here today anyway."

"Can I ask you something?" Anna says, a serious expression on her pretty face. I already know what she's going to ask, but I nod my head anyway.

"What happened between the two of you? You were the best couple. I've never seen young love like that in my life. Everyone thought you'd get married."

So did I, but life doesn't always turn out how you expect it.

I lick my suddenly dry lips. A few words flow through my mind.

Utter devastation.

Heartbreak.

Tragedy.

Pain.

A lot of fucking pain.

"I guess it just didn't work out," I tell them, shrugging simply. Understatement of the fucking year.

THREE

NEXT weekend comes around faster than usual. Lana texted me a few days ago and asked if I could meet them at Rift, which was the last place I wanted to be. When I told her as much, she told me that we could meet at a bar called Knox's Tavern instead. Tia offered to keep Cara for the night so I could go out and enjoy a night with my old friends. Still, I'm feeling a little unsure.

I love Anna and Lana, but being with them brings back so many memories. Having them in my life brings back Adam. My Adam, not the biker badass known as Rake. The Adam I loved, before he broke me. I keep trying to find a love like what we shared, but it just never measures up. And it makes me hate him even more. I need to get over it, I know. But I've tried and I can't. I don't think I'll ever be able to get to the point where I can see him and not feel anything, good or bad. I wish I could.

I'd love to see him and feel absolutely nothing, to be numb. For my heart not to race, for my chest not to get tight. For me to be able to breathe freely, not feel like tears are about to drip down my cheeks.

Maybe one day.

I glance at my reflection in my full-length mirror, looking from side to side. My dark hair is down and curled at the ends, and I'd done a red lip and winged eyeliner. My brown eyes are nothing special, but I'm lucky to be blessed with thick, long lashes. Lashes that Cara inherited from me. With a final inspection, I grab my black clutch and slip my feet into my black strappy high heels.

Then, I call a taxi.

"Do they only hire sexy men here?" I ask with wide eyes, as I take in the hunks around me. "And twins. Seriously?"

How are they real?

Was being sexy a requirement for working here?

Anna looks toward the bar and laughs. "I used to work here. Reid, Ryan, and Tag, they're all good guys. Reid can be a pain in the ass though."

She says that fondly.

"He can be a pain in *my* ass any time he likes," I say, leaning my cheek on my palm and studying him from the safety of our booth. When Lana and Anna break out in laughter, I realize how what I just said could be interpreted. If you have a dirty mind, which these girls clearly do.

"That isn't what I meant," I say, giggling. I then blurt out, "I'm still an anal virgin."

They laugh harder.

I roll my eyes and suck on my straw, letting the chilled drink fill my mouth and slide down my throat. When I notice a rough-looking man standing by the door watching us, I ask, "Who is that guy?"

Anna looks at the man and purses her lips. "That would be my compromise. Bringing him along was the only way the men would let us out without them."

"I see," I reply, checking the man out. "He's hot though."

Lana leans back in the booth and grins. "His name is Ronan; he was just patched in. The men have started calling him Shark, although no one will tell us why."

"So do you call him Ronan or Shark? It sounds confusing."

"We call him Ronan because we're used to it," Anna replies. "I don't get the whole road-name thing either. There obviously aren't any rules to it, because we still call Vinnie, Vinnie."

Lana's brows furrow in though. "Vinnie's road name is Wolf, didn't you know that?"

Anna looks confused, wrinkling her nose adorably. "How the hell do you know that?"

Lana shrugs her shoulders, pushing her glasses up on her nose. "I pay attention when people talk."

"So do I," Anna says easily. "I don't know how I missed that. That's interesting information."

"Yeah and his first name isn't even Vinnie. Vincent is his middle name."

"What's his first name then?" Anna asks, absorbing all the new information.

"Tyler."

"Hmmm. I can't picture him as anything except Vinnie," Anna says.

"I like your hair, Bailey," Lana says, pointing to the curls at the ends.

"Thanks," I reply, lifting a curl between my fingers. "I thought I'd try something different."

"It looks good," Anna agrees.

The sex god with the scar on his face walks up to our table, and I try not to hyperventilate. His biceps are so sculpted, and I can almost see his six-pack through his white T-shirt. Or is that just my pervy imagination? His face is chiseled perfection too. The scar only adds to his appeal.

I squirm on my seat.

"Anna," he says, lifting his chin, his firm lips twitching. "Back at the old stomping grounds, I see. What trouble will you be causing me tonight?"

"None at all, Reid," Anna replies with a grin, trying to look innocent and failing.

"Right," he murmurs, turning his attention to Lana. "You keep her in line for me, will you, Lana?"

Lana nods her head. "Always."

"It's good to see you too, Reid," Anna says, rolling her eyes. "I see you're your usual charming self."

Reid smirks in response. "You know me, I never change."

His gaze turns to me then. "And which one are you?"

"Bailey," I tell him, waving my fingers at him.

His eyes narrow as he studies me. "You going to be a pain in my ass too?"

The other girls giggle, obviously remembering our previous

words. "Only if you want me to. Knowing these two though, probably."

Yeah, this is my awkward way of flirting.

Reid actually grins then. It's fucking devastating. He turns to Anna. "Why did you have to come here tonight of all nights? Next time call up and let me know you'll be here so I can keep my ass at home."

"Why?" she replies, perking up and looking around the bar. "What's happening tonight? Male dancers on the bar? A pole-dance show? Morning Alliance playing here? Oooh, that would be awesome."

Reid cringes and tells Anna to slide over so he can sit down.

"None of the above. Summer decided she wants to have a weekly karaoke night."

"And it's tonight?" Anna asks, doing a crazy little happy dance. "Fuck yeah! We're all over that!"

She glances at me. "Bailey?"

"I'm in," I look to Lana. "Lana?"

She picks up her glass. "Few more of these and why the hell not?"

Reid scrubs a hand down his face. "I'm going home early. I knew I shouldn't have come in tonight. I told Summer that listening to people try to sing all night isn't a fun time, but you know her."

Anna wraps an arm around him. "Aww, come on now, Reid. You can do a duet with me. It'll be great. Where is Summer anyway? I haven't seen her in ages, and I think we're due for a catch-up." She looks at me and explains, "Summer is Reid's babe of a wife. She's great; you'll love her."

"She'll be here in an hour or so," he says, glancing down at his watch. "She keeps trying to come to work, and I keep telling her to stay home. We finally agreed on her only coming in during peak time and then going home to relax."

"Excellent," Anna says, looking to me and Lana. "We should make this a weekly outing, girls. Karaoke night at Knox's Tavern! We can bring Faye next time. She'll love this shit."

We all cheer.

"Try to keep your men at home," Reid suggests, raising his eyebrow at Anna. "Generally where you are, they follow, and with them comes even more trouble."

"Oh, please, we've all been so good," Anna says, waving her hand in the air. "Nothing's been going on recently. I know you keep up to date with the gossip, Reid, so you would know."

"Men are such gossips," I throw out there.

"It's true," Lana agrees.

"I own a bar," Reid says drolly. "People like to talk. Unless it involves me or mine, I generally don't give a shit, but yeah, I do hear a lot of stuff. That doesn't mean I repeat it though."

Anna nods her head. "True. Hey, you know, you should host a ladies' night with shirtless male waiters and male strippers."

"You'd probably make a heap of money," Lana says, grinning. "We could come here for all the bachelorette parties."

"Maybe you could take your shirt off too," I blurt out.

Lana and Anna start laughing. Reid stands up and walks back to the bar, his shoulders slumped.

Poor guy. I wouldn't want to deal with us either.

"Another round?" I ask, which is greeted by more cheers. I walk to the bar with a smile on my face. Some things don't change; these two always knew how to have a good time.

There's something nice about going out with friends who actually care for you, ones who won't leave you stranded at the end of the night. The only good friend I have is Tia, but one of us usually stays home with the kids, so we rarely get a night out together.

"Can I get three screwdrivers, please?" I ask Reid's twin.

He smiles, eyes crinkling. "Sure thing, sweetheart."

His friendly demeanor gives off a completely different vibe than that of his brother. Reid makes you sit up straight; Ryan makes you want to relax in the chair.

"Thank you," I tell him as he starts to make the drinks. I open my bag and pull out a fifty-dollar bill.

"It's on the house," he tells me, waving away the money.

"Oh, no, I can't," I say, feeling a little awkward, but he just winks at me.

"Anna and her friends get free drinks. It's one of the rules," he says in a no-nonsense tone.

"That's a terrible business decision," I advise him, which makes him laugh.

"It is, but sometimes life isn't always about business, is it?" he says, eyes shining with humor.

"I guess not," I reply. "But I'd still feel better if you let me pay."

He just shakes his head. "Come on, I'll help you carry the drinks."

He takes two glasses in his hands, and I carry the third back to the table.

"What great service they have here," Anna teases as Ryan places the drinks down. He sits down in the same place Reid did.

"Best bar in town," he replies with a smirk. "Haven't seen

you in a while, Anna. You've been ditching us for Rift, haven't you? That hurts, Anna."

"You should be happy about that," Anna says, bringing her glass toward her. "Less drama for you."

Ryan shrugs his broad shoulders. "Those sound like Reid's words. I like it when things get a little interesting around here."

"I'll drink to that," Anna murmurs, lifting her glass in the air. We clink our glasses together, then take sips. "Ryan, you met Bailey, right?"

"Met her, didn't know her name," he says, nodding his head at me with a smile. He then looks back at Anna. "Where did you find this one? I always see you out with the same people, now all of a sudden you have a new friend?"

"Why does everyone say that? Bailey is an old friend. We went to school together, actually," Anna replies. "And she's Rake's ex-girlfriend. So he doesn't need to know she was here."

Ryan grins. "See? Trouble. My lips are sealed. It's not like I talk to Rake unless he comes in here anyway."

"I'm telling you just in case," Anna says, stirring her drink with the straw.

"Well in that case, noted. And how have you been, Lana?" he asks, turning his attention to her. "Punch any women in the face recently?"

Anna slaps his arm. "Dude, don't speak ill of the dead."

My eyes flare. "Wait, what?"

"I'll tell you later," Lana says to me, sighing, then looks to Ryan. "Thanks for bringing that up, Ry. But I'm good. Same old. Why don't you have a drink with us?"

Ryan raises an eyebrow at Lana. "Trust me, I would, but it's going to get busy as fuck any minute now and it wouldn't be the greatest idea to get comfortable."

He kisses Anna on the cheek, then glances at me. "Hope you all have a good night. Let me know if anyone harasses you." He smirks. "So I can send Reid."

We all laugh at that.

He stands, then flashes us one last cheeky grin. "I expect to see you all on the microphone."

"You won't be able to tear it away from us," I tell him, then check out his ass when he walks away.

Anna makes a sound of amusement. "He's so very taken."

"The good ones usually are," I say with a huff. "I can still look from afar. You guys are used to seeing all these men, but I'm still wondering where they all came from, and where they've all been hiding."

"The good ones are faithful," Lana agrees, taking an ice cube out of her glass and placing it on her tongue. "All you can do is hope you can catch a man who will be the same to you— ridiculously loyal, physically and emotionally."

"The two of you have," I say, trying to keep the wistfulness out of my voice and failing. They'd been telling me about their men all night. Who knew bikers were the way to go? It's probably just these bikers, which makes the women even luckier. Would Adam and I be at a different place if we had that kind of trust between us? It's going to be hard to completely trust a man again, because in my experience all they do is let you down in the end.

"You'll find someone worthy of you," Lana says sincerely. "It happens when you least suspect it."

"Then bam!" Anna pipes up, slamming her fist on the table

for emphasis. "He comes into your life and nothing is the same. He takes up every thought in your mind and there's nowhere you'd rather be than in his arms."

Lana nods. "You're a goner. Then you realize you never really stood a chance at all. If love is out to get you, you might as well stop trying to fight it and just go with it."

I roll my eyes. "I don't think it's going to happen for me, to be honest. I think I'm actually okay with that now though. But enough talk about me and my singleness, let's have another drink and get ready to sing our asses off!"

FOUR

AFTER our terrible rendition of "Man Down" by Rihanna, we give up the microphone to others. I meet Summer and Taiya, Reid's and Ryan's wives. Both are so beautiful and charismatic, I can see why the men chose them over all others. They could clearly get any women they wanted, but they're obviously in love with these two incredible ladies.

"That was fucking horrible," Reid says as we sit back down at our table. He sounds extremely amused, and I can tell that he really doesn't mind the fact that we're here, no matter how much he tries to pretend otherwise.

"That was fucking great!" Summer disagrees, hugging her baby bump. She's five months pregnant and dressed in a cute black baby-doll dress. After watching Reid with her all night, I feel a pang in my chest. He's so protective yet sweet. Gruff, but to her he turns into someone completely different. Yeah, that's love all right.

"I'd like to see you do better," Anna challenges back. Reid

simply grins and shakes his head, wrapping his arm around Summer and affectionately kissing the top of her head.

"Wouldn't want to make you all look bad," he says smoothly.

"Cop out!" Anna calls out.

"Come on, Reid," Summer says to him. "We won't even give you shit for how terrible you're going to be."

He kisses her to shut her up and it works.

We all try again to get Reid to get up onstage to sing, but he turns us down flat.

"No way in hell I'm getting up there," he says, standing up. "And my beautiful wife and I are going to make an exit before you guys get back up there again. I'm pretty sure Rihanna is fucking crying right now after hearing you annihilate her song."

"I'm not going anywhere," Summer says, moving to the music. "I want to stay with the girls!"

"Summer," Reid says, waiting until she looks at him. "You're pregnant and tired. Let's go home and rest; you can see the girls another time. You know we can't get rid of them, they're bound to come back."

Summer glances at all our faces. "Will you come back and see me?"

We all agree.

"And I like the ladies' night idea," she says, winking.

Reid groans and shoots Anna a look that promises retribution.

Anna simply gives him a thumbs-up.

The two of them head off, leaving us to our own devices.

We're talking about the good old days when Lana suddenly stands up and points. "Holy crap, look who's here."

We all look in her line of sight.

I see a tall, lean man with shaggy white-blond hair coming toward us. Next to him is a larger, scarier-looking man dressed in leather and sporting a Mohawk. As they come up to our table, I see the blond man has beautiful green eyes, while his friend's are dark and ominous.

"Talon!" Anna squeals, jumping into his arms. Talon wraps her in his embrace, his muscled, tattooed arms holding her almost tenderly. Who exactly is this Talon? I glance at Lana, but she's too busy smiling up at the man. He lifts Anna in the air before putting her down, then hugs Lana.

When he lets her go, he looks down at me. "And who do we have here? Did you two finally find a new friend?"

Gently pulling me up from my chair, he pulls me against his chest. "I'm Talon."

Feeling a little awkward at being held by a complete stranger, yet oddly attracted to him, I look up at his face and say, "Nice to meet you. I'm Bailey."

"Slice, I'd say it's nice to see you again, but that would be a lie," I hear Anna tell Talon's friend.

Slice laughs deeply in return. "Don't be like that, Anna."

"Let her go, Talon," Anna chastises, grabbing my arm and pulling me away from him. "She's off-limits."

"Ah, come on," Talon grumbles. "You just made her forbidden. Do you know what that does to a man like me?"

I look at Anna. "I thought you said no bikers were going to be here tonight beside our guard?" I look toward the door. "Speaking of . . ."

Where is that guy?

"I meant no Wind Dragons," Anna replies, nodding her head at Talon. "These guys just seem to pop up everywhere."

My brow furrowing, I ask Talon, "You're not a Wind Dragon?"

Talon scoffs, sitting down next to me and laying his arm on the back of my chair. "Definitely not, gorgeous."

The men aren't wearing any *cuts*, a word I'd only learned tonight, but they sure do look like bikers to me. If he isn't a Wind Dragon, I guess he's with a different club, or something like that.

"What the hell did you do to him?" Anna asks, glancing around the bar.

"He's currently being distracted," Talon replies, flashing me a wink.

"Talon, I swear to God—"

"He's fine," Talon interrupts. "I just wanted to see you. It's been a while."

Anna's expression softens. She sits down, Slice next to her. "Yes, it has. How have you been?"

"Good," he says, then looks at me. "Even better now."

Anna does not look happy, her eyes narrowing and her mouth tightening. At her suddenly sober expression, I can't help thinking that she needs another drink or two. "She's Rake's ex."

Talon's eyes widen at that, and all of a sudden, I'm feeling a little sober too. Why did she have to bring up his name?

"Well, if she has such bad taste in men, I'm sure I'm right up her alley," he says, lips twitching.

Slice chuckles at that, sending an amused look in my direction. "Ain't that the truth."

I hold up my hand. "In my defense, it was years ago. I like to think I've grown since then."

"All is fair in sex and pussy," Slice adds, then sends a flirty look in Lana's direction.

"Tracker will murder you," Anna grumbles, crossing her arms over her chest. "No, he's going to murder me, and so is my brother and my man when they find out how tonight turned out."

I gape. "You said Rake wouldn't find out!"

She cringes, then tries to play if off by waving her hand in the air. "It will be fine. I can handle my brother."

I open my mouth and then close it. It is what it is. "If shit is going to start over this, we might as well go out with a bang."

When Talon murmurs his approval, I narrow my gaze on him. "Not that kind of a bang. Drinks and dancing maybe. Either of you two up for some karaoke?"

Slice looks like I've offended him with just the thought, but Talon throws his head back and laughs. "I like you, Bailey. I'll tell you what. One kiss and then I'll sing any duet you want."

Unconsciously, my eyes lower to his delicious-looking, full lips.

He's handsome, yes, but I feel nothing.

Why do I feel nothing?

Am I broken?

When was the last time I had a proper kiss? A consuming, melting, mouthwatering, panty-wetting kiss? The sad thing is, the last person to kiss me like that was Adam.

Fuck it.

"Deal," I blurt out.

Four pairs of eyes, suddenly all on me.

"What?" I say, shrugging my shoulders. "He's cute."

"So are you," Talon rasps, his tone making me look at him. He licks his bottom lip, his eyes smoldering. "Come here."

"How about you come here?" I say in a sultry voice I didn't know I possessed.

Talon grins, eyes heated, and comes closer.

"Bailey!" I hear Anna growl over Slice's laughter and Lana's soft "Uhh, Bailey?"

I ignore them all.

If I want a kiss, then I'm going to get one. I'll let future me worry about any possible consequences. When Talon grabs my face in his large warm hands and slants his lips on mine, I block everything else out.

Everything except his lips.

His spicy scent.

His tongue.

Yeah, it's a good kiss.

Great, even.

But it's not an Adam kiss.

Not for the first time, I think that maybe the man has broken me. Ruined me for any other. Determined not to let the bastard win, I deepen the kiss with Talon and let my hands wander over his muscled back. He makes a deep growling sound, which brings me back to reality, reminding me that people are indeed watching us make out right now.

Then I hear a familiar voice, and I just *know* I'm now in deep shit.

And I've brought everyone down with me.

"What the fuck?" I hear Adam growl. I pull away from Talon and look up into the angry eyes of Adam, Arrow, and Tracker.

Fuck.

His gaze doesn't leave mine. A muscle in his jaw repeatedly tenses, and his hands are clenched to fists.

He looks pissed.

And I mean *pissed*.

Yeah, tonight was one huge fucking mistake.

Adam didn't want me around his family, and no matter what Anna said, tonight shouldn't have happened. I don't want to cause a rift between the two of them. And I don't want to fight with Adam, because I just know that old shit is going to resurface. That's the last thing I need. And, I definitely shouldn't have kissed Talon knowing he has some beef with Adam.

I should have sat my ass at home and played Monopoly with Cara, Tia, and Rhett.

"Pretty sure I told you to stay away from my family," Adam growls at me. He glances next to me, his mouth tightening at Talon. "And you. I let you live because of Anna, but don't fuckin' push me."

Talon simply raises an eyebrow, looking . . . amused? Are these men all insane? "I'm sitting here enjoying the company of a beautiful woman who isn't with any of the men in your club. I fail to see what you're so fucking angry about, Rake."

Anna stands up, her face pale. "Rake, wait. I'm the one who—"

"Stay out of this, Anna," Adam growls, eyes steady on me. The way he is—his body posture, the menace pouring off him—it's like the Adam I used to know times a hundred.

I don't miss the way Arrow scowls at Adam's tone when addressing Anna, and takes a protective step in her direction.

That right there is what I wish I had.

But no one is going to protect me.

I see the sexy bald guy from the bar storm up to us. "Take this outside, now. Or Reid will be here to kick everyone's ass."

Arrow looks at the man, who takes a step back. Yeah, I

wouldn't want to mess with Arrow either. Still, I guess the men respect Reid and his bar, because they grab their women and make an exit. Thinking I'm now free to jump in a taxi and get the hell out of here, I jump in surprise when Adam grabs me by the upper arm and pulls me to his side.

"Let go of me," I say so only he can hear.

"Not a chance," he growls under his breath. "You came back here, into my fuckin' territory, with my people, now you and I are going to have a little chat."

"You don't own this bar," I say snidely, narrowing my eyes on him. "How is this your territory? Just let me go. I'll go home and we'll pretend this never happened."

"Yeah? Think I'm going to forget you kissing a guy I can't fuckin' stand any time soon? You know nothing about loyalty, do you? Maybe hanging with Anna and them will be good, maybe you'll even learn something."

He's such a dick.

I kick him in the shins. He looks down at me but doesn't even flinch, so either it didn't hurt, or he's just not giving me the satisfaction of knowing that it did.

"Mature, Bailey."

"So much bad shit to say about me, yet you're still holding on to me. Why?"

"Like I said, we need to talk."

"Talking is the last thing we need to do," I fire back. The time for talking is over.

"Bailey!" Talon calls, taking my attention away from Rake. Rake stiffens as he approaches us. He and Talon stare at each other, the tension between them making the air feel thick and uncomfortable. I can tell that this has to do with more than me. I try to pull my arm from Adam's grip, but he just holds on tighter. Slice steps up next to Talon, having his back if anything goes wrong, I guess.

"Do we have a problem here?" Adam asks.

Talon tilts his head to the side. "You tell me."

"Rake, let's go!" Arrow calls out, turning to Anna and saying something in her ear. Was he doing Anna's bidding? Something about that amuses me, the big, scary-as-hell man trying to appease his woman.

"Let me go," I mutter, tired of their posturing. "I need to go home."

They both look down at me, as if they only just remembered that I'm here.

"I'll take you home," Adam commands, then looks at Talon. "This isn't over. I don't want to ever see you near her again, do you fuckin' understand me?"

Talon however, ignores him and looks at me. "You can go with him, or I can take you. Say the word."

The air thickens again.

Shit.

I don't want a fight to break out because of me, and I don't want Talon to think I like him more than I do. He's a nice guy, but I have no intention of sleeping with him, or dating him.

"Thank you, Talon," I tell him. "I'll be fine. I don't want to cause any more trouble."

Talon nods slightly, his eyes telling me that if I need him, all I have to do is speak out.

But I don't.

I wave 'bye as Adam pulls me to his bike.

Talon and Slice don't leave though—they stand there watching.

I'm handed a helmet, which I put on. Adam makes sure our hands don't touch.

"Get on," Adam demands, without bothering to help me up. I've never been on a bike before, and I'm pretty sure he knows this.

"I've never ridden on the back of a bike before," I admit quietly, not knowing how to feel about it. Is it safe? As a single parent, I can't exactly afford to do anything reckless. My daughter needs me, and if she doesn't have me, she has no one.

He licks his bottom lip. "So? The old Bailey would have loved this shit. The old Bailey made Anna look like a saint. Have you changed so much?"

I stare daggers at him. "I grew up, Adam, perhaps you should try it?"

He makes a scoffing noise but says nothing while I awkwardly straddle the bike and reluctantly wrap my arms around his waist.

I have one question running through my mind.

Why did he want me to leave with him?

FIVE

WHEN we come to a stop, I almost want to kiss the ground. Anna and Lana come over to me as I fumble off the motorcycle and take off my helmet. They obviously made it here before us.

"You okay?" Anna asks, glancing between Adam and me.

"She's fine," he answers for me.

The jerk.

"*She* can speak for herself," I snap, turning my back to him and facing the girls. "I'm fine. I just want to go home. Could you give me the address for this place so I can call a taxi?"

Anna and Lana turn their heads to look at each other.

Are they not going to help me? It's Anna's fault I'm here in the first place.

"They can't save you, Bailey," Adam rasps, coming up next to me. "I warned you; you didn't listen. Now you gotta deal with me."

I lift my head to look at him. Was he always this damn tall? "I don't have to do any damn thing I don't want to, *Rake*."

I need to remember that that's what he goes by now. Also so I remember that I don't know the man standing next to me.

He laughs without humor.

And I've had enough.

I turn and start to walk down the road, pulling out my phone. There has to be a street sign somewhere around here. Suddenly I'm grabbed around the waist and pulled back into a hard body.

"We're going to talk, Bailey. Then I'll take you home, all right?" he murmurs in my ear.

"We don't have anything to talk about," I reply, tilting my head away from his lips.

"Yeah," he whispers. "We do. So you can come inside of your own accord, or kicking and screaming. At this point, I don't care which one you choose."

He wraps his fingers around my nape and squeezes firmly. "What do you have to lose? I never told Anna what happened that night. In fact, I never told a single soul. Trusting you is my burden to bear, and not a mistake I'll ever make again."

His comment sends me straight back to that night, just the place where I didn't want to go.

"Fuck you," I grit out, turning around to face him. "You don't know shit, Adam. Just let me go. I won't see your sister, or anyone connected to you again."

He studies me and rubs his palm along his jaw. Then, in a simple move, he bends down and throws me over his shoulder.

"Adam!" I yell, squirming around. "Put me down, you asshole! Anna, I'm going to kill you!"

I ignore the men's catcalls as he walks with me through their clubhouse. From upside down, all I can see is scary-looking leather-clad men, and all I can hear is music and laughter. All I can feel is anger and embarrassment. I'm wearing a fucking dress, and who knows what everyone can see. I punch the back of Adam's thighs, but all he does is slap my ass once and I freeze.

"No one better have seen that," I growl, trying to push my hair out of my face. A door is opened, a light is turned on, and then I'm tossed onto a bed.

His bed.

His very large, black, could-be-a-porn-set bed.

Images rush through my mind, me on that bed, underneath him, but I shake my head and push them away, knowing that they have no place being there. I look away from the bed and study the man in question instead, causing more memories to flash through my mind. I miss the old Adam. Before everything went to hell. The Adam who I would lie with in bed, staring at the ceiling, just talking for hours. The Adam who was my best friend in the world. He paces the room, stops, gives me a cutting look, then takes off his jacket and throws it on the ground, bringing me back to reality

"I never wanted to see you again," he says, running a hand through his short blond hair. "Yet here you are. In my fuckin' clubhouse. Christ."

"You brought me here," I remind him.

"I know," he grits out between clenched teeth.

I cross my arms over my chest, hugging myself. "Anna and Lana wanted to see me. I didn't seek them out. And I didn't want to say no, even though I knew I should have. I couldn't hurt their feelings. I still care about both of them."

"I know you do, but this isn't fuckin' working, Bailey," he says, shaking his head. "It's too fuckin' much. You're in my territory, everywhere I go, when all I want to do is forget that you even exist."

Ouch.

Why do I do this to myself?

I can't have everything I want, and it looks like a friendship with my old friends is going to be something to add to that list. I totally see where he's coming from. Anna and Adam are a package deal. I can't be in her life without being in his. It is too much. Too much everything. Pain, emotions, memories. Just everything.

"I'll stay away," I say in a small voice. "I don't want to be here either."

Being reminded of everything I lost, everything that happened, isn't a good time for me. I understand when he says he wants to forget. When you're stuck in a place where you can't go back, when you can't fix the past, you need to let it go or it will eat you alive.

He looks at me then, I mean really looks at me. Looks inside me. "Why?"

"Why what?" I ask softly, swallowing hard at the emotion I see flashing in his green eyes.

"I mean," he says between clenched teeth, "why don't you want to be around me? You're the one who fucked everything up, and now you're acting like I'm the one who did something wrong, when the only thing I did was trust a woman who obviously couldn't keep her legs closed."

Before I know it, I'm on my feet, and I slap him right across his face. No one talks to me like that. No one.

His eyes narrow, but he doesn't even flinch or lift his hand to rub his face. Instead, he just stares at me with heat in his eyes.

"I want to go home. Now," I demand, touching his chest with my hand. "If you ever cared about me at one point in your life, you will get me out of here."

His throat works as he swallows. Did he realize the line he just crossed? "All right, let's go then."

I exhale in relief, then follow him out of the clubhouse.

I don't look anyone in the eye.

I don't say good-bye.

I just get the fuck out of there.

I hand Adam his helmet, then walk down my driveway without looking back.

"Bailey," he says, making me stop and turn to him.

"What?" I ask quietly, just wanting tonight to be over with. I like to think that I'm a strong woman, but there's only so much I can take.

I'm surprised when he walks down my driveway and stops in front of me. "You know, I try not to be an asshole to you, I really do. But when I see you, my mind is fuckin' clouded and I can't control my emotions." He sighs. "You're the only person who it happens around, and it's a weakness."

"A weakness?" I ask, not sure what he means by that exactly.

"Showing emotion is showing weakness," he says, looking into my eyes. "If two people are angry, and one stands quietly while the other rages and breaks shit, who do you think is the most powerful, mentally?"

"Does it matter who is most powerful?" I ask, tilting my head to the side. "I guess the quiet one would be, but then he would hold it all inside, and it would slowly eat at him. The man who raged and reacted may have less control, but he gets all the emotions out, so they don't destroy him."

"Yeah, well," he says, looking down at his feet. "You make me rage. You make me feel shit I don't want to feel."

I swallow hard at the emotion in his voice.

"I'll wait until you get inside and lock the door," he says, but I don't move. I just look into his eyes, seeing how much of my Adam is still in there.

"Bailey, go," he whispers, eyes narrowing.

I nod and slowly walk to my front door.

I'm about to close it when I hear him say, "It would help if you weren't so fuckin' beautiful."

But that must have been my imagination, right?

I close the door, lock it, turn around, and collapse against it. My breaths come in pants, in and out, in and out in quick puffs. I squeeze my eyes shut, emotions running through me. Ghosts from past pains, past wounds that are now being split back open. Why did this have to happen? I don't want to deal with all of this. I was finally in a good place, and now . . . I won't let him ruin that. He made me so angry, but then when we just spoke . . . he made me feel something else. Something I need to bury. The anger, yeah, I can understand that. The other emotions—no, I don't need to concentrate on those. They don't exist. I need to learn how not to let him get under my skin.

It's been years, I tell myself over and over again.

The past can hurt me only if I let it.

I need to be stronger.

When I get my breathing under control, I pull myself together, have a long, hot shower, and then go and pick up a sleeping Cara from Tia's house. I put her in bed next to me, cuddling close.

But even then, sleep doesn't come.

All I do is replay his words in my head, over and over again, in a loop.

The only thing I did was trust a woman who obviously couldn't keep her legs closed. The only thing I did wrong. The only thing.

He has no idea, and it's my fault he doesn't.

The truth is, I've been protecting someone who doesn't deserve it. Adam's anger, bitterness, and venom—I don't deserve them.

Why don't I just tell him? I don't want to go back there, but I can't keep going on like this either.

The truth will set me free, but it will enslave Rake.

I don't want to hurt him, but right now all I'm doing is hurting myself.

What the hell am I going to do?

The next time I see Adam is several weeks later. In the wrong place at the wrong time, again.

After picking up Cara from school and then taking her to her dance class, I was too tired to cook, so I decided to stop at one of the diners we pass on the way home. Had I paid attention and seen the two bikes out front, I would have turned around. But I didn't. So here I am, sitting across the booth from my daughter, waiting for our orders, while Adam and one of his biker friends sit with two women, eating, laughing, and being generally obnoxious. They haven't seen me yet, and I hope to keep it that way.

"How was your class today, Mom?" Cara asks me sweetly.

My expression softens as I look at her, my worries fading away. "It was great, Cara. My students learned a new letter of the alphabet. How was your day?"

"Good!" she beams. "It was library day, so I got a new book."

"Which book did you get?" I ask her, just as a waitress brings us our drinks.

"Thank you," I tell the young girl, then look at my daughter expectantly.

"Thank you," Cara tells her, then starts to sip on her milk shake.

"You're welcome." The girl smiles, then leaves our table.

"It's a book about a unicorn," Cara continues, wiping the milk off her lips with the back of her hand. "Can we read it tonight?"

"Sure," I tell her, playing with the straw in my juice. "After dinner and bath time."

I suddenly feel eyes on me, and I try my hardest not to look in their direction. From their angle, they can see me but not Cara.

Maybe he'll just pretend that he doesn't know me.

Or is that just wishful thinking?

I hear Adam's friend, the bald guy, call out, "Where are you going, Rake?"

Shit.

Is he coming over here?

I don't want to look over and check.

Would he be rude to me in front of my daughter?

I'd kill him if he did that, but to be honest I don't think he would.

"What are you doing here, Bailey? Why are you there every time I turn around?" I hear him growl. I can now feel everyone in the diner staring at me. Goddamn the man. Did he have to be so loud? Adam never did care what people thought, but I don't want to get attention like this with my daughter here.

I don't even lift my head. "What? Do you own this diner too?"

"Cute," he replies, voice closer now. "I could if I wanted to."

Egotistical bastard.

I look up to see him almost at our table. "Well, until you do own it, you should probably just leave me alone."

"Who are you here with?" he asks, then comes to a stop when he sees Cara sitting there, peering up at him with curious brown eyes.

"Who's the hottie, Rake?" his friend calls out.

Adam turns to his friend and says, "Shut the . . ." He turns to look at Cara, an apologetic expression on his face, then takes a seat next to me, opposite her.

"You never told me you had a kid," he says to me, tone gentler now as he studies her intently.

"How do you know she's mine?" I ask him.

"She looks just like you," he says, giving Cara a little smile. "I'm Ra— I'm Adam. What's your name, sweetheart?"

"Cara," my daughter replies, flashing Adam an unsure look.

"That's a pretty name," he tells her sincerely. "And how old are you, Cara?"

I know exactly where Adam is going with this, but he's wrong. Cara isn't his child.

"I'm six."

I can almost see him mentally calculating how long it's been since we were together. If she were Adam's, she'd have to be at least seven years old.

"She's not yours," I say under my breath, so only he can hear me, trying to put him out of his misery.

"Of course she isn't," he says in a soft, yet bitter tone.

He has no idea. None.

Let him be bitter—I couldn't care less. I owe him nothing.

Or at least that's what I tell myself.

Our food arrives, and Adam waits quietly as the waitress sets it down.

"Thank you," Cara tells her politely, while I do the same. She smiles, then winks at Adam before she leaves. I ignore the stroke of jealously that hits me, because it has no right to be there.

"Listen, Bailey," he starts, looking a little uncomfortable. "Anna and Lana haven't spoken to me properly since that night. . . ."

He rubs the back of his neck, then watches Cara as she picks up a fry and pops it in her mouth. "Would you like some, Adam?" she asks, always considerate.

"No, thank you," he tells her, smiling. "You're a polite little thing, aren't you? Your dad must be proud."

Cara's face suddenly drops, and I kick Adam's leg with my left foot.

"I don't have a dad," she whispers sadly.

Adam's expression softens. "Well, then it's his loss, because you are one pretty, kind little girl."

Cara lifts her face. "That's what Mom says too."

"Your mom is right," Adam says, then turns to me while Cara continues to eat. "My own sister won't give me the time of day. Lana gives me evil looks I didn't even know she was capable of. They want to see you. I'll stay away, all right? You have your girls' nights, or whatever. As long as a few of the men are there with all of you, I won't cause any shit."

"It's fine—"

"Bailey," he says, sighing. "They want to be around you as much as you want to be around them."

I nod my head, giving in. "Okay then. I'd like that."

"And Bailey?"

"Yes?"

I don't miss the way his jaw tightens. "Stay away from Talon."

I open my mouth but then close it. I'm not going to justify that comment with a response. I will stay away from Talon because I don't like him like that, not because he tells me so. I also don't want to start any unnecessary trouble with everyone, especially for Anna and Lana.

He nods his head, like he knows he's gotten his point across, then looks to my daughter. "Nice to meet you, Cara."

"You too, Adam."

He pushes back his chair, stands, and returns to his table. The four of them leave moments later.

I try not to look at the beautiful woman by Adam's side.

Every time I've seen him, he's been with a different woman. Are they so replaceable to him? Just like I was. It hits me just how much he's changed, how much I don't know about him anymore.

He really isn't Adam anymore.

He's Rake.

When Cara and I finish eating, I go to pay the bill, only to find out it's already been settled.

Is that his way of saying sorry?

I don't know.

I don't want to think about him at all.

SIX

ANYONE who says men don't gossip is lying.

After getting phone calls from both Anna and Lana, demanding to know why they had to find out from Rake that I have a daughter, I told them I'd meet them tonight to catch up. Not over alcohol, but dinner instead. I told them I'd cook, so they could come over to my house.

I decided to make sushi, because I remembered Anna loved it, and some homemade spring rolls and a few other bites. Cara and I often cook together, trying new recipes. She loves to help bake cakes and other sweets, so we both made a red velvet cake with cream cheese icing for dessert. After finishing up in the kitchen, I take a quick shower and get dressed in jeans and a black T-shirt that's tight around my boobs and a little loose around my stomach. I give Cara a bath and put her in her favorite pink pajamas.

"Your hair is getting so long," I tell her as I gently brush it.

"I know," she beams. "I like it. It's like yours, almost."

I smile at that. "It is. Maybe it will get even longer than mine."

A knock at the door has me standing up and putting the brush down. "That will be them. Perfect timing."

I walk to the front door with Cara next to me. Unlocking the door, I open it to see the beautiful faces of Anna and Lana, one of them carrying a bottle of wine, the other a wrapped gift.

"Hello," I say, smiling and opening the door wider. They step inside, each giving me a warm hug and a hello before turning their attention to Cara.

"Aren't you beautiful? I'm Anna, and this is for you," Anna says, giving Cara the gift. Cara, with wide eyes, thanks them, then turns to me for approval.

"You can open it if you like," I tell her, trying to hide a smile. "You guys didn't have to do that."

"We wanted to," Lana says, holding up the bottle of wine. "We bought red wine too."

"I can see that." I laugh. "Come on, let's go sit down. Do you want something to eat now? Or do you want to wait until later?"

"What did you make?" Anna asks curiously, checking out the inside of my house.

"I made your favorite," I tell her, smiling and nodding my head toward the kitchen.

Her perfectly arched eyebrows lift. "No way. You made sushi?"

I grin but don't say anything, so she runs into the kitchen to find out for herself. I hear her cheering, which makes me laugh and Lana shake her head in amusement.

"Look, Mom! A new doll! She's so pretty!" Cara calls out from the floor, surrounded by a pile of ripped wrapping paper. "Thank you, I love her!"

"You're welcome, Cara," Lana says, sitting down on the couch. "She's gorgeous, Bailey, looks just like you. Rake said as much."

"He did?" I ask, getting caught off guard at her bringing him up so soon.

"Yeah," Anna says, walking into the living room with a plateful of sushi. "He couldn't stop raving about her. And holy shit, this sushi is amazing." She pauses and cringes. "I mean, holy crap."

"Make yourself at home Anna," Lana says, sarcasm lacing her tone.

I laugh. "My home is your home, as always."

Anna sits down and picks up a piece from her plate. "This place is great, Bailey."

I look around at my white walls and cream furniture. "Thank you. How have you guys been? Adam said you were giving him a hard time."

Anna smirks, a devilish look taking over her expression. "He can't choose who we're friends with. You're not just some random chick; you're an old friend, and he's just going to have to get used to the fact that you're going to be a permanent fixture in our lives now."

"You guys . . ." I say softly, a rush of emotions hitting me.

"Oh, don't get all mushy on me," Anna says, smiling. "Lana, I think we need some wine."

I stand up. "I'll get some glasses."

I head into the kitchen and return with three wineglasses, a corkscrew, and a juice box for Cara. I turn the radio on for some background music, then return to my seat.

Lana pours the wine. "To not letting men win!"

We clink glasses, then each take a gulp.

*   *   *

After Cara falls asleep and I carry her to bed, the interrogation begins.

"Why didn't you tell us you had a daughter?"

"Who is the father?"

"How long were you with him for?"

"Is there any chance she's Rake's?"

I hold my hands up. "Calm down, both of you. I didn't tell you because I knew I'd have to answer a million questions about who her father is, and to be honest I wasn't ready for Rake to find out."

Lana looks a little contrite, but Anna simply says, "Tell us!"

I put my glass down on the table. "After Adam and I broke up, I moved away from home and did a little traveling. Worked in bars, or whatever I could find at the time."

Really, I'd been fucked-up. I was in so much emotional pain. I would do anything to get rid of it, anything to distract myself. Usually, I found my distraction with other men.

"I ended up in a town called Channon. It's a country town about ten hours from here. Anyway, I met this guy, Wade. We ended up sleeping together a couple of times, and I got pregnant with Cara. Things didn't work out, so I moved back here. That's it. There's no big story, and she isn't Adam's child."

Anna looks slightly disappointed, like she expected a better story.

"Sorry to disappoint you, Anna," I tell her, laughing quietly.

"Where is Wade now?" Lana asks, studying me curiously.

"In Channon," I explain. "He doesn't have any contact with Cara. Just another deadbeat dad."

Lana and Anna both nod in understanding. I know neither of them had their fathers in their lives when they were growing up either, just like Cara won't. I had my dad with me all the time, up until I was thirteen, when he and my mom divorced. After that, he visited every weekend until he passed away from a heart attack when I was sixteen.

"I was kind of hoping she was Rake's," Anna admits, cheeks flushing guiltily. "I don't know why, but I was."

I roll my eyes at that. "She isn't."

This isn't some romance where everything works out in the end, and the hero and the heroine end up together in a happily ever after only someone with a big imagination could formulate.

"She looks just like you," Anna muses out loud. "She's stunning."

"Thank you," I tell her, smiling. "She definitely is something. Do you two want something else to drink?" I ask, looking at the now-empty bottle of wine.

"What do you have?" Anna asks, standing up.

My lips kick up at the corners in a wolfish grin. "We could make some cocktails."

"I like this idea," Lana says, rubbing her hands together. We all head into the kitchen, and I pull out whatever alcohol I can find, while the girls look for other ingredients in the fridge.

"Remember when we used to do this before parties in high school?" Anna says, washing the fruit. "Everyone had to make a drink, and then we all had to taste it, to see who could come up with the best one."

"Except Adam used to make them disgusting on purpose, just so we had to drink it," I say, smiling fondly. "He'd put peanut butter and stuff like that in them. It was gross."

Anna and Lana laugh. "Yeah, but he used to drink yours for you, Bailey, so it was only us who had to suffer!"

I open the half-filled bottle of vodka and smirk. "Girlfriend benefits."

"I'm his sister!" Anna fires back, her shoulder shaking with laughter. "Where's the loyalty?"

"Exactly," Lana adds. "His job was to harass your life."

"Well, he succeeded," Anna grumbles, but the smile playing on her lips says otherwise. Adam is a great big brother, there's no doubt about that. He always treated Anna like gold.

"Do you have any mint?" Lana asks, concentrating on slicing the lime thinly.

"I don't think so," I reply. "Do you feel like Anna has the upper hand here? She used to work at Knox's Tavern and she's a scientist."

"And she drinks the most out of all of us," Lana says, nudging Anna with her shoulder. "Yeah, she has us at an advantage."

"Wait, did this turn into a competition? I thought we were just talking about old times, but if we're going to relive them, game on!" Anna cheers.

"Who is going to be the judge?" I ask, finding the whole thing amusing.

"Arrow—"

"Hell no," I cut her off. "That's not fair."

"Well someone has to come and pick us up," Lana says, shrugging. "Whoever it is can be roped into being the judge. We won't tell him whose drink is whose."

"Deal!" Anna calls out, doing a little dance.

"We're so mature," I muse out loud, pulling out the blender and mentally selecting ingredients. If it's Adam picking them up, I know he loves citrus flavors, so I'll definitely do something with orange or lemon.

"You're a teacher," Lana points out. "Educating the youth of today to become tomorrow's leaders."

"Yeah, well, I'm off duty," I huff.

"And you're about to get schooled," Anna teases, then tilts her head to the side, her blond hair falling over her cheek. "I feel like we need a time limit or something. This competition is getting fierce."

"Ten minutes!" I call out, slamming my hand down on the table. "And tell whoever is picking you up to get his ass over here for taste testing."

"Wait," Lana says, pushing her glasses up on the bridge of her nose. "What does the winner get?"

Anna looks contemplative. "One favor. The winner gets one favor from each of the losers."

"Like a marker?" Lana asks, smirking. "You've been hanging around bikers too long."

Anna rolls her eyes. "Look who's talking. Come on, with the amount of shit we get into, these will be useful."

"And will probably get you into trouble with your men," I add casually.

At least it will if I win.

We all look at each other and nod.

Game on.

When Adam comes to the door to pick up the girls, I'm not surprised. While having him in my space makes me feel a tad uneasy, the fact that he's the one who came definitely works to my advantage.

"You want me to do what?" he asks, eyeing us all individually, then staring skeptically at the three glasses in front of him. When he first hesitantly stepped into my house, he looked around, taking in the place. Now, however, he has an *Are you fucking kidding me?* look on his face, one I shouldn't find sexy. But I do. In fact, his adorably confused expression makes me almost want to forget that I hate him and fall into his arms. Almost.

"Fuck. I feel like I'm back in high school. You're all fuckin' nuts," he says, running his hand over his jawline. I see the way his lips twitch though, and I know he's finding this amusing as hell. So we ignore his complaints and just stare at him expectantly.

"What did you guys bet?" he asks, gaze lingering on me before picking up the first glass.

"Don't you worry about that," Anna says in a saccharine sweet tone. "It's between us women. Just take a sip of each, you don't have to drink the whole thing."

"Like I would," he growls, then takes a sip of the pink liquid. I watch his throat work as he swallows, then he wipes his mouth with the back of his hand. He places the glass down, then picks up the second one, which is mine. The orange liquid swishes around the rim of the glass as he takes a small sip, then a bigger one. I try to hide my smile, knowing that there is no way I'm losing this stupid, childish, yet hilarious bet. The third glass is Lana's. Adam sips it, then puts it down, making a face. He points to my glass. "This one is hands down the best."

Anna and Lana yell "Come on!" and other shouts of complaint while Adam and I just watch each other. Amusement dances in his eyes, and he knows that I know exactly what he likes, and I used it to my advantage.

"Hope you won something good," he rumbles, then looks toward the hallway. "Where's Cara?"

Why did he want to know?

"Asleep," I reply a little hesitantly. "She's fast asleep."

He nods once, then looks away, giving me an unguarded moment to stare at his handsome profile. His five o'clock shadow has me wanting to run my fingers over his cheeks and his jaw. He's the same, but he isn't. More angled. More ripped. He's harder. And not just on the outside.

What has your life been like, Adam?

"Women, let's go," he says, looking around my living room once more. "I'm hungry. I say we stop for food."

"Bailey made us the best dinner," Anna tells him. "You would have loved it."

He mutters something under his breath, then walks outside. I guess he's done waiting.

Anna and Lana both hug me at the same time, and I wrap an arm around each of them.

"I'll see you soon?" I ask quietly, looking from one to the other.

They both assure me that they will.

I'm glad, because now that I have them back, I don't think I can lose them again.

Rake

I walk outside and check out the front of Bailey's house, not feeling satisfied with the level of her security. Pretty much anyone could break in, so I make a mental note to sort it out.

Her house, it's so her. Warm and inviting. Cozy. And she cooked for them.

I scrub my hand down my face. Am I feeling jealous because she cooked for them and I didn't get anything?

Yeah, I fuckin' am.

Everyone gets her, except me. And I'm the one who knows how amazing she is to be around.

I'm losing my shit.

Anna and Lana say their good-byes, laughing and carrying on. I move so Bailey's door is in my line of sight, and get one last peek at her before she closes the door.

"Can you two hurry up?" I grumble as they take their sweet time getting into the four-wheel drive.

"Why are you so grumpy?" my sister asks, sliding into the passenger seat.

"I'm hungry," I tell her. "Not all of us have eaten."

"So let's stop somewhere on the way," she suggests, studying me. "Are you sure that's the only reason you look like someone stole your motorcycle?"

I throw her a warning look, which she heeds, turning to stare out the window.

I put on some music and drive to the diner to grab some food.

It doesn't taste as good as I know Bailey's would.

SEVEN

Bailey

"I FEEL like my life is a series of awkward events," Tia says as she blows on her coffee the next morning.

"What happened now?" I ask, running my fingers through my hair, trying to tame it a little. It was the next afternoon, and we'd both just gotten home from work. Our kids were doing their homework in Cara's room together.

"Dentist guy asked me out on a date," she grumbles.

I gasp. "You said no, right?"

Tia worked as a dental assistant, so going out with essentially her boss would be a pretty stupid fucking idea.

"Of course I said no," she says, waving her hand in the air. "So we just had sex on the patient chair instead."

My jaw drops open. Did she just say. . . ? "Tia, what the hell were you thinking? So now you have to face him? It's going to be awkward as hell."

"It won't be that awkward for me," she says, sipping her coffee casually. "I'd be more embarrassed if I were him, and had a penis that small."

I cover my face with my hands. "You didn't tell him that, did you? Because if you did, you're probably currently unemployed."

"No, of course I didn't. I'm not that mean. I was all . . . 'Oooh your cock makes my mouth water' and afterward, I even pretended to be sore."

Oh my god.

I blink slowly a few times, processing this extreme amount of too much information. "How are we friends?"

Tia laughs, her blue eyes sparkling with humor. "Because of the no-judgment clause in our friendship agreement."

My lips twitch at that. "You aren't going to sleep with him again are you? It's the worst idea you've had, and you've had many. You're not supposed to shit where you eat."

She wrinkles her nose. "Is that a real saying?"

"Yes."

She sighs, putting down her mug. "I told you, he has the tiniest penis, so no, I won't be going there again. It looked small in his pants, but I thought that maybe he was a grower, not a shower, you know? But he's neither."

I want to laugh at the look on her face. She looks so sad about the whole thing. "It happens. Maybe he's a really nice guy. Or maybe he's good with his hands and mouth. You can't be penis racist. Penis discrimination! It's a thing."

She rolls her eyes. "Everyone has things they aren't willing to compromise on. For some it might be height, or money, or whatever; for me it is penis size. Don't judge me, Bailey, just accept me as I am. And for the record, he isn't talented with his hands or mouth either. I usually find men are either good at fucking or with their hands or mouth—either or. But this guy wasn't good at anything. Such a shame."

I try to contain my laughter but fail this time. "You're fucking hilarious. I don't have a deal-breaker thing, I don't think."

"Yes, you do," she replies drolly. "It's height. You never go near short guys. That's your thing."

"Well, aside from that, I'm not shallow!" I reply a little defensively. Yeah, I wasn't feeling the short-guy thing. I was about five feet seven inches and I wanted a guy who was at least six foot.

Adam is about six three, my mind reminds me.

Yeah, true. But he's also an egotistical asshole.

"I bet Adam has a huge cock. Doesn't he? You can tell me. I won't announce it on social media like I did with the dentist," she says, wiggling her eyebrows.

Did I mention his name out loud? I don't think I did. It must be a coincidence she said his name as I thought it. Only then do I realize what Tia just said.

I gasp. "You didn't!

She shrugs.

Christ, this woman!

"Does he? Spill!" she almost yells.

I puff out a breath, an image of Adam's cock filling my mind.

Long, thick.

Fucking perfect.

"Yeah," I admit sullenly. "It's the prettiest cock I've ever seen in my life."

The man could be a porn star if he wanted to.

Like Bruce Venture.

Okay, no one's penis is *that* nice.

"I knew it!" she says, slamming her palm down on the table. "Maybe I need to get me one of those bikers."

I'd normally advise against something like that, but Anna and Lana seem happy enough.

"Can I ask you something?"

"Sure," she replies. "What's up?"

"When Adam took me back to his clubhouse on his motorcycle that night he made a comment about the 'old Bailey' and pretty much said I used to be up for anything, which was true. I had a wild streak a mile long and was always up for an adventure. Do you think I'm boring? I know having Cara changed my outlook on the world, but that didn't mean I had to change who I was, you know?"

Her eyes soften on me. "Bailey, you were a young mother, managing on your own. You had to be responsible. And I don't think you're boring at all; you're a wonderful woman and a great mother. Just because you paused before jumping on the back of a motorcycle with your ex doesn't make you boring, it makes you smart."

I nod. "Yeah, I guess you're right."

"Mom, I finished reading my book," Cara says, walking into the kitchen. "There was one word I didn't know, so Rhett helped me."

"Good girl. What was the word?" I ask her as she sits down in between me and Tia.

"*Enormous*," she says, holding her hands out wide.

Tia and I quickly glance at each other.

And then burst out laughing.

"Remember the time we rented that hotel room out and you flooded it?" Anna says to me. It was time for our monthly catch-up, and this time we were having dinner at an Italian restaurant after seeing a movie at the cinemas.

"Why do all the stories about me come out?" I grumble, poking my pasta with my fork.

Anna laughs, closing her eyes. "We were drinking gin with orange juice. I remember because we were singing that rap song that goes with it."

Lana covers her mouth with her hand. "Didn't she pass out in the shower? Blocking the shower drain?"

Anna nods. "Yeah, we woke up to soggy carpets. We had to pay a shitload."

I cringe. "I've never drunk gin again, to this day. Besides, Anna, that whole hotel setup was so you could hook up with that guy you liked without Adam finding out."

"Which he found out anyway," Lana adds, eyes twinkling.

"If he hadn't joined the Wind Dragons, he should have been in the FBI," Anna grumbles, sitting back and rubbing her full tummy. "I think I need a break before dessert."

Lana looks up from her meal, eyes on the door. "Looks like we have some gate-crashers."

I follow her line of sight to see Arrow and Tracker walking up to us. With them is a guy I don't remember seeing before, with dark hair and a scar slashed down his jaw and neck. Arrow walks straight up to Anna and kisses her hungrily in front of everyone, not caring who sees. Tracker lifts Lana in the air and sits down in her chair, putting her on his lap. He then too kisses her like they're both alone. The other man sits next to me and smiles, flashing straight, white teeth. I think the smile is meant to reassure me, but to be honest, it kind of scares me.

"I'm Irish," he says, tilting his head to the side. "Looks like it's just you and me tonight."

I glance at Anna, who rolls her eyes. "Irish, don't scare her. Bailey, ignore him."

Shifting in my seat, I feel a little uncomfortable. If I'd known I was going to be a third wheel tonight, I wouldn't have come out.

"What are you guys doing here?" Lana asks Tracker, making me feel better that they didn't know the men were going to show up.

"We were on our way to Rift, wanted to know if you all wanted to come," Tracker says, nuzzling Lana's cheek.

Irish moans. "Just *tell* them to come and let's go. I need a fuckin' drink."

The women both look at me. I guess they're letting it be my choice.

"Pretty sure Adam told me never to step back into that place," I mutter, crossing my arms over my chest.

"Adam?" Irish asks, looking confused. "Ohhh. Rake. Why doesn't he want you there? You're a sexy woman. He should be all over that shit."

"Been there," Tracker says, looking amused.

I throw him a dirty look, for which he replies with a wink.

Irish puts up his hand. "Wait a damn second. Rake has fucked her and doesn't want her at the club? Which means . . ."

"He actually cares about a woman other than our women? Yeah," Tracker says, grinning wolfishly. "Another one bites the motherfuckin' dust."

I shake my head. "How does his not wanting me there mean he cares? That makes no sense."

"Makes perfect sense," Arrow says in that gruff, deep voice of his. "If he didn't care, he wouldn't give two fucks about where you showed up."

I roll my eyes. "You're wrong. And it doesn't matter. Is he

going to be there? If he isn't, I'll come; otherwise you guys can go and I'll take a cab home."

Tracker studies me, a little too closely for my liking. He pulls out his phone, hits a number, then puts his phone to his ear. "Rake. Where are you, brother?"

He listens, then replies, "I want to take the women to Rift with me. That gonna be an issue?"

Tracker glances at me then, those blue eyes looking directly into mine.

"Yeah, I've got you. All right. 'Bye."

"Well?" Anna asks, looking at him expectantly.

Tracker grins at Anna. "All good, Anna Bell, so we going or what?"

Irish puts his arm around me. He smells good, like leather and mint. "We're in, right? Let's go. My dick is hard and I need to find someone to take care of it. Unless Bailey is offering?"

"Ummm. Yeah, probably not," I mutter, taking his arm off me and standing. "I guess we're going dancing."

"Don't say probably," Lana suggests, narrowing her eyes on Irish. "Say no. They don't take subtle hints; you need to be firm. Let him know you're not playing games, which is what most women try to do with him."

I look at Irish, who is busy flashing Lana an amused look at her analysis.

"Irish," I say, getting his attention. "No way in hell will I ever be taking care of your dick. I don't care how hard it is. Guess we better go to Rift so you can find a substitute."

Everyone except Irish laughs.

Lana nods in approval.

Rift, here we come.

EIGHT

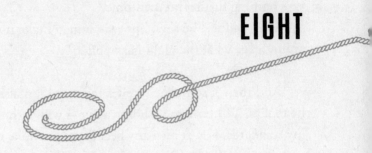

"W HAT'S your real name?" I ask Irish, watching as he sips his
beer. I pick up my Coke and take a sip, waiting for him to
answer. There's no way I'm drinking tonight, not when Cara has
dance class in the morning.

"What makes you think it's not Irish?"

I make a face. "My common sense?"

He smirks, then licks his lips. "How about a kiss? I'll tell you
then."

I purse my lips and wrinkle my nose. "I already fell for that
one with Talon."

Irish scowls, his fingers tightening on his bottle. "You kissing
men from other clubs now? Where's the loyalty, Bailey?"

"I don't belong to anyone, and I wouldn't have even met any
other bikers if it wasn't for Anna and Lana, so you take that up
with them," I reply in a curt tone. Speaking of . . . I look to see
both of them on the dance floor with their men. Arrow isn't
dancing, just watching Anna shaking her ass in front of him, but
Tracker's grinding behind Lana, pressing his penis against her ass.

Not one shit is given.

"What happened to you finding a woman?" I ask when he says nothing further on that topic.

"I'm looking," he says, lips twitching. "I take my time, look around. See what the night has to offer."

"And then?"

"And then if someone catches my eye, I'll make my move," he replies. "If I have to go home alone, I will, rather than lower my standards. I don't own any beer goggles, unlike most men."

I put my drink down on the table. "Has anyone ever told you that you're an asshole?"

"All the time."

"So what happens after you've screwed her? Bone and bail? Even though she apparently meets your very high standards?" I ask, tapping my short red fingernails on the bar.

He shrugs and tilts his head back, downing his drink.

Jerk.

"Have you heard of the term *fuckboy*? There's some new lingo for you," I continue, standing up from the barstool when I hear "One Last Time" by Ariana Grande play.

"Not a boy, lady," Irish replies gruffly. "I'm a man. I don't play games. Women know what they're getting with us: there are no lies or pretty words involved. And when I meet the woman who's meant to be mine, I will treat her like a fuckin' queen. Until then though, everything is a game."

I nod my head, acknowledging that as the truth. "You're right, I guess."

Besides, who am I to judge?

I turn my head back to the dance floor, mouthing the lyrics to the song. Anna spoke to the DJ, who started suddenly playing songs I can't imagine bikers liking. The way Irish cringes tells me that I'm right. I love how the men give in to the women, at least over things like this. And it's the little things that matter.

"I love this song," I say, starting to move my hips to the music.

"You would," Irish grumbles from beside me.

Tracker walks up to me and grabs my hand, pulling me to the dance floor. When I resist, he simply grins. "Come on, if I have to dance to this bullshit, then so do you."

"I like this song," I tell him, letting him pull me along behind him. He stops next to Lana, putting me in between them, then starts to dance. Looking into Lana's amused gaze, I dance, a little awkwardly at first, until I get into it. By the time the next song starts, Lana and I are practically grinding on each other and I can feel Tracker's warmth behind me. Still, he doesn't touch my body or cross any lines. When Irish comes and pulls me by my hand, I go with him, dancing with him without our bodies touching. He spins me around, and even though he's not as good of a dancer as Tracker, he's not bad either.

"Ardan," he says into my ear, making me jump a little.

I glance up at him. "What?"

"My name"—he smirks—"is Ardan."

I smile widely. "Nice to meet you, Ardan."

We dance for another song, until a woman with a seriously nice ass catches his eye, then he leaves me with Tracker again to make a play for her.

"She's hot," Anna says, grabbing my waist and dancing behind me. "Should we get a drink?"

I nod, desperately wanting some water. We walk back up to the bar and order some water. When I hear Anna mutter "Oh fuck" under her breath, I turn around, bottle of water in my hand, and look in front of us.

Adam.

Why is he here? Tracker told him . . .

When I see the woman with him, my body instantly goes on shutdown. On protection mode. My emotions disappear. Anything for self-preservation. How much of a dick can he be? I instantly feel bad for being so hard on Irish, when it's clear Rake is the real asshole here. He knew I was here; he knew. Yes, I wasn't meant to be here, but he could have made this pleasant by staying away. I guess that isn't really fair though: he's allowed to be with any woman he wants; it doesn't really make him a bad person. I think the fact that it still hurts me is more concerning, and I have a feeling that if the situation was reversed, and I was here with another man, he wouldn't be reacting by ignoring me.

How does he still have the power to hurt me after all these years? They say time heals everything, but it doesn't. It dulls the pain, yes, but seeing this right here, rips open all the old wounds. Keeping my expression as blank as I can, I avoid Adam's eyes, even though I can feel them on me, and turn around to face the bar again.

He isn't mine.

And I don't want him to be.

Then why does this hurt so much?

"Do you want to dance some more?" I ask Anna and Lana, who are both studying me a little too closely for my liking.

Don't show weakness.

I have two rules in my life. First, never let them see you bleed. And two, always have an escape plan.

"Yeah," Lana replies. "Are you sure you don't want to go?"

I shake my head.

Leaving now will give him power, will let him know that he still has a hold on me. I don't want that. I should hate this man with everything I have, but I don't, which kind of makes me hate myself.

I'll never forgive him for the past, so it's best to let things be. What I feel for Adam, what I'll always feel for him is irrelevant. It's warped. It's wrapped in anger, hate, and distrust. Underneath all that, yes, there is love, but love isn't enough, at least not this time. What could have been a fairy-tale love has now turned into nothing but pain and harsh cold reality.

"No, why would I?" I say, my poker face being tested now more than ever before. "I love this song!"

I wrap an arm around each of them and head back to the dance floor without looking in his direction.

A few songs later, when the girls return to the bar for another drink, I can't exactly avoid him anymore. He speaks to them, while I stand on the other side, scanning the bar, looking anywhere except at him. The woman who was with him has disappeared; hopefully she left. Realistically she's probably in the bathroom or on the dance floor. When a figure appears on my left side, I know it's him, so I don't look up.

"You gonna ignore me all night?" he asks, elbows on the bar. "I think I'm being pretty cool, since I told you I didn't want to see you here again."

I turn my head and narrow my eyes. "You said I can hang out with the girls, and everyone wanted to come here, and they wanted me to come with them. Maybe you should stop being so petty and just let it go. You didn't have to show up here tonight."

"It's my club," he fires back. "I'll show up here whenever the fuck I like."

"Okay, fine," I say, shrugging. "You own the club, but you don't own me, so why don't you just pretend like you don't know me, and we can both have a good night. Just like I was doing before you decided to talk to me."

"I'm not the boy you knew, Bailey. You can't lead me around by the dick anymore. You have no idea who I am now, and it's only because of our history that I'm cutting you some slack, but if you're going to be hanging around my family, perhaps you should learn some fuckin' respect."

I make a sound of amusement. "I respect everyone else here."

"Pretty sure you weren't always such a bitch."

"Like you said, we are different than who we used to be. You have no idea who I am now either. And I'm pretty sure you weren't always such an asshole," I fire back, then turn to leave, but he grips my upper arm in a firm hold.

"All you better do here tonight is dance and look pretty. You go near a man, I will end him, do you understand me?"

So he can flaunt his women around, but he expects me to stay away from men? Not that I'm on the prowl or anything. I'm legitimately here to dance and have a good time with my friends, but who does he think he is to decide that for me?

"Like I said, you don't own me. If I want to hook up with a guy, I will. But don't worry, I'm not as easy as the women you're used to."

Green eyes turn murky, and he stares at me like he wants to kill me. "Well, you set the standard, didn't you? Apparently I just have shit taste in women."

That line hits like a blow, and I can't hide the wince that appears on my face.

"I hate you," I say quietly. He flinches, but I don't give a shit. "I don't want to talk about anything to do with us. Ever. And you need to stop bringing it up."

"The past is all there is between us," he replies, looking away from me. "Every time I see you, all I see is what was, so how can you ask me to do that?"

"There is nothing there for us in the past!" I yell, turning away from him. "Nothing."

"There's nothing for us in the future too," he adds simply.

I need to leave, to get away from him right now.

Because I am going to lose it.

My nose is tingling, a sure indication that I am going to cry. And I can't let him see me break.

He makes me weak, and I hate it.

"Why don't you just leave me alone? Flaunt whoever you want in front of me—I don't give a shit. All I want is to try to have a good night without all the shit you bring to my life."

"You probably should have thought about that before you broke my fuckin' heart," he snarls. "Fuckin' hell, Bailey. It still hurts to see you. I can't fuckin' see you, don't you get it? Yet at the same time, I can't stay away. Knowing you're here, it brings me here. It's like I'm a sadist or something, asking for the pain of our fucked-up memories. I can't help it."

It hurts me too, and I know it's my fault for not being honest with him about it. If I'm being honest with myself, half of me wants to protect him from what happened.

Okay, maybe more than half.

The rest of me doesn't think he deserves to know the truth. Why should I bare my soul to him? He didn't bother to talk to me, to even hear what I had to say after that night. He just cut me out and moved on. How am I supposed to tell him what happened? How is he going to look at me after? If I say it out loud, it becomes real.

I don't want it to be real.

I pull my arm out of his hold and walk to the bathroom, needing to gather myself. When the girls come after me, I put a smile on my face and pretend everything will be all right.

It has to be.

When midnight hits, like Cinderella, I figure it's time to go home, since I have to be up at eight. After Adam disappeared into the VIP room, this time with two women, I didn't see him again. He made a big show of it, making sure I saw, which made my blood boil. I wanted to go home then and there, but I stuck it out, not wanting him to win, and I tried to enjoy my night with the girls, to forget he was even here, even though all I could do was replay his words over and over in my head and picture what exactly he was doing to the two women in there with him. He's definitely right about one thing—he's changed, and I need to realize that so I can let everything in our past go. He's not Adam, the sweet boy who stole my heart. He's Rake, the man-whore asshole. As I'm about to call a taxi, Tracker tells me that one of the MC members can take me home.

"I can just take a taxi," I tell him. "Don't worry about it, Tracker."

He shakes his head. "We always have someone here sober just in case. You're not going home alone in a taxi, Bailey."

Apparently his word is law, because he turns his back to

me and yells out for one of his men. I hear a rumble of motor-cycles and turn my head toward the parking lot, where ten bikes pull in. Just how many men did they have in their MC? When Tracker and Arrow stand in front of Anna and Lana, as if protecting them, I have to wonder what the hell is going on. The tension in the air spikes as the men get off their bikes and approach us.

Irish grabs me and puts me behind him.

"Don't say anything, and do as you're told," he commands me quietly. I nod, fear rendering me speechless. It's clear that this is no macho posturing—something's going down, something serious. I make myself as invisible as I can, sinking behind Irish and holding my arms around myself. Did stuff like this happen a lot? What am I supposed to do in these situations?

The other men advance until they're mere feet in front of Irish and the rest, who are now standing shoulder to shoulder in front of me and the other girls.

"Any reason you're at our club?" Arrow asks, in a calm yet deadly tone. I slowly peep around Irish and see that these men aren't Wind Dragons. They have a different emblem on their cuts, and I've never seen any of them before.

"Just in the neighborhood," one man says, stepping in front of the rest of his men. He looks to be in his early forties, with dark hair and olive skin. He looks over each man, before stopping on Arrow.

"Yeah, *our* neighborhood," Tracker replies, sounding pissed off. "Get the fuck out of here, unless you want to have a problem."

The club doors open and Adam comes out with a bald guy—Wolf, I think I heard one of the guys call him. Adam looks around almost frantically until he sees me, then storms in my direction, taking his place next to Irish, right in front of me. Wolf stands on the other side, next to Arrow.

I'm suddenly wishing I'd taken my ass home when Lana offered.

"We have a fucking problem, all right," the man roars, staring daggers at . . . Adam? I can only imagine what Adam did. "You don't have enough whores in your club? You need to fuck my old lady?"

Fuck.

Adam slept with the man's woman? Is he crazy? Is this who he's turned into? A walking dick? I feel like slapping Adam myself. When he was with me, as young as we were, he claimed he was always loyal. I saw him flirt, sure, and I saw women trying to get his attention plenty of times. It made me jealous as hell, but I never saw him act on it.

In high school, the rumors of his cheating followed us around and I'd get angry with each one, not knowing in my youth and inexperience how to handle the situation or my emotions. Looking back, I know I added a lot of unnecessary drama to our relationship. I had trust issues, and Adam had a huge ego. Apparently that hasn't changed, plus *Rake*'s life is like a free-for-all, smorgasbord of pussy. And this is the man I once thought I'd marry? I can't help but feel disappointed.

Focus on the issue at hand, Bailey.

I can actually feel all the Wind Dragons look in Adam's direction.

"I haven't fucked anyone who mentioned being an old lady," Adam replies, looking the man in the eye. "If you can't control your bitch, pretty sure that's not my fuckin' problem."

I cringe, then look at Anna and Lana, who are wearing similar expressions on their faces. The men are outnumbered, but they don't seem scared in the least. I, on the other hand, want to run back into Rift and hide. From the corner of my eye, I see Arrow saying something to Anna under his breath and her slight nod in response. I'm too busy watching them to see the man from the other MC step forward and throw the first punch at Tracker. Adam pushes me backward, and then Anna grabs my arm and pulls me back into the club, Lana by our sides. She yells for the bouncers, telling them to lock the club doors so no one can get in and out. Her demands are met instantly.

"What do we do now?" I ask, unable to hide the panic in my voice. "Just watch them get beaten up?"

I look outside to see Adam punch a man in the face and then in the stomach.

"They'll be fine," Anna replies confidently. "It's only two against each of them. They can handle it."

Lana nods her head, not looking as confident as Anna but still standing strong. "They'll be fine. And now they don't have to worry about us being safe, so they can concentrate on kicking those dickheads' asses. Knock him on his ass, Tracker!"

Christ.

What happened to the innocent little Lana I knew in high school?

I take a few steps away from the glass door and wrap my arms around myself.

I really just want to be at home with Cara right now. I didn't sign up for this.

NINE

T HE cops eventually show up and everyone is taken in. With the camera footage from the club, Anna tells me it will show who started the fight, so "our" men will be fine. Sin rocks up with his wife, Faye, who heads to the police station to sort the men out. Sin takes the rest of us home, fuming the whole way about how he wasn't there when "shit" went down. To me, it sounds like he's just angry he missed out on a fight.

"They're lucky none of you got hurt," he rumbles, fingers clenching on the steering wheel. "All this because Rake fucked someone's old lady? I guess it was only a matter of time before his dick got us all into trouble."

I ignore Anna's and Lana's pitying glances.

Adam can fuck the whole world if he wants to; it has nothing to do with me anymore.

It doesn't hurt.

Nope.

Not. One. Little. Bit.

Let him man-whore around town.

Bastard.

"What's going to happen now?" Anna asks, looking in Sin's direction. "You guys going to fight with the other MC every time you see each other because of some unfaithful woman and my slutty brother?"

Sin chuckles darkly. "We'll see how it goes. Them coming into our space is asking for trouble and lacks some damn fuckin' respect, although the men already taught them a lesson, even being outnumbered. I heard their president is in the hospital."

He sounds proud.

Yeah, they're all batshit crazy.

"Did you see the guy with tattoos all over this face?" Anna asks, making a face. "He looked scary as shit."

"I saw Tracker punch him in the nose," Lana says, smirking. "That was probably the only reason why. Otherwise I was too busy checking out my man to even notice the opposition."

Sin snorts with amusement from the front.

Anna puts up her hand. "Hey, I checked out my man too. I also sussed out everyone else. I even picked out a few weaknesses in their fighting technique."

We look at Anna with different expressions on our faces. Lana looks impressed, and me? I think my expression must hold a mixture of both shock and wonder.

"All the men should marry nerds," Sin says, chuckling. "The women are becoming a force to be reckoned with."

"Damn straight," Anna calls out, resting her head back against the seat.

Lana glances at me out of the corner of her eye. "Strength comes in different forms. All of them are valuable."

I don't know why, but I suddenly avoid her gaze.

I get dropped off first. "Thanks for the ride, Sin."

"No problem, Bailey," he says, turning his head to me and giving me a look I can't interpret.

"I'll walk you to your door," Anna says, getting out of the car. Silently we make it to my front step. I pull my keys out of my handbag and unlock my door.

"Well, this has been . . . fun." I cringe, then flash Anna a sheepish look. "I hope the men don't get into any trouble."

Anna sighs and rubs the back of her neck. "They'll be fine. Listen, I'm sorry you had to be there tonight. Just know that no matter what, you would have been safe, all right? The men would have had your back just as they would have had ours. You're family."

I smile and wrap my arms around her. "Thank you, Anna. It was definitely a night I won't be forgetting soon."

"I couldn't help noticing who Adam's first instinct was to protect tonight," she murmurs, looking contemplative. "Interesting, don't you think? It sure as hell wasn't his own sister."

I roll my eyes at that. "Probably because he knew Arrow would have it covered. And Tracker would protect Lana. That leaves only me."

"Keep telling yourself that, Bailey," Anna calls out as she walks back to Sin's car. My smile drops as I step inside and close the door.

If he really cared about me, he wouldn't have fucked those two women tonight, not that I care. Nope. Not at all.

After a few hours' sleep, I get up and take Cara for her dance class, followed by some grocery shopping and a few other errands. When we get home I'm tired and in no mood to cook, and Tia and Rhett have gone to visit her family, so I decide to take Cara out for dinner.

"Can we eat at the same place we did last time?" my daughter asks, pushing her dark hair out of her face.

"Why?" I ask, not so sure about going to the place we ran into Adam last time.

"Because the food I had was so yummy!" she says, beaming. "And the milk shake. And the nice man was there."

Great.

Cara getting attached to Adam is the last thing I need right now.

"Why don't we try a new restaurant?" I suggest, adding, "There's a pizza place down the road we haven't tried. I'm sure you can try all their different pizzas."

"Okay!" she cheers, and I exhale in relief. I don't want to have to face Adam after everything that happened last night. I wonder if he felt bad about sleeping with another man's woman. Probably not. Though if you look at it from his point of view, he doesn't owe the man loyalty, the woman does, and he said he didn't know she was his.

Great, now I'm defending him.

Cara and I decide to walk to the pizza place, since it's so close by. When we get there, I find it has a welcoming, family feeling to it, and am so glad we didn't go back to the diner Adam frequents. I wonder how long they spent in jail last night, or if Faye was able to get them out quickly. It's clear that hanging around the MC isn't the best idea. I love the girls, and even the men are growing on me, but I need to think of Cara.

What if something had happened to me last night? Cara would have become an orphan. I know it's pretty morbid to think of things like that, but I do. I don't want Cara to have no one. With her father not in the picture, that leaves only my side of the family. My own father is dead, and my mother moved away with her new husband. Cara, Tia, and Rhett are all I have.

I push the thought aside as we enter, and concentrate on the more cheerful subject of pizza. The place is as inviting as it seemed from the outside, and soon Cara and I are gorging on delicious slices of cheesy goodness.

"Have you had enough to eat, Cara?" I ask her as she sits back in her chair. It looks to me like she's in a food coma.

She nods eagerly and touches her belly. "I'm full. It was so yummy!"

"So no room for dessert then?" I tease, grabbing my bag and sliding it over my shoulder.

She pouts. "I always have room for dessert."

I grin.

We order ice cream.

TEN

TIA and I intertwine our arms as we leave the bathroom and re-take our seats. Tonight isn't something that happens very often for us, but Tia's mother is visiting for the week and offered to stay at home with the kids so we could enjoy a kid-free night together. After drinking a bottle of red wine and watching movies, we decided we might as well make the most of it, so we got dressed up and jumped in a cab. When the driver asked us where we wanted to go, I realized that I only know two places, Rift and Knox's Tavern. There was no way in hell I was going to the former, so here we are at the latter, enjoying a drink and enjoying the view.

"Why haven't I been here before?" Tia asks for the fifth time, flicking her blond hair over her shoulder and giving Ryan Knox her "sex eyes."

"They're all taken, Tia," I tell her, scanning the bar, just people-watching.

"All the good ones are," she grumbles, wrapping her arm around me. "I'm glad we're out of the house though. It feels good to let loose a bit, doesn't it?"

"Since getting back in touch with Anna and Lana, I've been going out more than I have in the last few years put together."

"That's true." Tia giggles. "It's great though. You can be a good mother and still get to have some fun. The happier you are, the best you give to your child."

I look at her with a raised brow. "I think you need another drink."

"I think you're right," she agrees, standing up. "I'll order them."

"He's taken!" I say, trying not to laugh.

"I can still look," she huffs, picking up her purse. "Nothing wrong with enjoying the view."

I roll my eyes as she walks to the bar, hips swaying.

"Looks like tonight is my lucky night," comes a sexy deep voice, making me jump slightly.

"Talon!" I say in surprise as he takes a seat, looking particularly happy with himself for some reason. I take in his extremely light hair, crystal-green eyes, and all black clothing, his shirt rolled up at the sleeves. Why did that instantly make men more attractive?

I like Talon, I do, but I know that hanging out with him isn't a good idea. I really don't need any more drama, and adding more bikers into my life is going to bring nothing but that. Still . . . It's not in me to be rude to someone who has been nothing but nice to me thus far.

"I'm surprised you're not at Rift," he says, nodding his head at a passing man.

"New stomping grounds," I joke, glancing around. "Where's your partner in crime?"

"Slice? He's around here somewhere," he replies, smirking. "Where are yours?"

"Anna and Lana? They're not here; I'm with another friend. My neighbor, actually. She's at the bar," I say, nodding my head in that direction. When I think about it, Talon is just Tia's type, another reason why I wish we hadn't run into him tonight.

He doesn't look in Tia's direction, keeping his green gaze locked on me. "Rake know you're here?"

My eyes narrow. Deciding to deflect, I ask, "What's the deal with you two, anyway?"

I had felt the tension between them. Adam didn't seem to like Talon, but I had no idea how Talon felt about him. To me, it seems like there's mutual respect between them, but something else simmering underneath.

Talon stretches his neck to the side. "No deal. Just seems to me that Rake thinks he has some kind of claim on you, and I don't want to cause unnecessary shit."

"He was my boyfriend in high school," I say drolly. "And it didn't end well. So I don't know how that can transform into him having a claim on me. No one has a claim on me."

Talon nods his head, looking contemplative. "I think you're a beautiful woman."

My eyes flare. "Well, thank you."

"I don't have a woman in my bed right now," he continues, making my eyes narrow. Sometimes men don't know when to stop.

"So, what? The position is open?" I ask, trying to keep my tone even.

He nods and licks his bottom lip. "I'd like nothing more than to take you home, spread those legs, and—"

"And who is this sex god?" Tia asks, sitting down with wide eyes. She slides my drink to me while still looking at Talon. "Fuck me. We're coming to this bar every chance we can from now on."

Talon grins, eyes running over my best friend. She's beautiful, almost ethereal, until she opens that mouth of hers.

"Talon," he introduces, reminding me that I'm kind of being rude right now. Before I can introduce Tia, she does it herself.

"Nice to meet you, Talon."

She slides her straw in her mouth seductively.

"This is Tia," I tell Talon, nudging Tia.

"What?" she asks me.

I sigh and sip on my drink. "So, Talon, what were you about to say before Tia returned to the table?"

I raise my eyebrow, a challenge.

He chuckles, eyes dancing with amusement. "I'm not shy, sweetheart. You sure you want to go there?"

I notice his gaze going straight back to Tia.

Interesting.

Tia is a beautiful woman, so I won't be surprised if he's attracted to her.

"I'm not shy either," Tia adds, leaning back in her seat and looking between the two of us. "What are we talking about?"

I'm saved when Slice walks up to the table and slides his large frame into the last available seat. "I think I've had all the pussy that's here tonight." He looks to me and Tia. "Well, almost."

I consider throwing my drink at him but decide it will be easier to put up with him if I just drink it.

"The women here must have pretty low standards," Tia throws out there.

Talon throws his head back and laughs. "You have no idea."

Slice smirks, not offended at all. "Don't knock it till you've tried it."

Tia tilts her head, like she's considering it. "I think I'm going to pass, but out of curiosity, what are you working with? Eight inches? I wouldn't want to waste my time on anything less than seven."

I scrub my hand down my face. "You can't ask a man how big his penis is as soon as you meet him, Tia. I'm pretty sure that's rude."

Tia shrugs and flashes me an innocent look. "Just making conversation."

She seriously has no shame.

"'Wasting a number'?" Talon asks, brows furrowing.

"Yeah, you know," Tia explains. "The number of people you've slept with. I don't want to waste a number."

This time Talon and Slice both laugh, their big bodies shaking.

Tia glances at me and shrugs, because she was just telling them the truth. She really doesn't want to waste a number on a small penis, like she did with dentist guy.

"How about you?" Slice asks me. "You not looking to waste any numbers?"

"She needs to add more numbers if you ask me," Tia says unashamedly. "I think she needs a good—"

"Tia!" I groan, covering my face with my hands. "Can you please not tell men you just met that I need a good fucking?"

Tia blinks slowly a few times. "Actually I was going to say you need a good man, not a good fucking. But now that you mention it . . ."

I look to the men and hold up my hand. "Don't you two even fucking say anything."

They both try to maintain straight faces but fail.

Then Slice says to Tia, "You won't be wasting a number."

She looks down to his crotch.

Talon slaps the back of his head. "Lay off, fucker."

"I'm just messing around," Tia says, grinning and sending Talon a sultry look. "But I like that you're jealous, Talon. I think we'll get on fine."

Talon glances at me, then Tia, suddenly looking uncomfortable and making me want to laugh. I actually think he likes Tia but doesn't know how I'd take it, both because I'm her friend and because he was hitting on me only moments ago.

Slice suddenly stands up, his chair almost falling over with the action. "I'll go get us a round of drinks. I know how you good girls get when you get some liquor into you."

"If we're the good ones, how bad are the bad ones?" Tia ponders out loud, watching Slice walk to the bar.

"Don't answer that," I tell Talon.

"Why do they call him Slice?" Tia asks, tapping her red nails on the table.

"I don't think you want to know that either," Talon replies, running a hand through his shaggy hair.

"How come I never see you wearing your MC cut?" I ask Talon, wondering if I'm even allowed to ask about such things.

He rubs his chest with his palm. "Reid has new rules on this place, which is fair enough. We come here to drink and hang out when we want a break from the clubhouse. He doesn't want any shit started, and neither do we."

"Wait, you're a Wind Dragon?" Tia asks, nodding her head in approval.

"No," Talon says slowly. "I'm the leader of the Wild Men MC."

My head snaps to him. "But you know all of them. You know Anna. Shouldn't you guys be enemies?"

No one tells me anything.

Talon wraps his arm around the back of my chair. "We have history. I'm not a part of that MC, but I care about Anna a lot. That's all you need to know."

"Leader?" Tia whispers, her eyes bugging out. "That's pretty fucking sexy."

I take the hint and don't press him further. I give Tia a look that begs her to stop eye-fucking Talon, but she doesn't pay me any attention. If Tia wants something, she'll go after it, and she's the same with men. If she wants Talon, he doesn't stand a chance, and I have a feeling that's going to start a lot of shit within the group.

Tia is in the same boat as me, a single mother, and maybe I can try to explain to her that being with a biker isn't the safest option, for her or for Rhett. I think it's different because I already know Adam, Anna, and Lana; I didn't go looking to be involved with something like this. They happen to be people I could never turn my back on again, no matter what. Slice returns with our drinks, placing them in front of us.

"Is this a Long Island iced tea?" I ask him, taking a sip and making a face. "Do you know how much alcohol is in this?"

He nods, his dark eyes looking almost playful.

Who is this man?

"Drink as much as you want, sweetheart," Talon declares. "I'll get you both home safely, you have my word."

"And untouched," I add, staring him in the eye. It takes him a few seconds to look back at me, because he's still staring at Tia.

"Speak for yourself," Tia mutters under her breath, causing Slice to bark out a laugh.

"I like this woman."

"Untouched," Talon repeats, the threat in his voice obviously for Slice. I don't know why, but I trust Talon. I shouldn't, clearly. He's a biker, and I've met him only once. But Arrow's a biker. And Tracker.

And . . . Adam.

We lift our glasses, clinking them in a cheers.

Talon gently takes the drink out of Tia's hand and puts it on the table. "I think you've had enough, Tia."

"Says who?" Tia asks, looking around, smiling boozily when her gaze lands on me. "Do you want to do shots?"

Talon and I shake our heads at the same time. "I don't think that's a good idea, sweetie."

"You're probably right." She sighs, looking down at her boobs and rearranging them in her bra.

"Her eyes are up there, Talon," I tease, making Slice chuckle.

Talon sends me a *Don't you start* look, then picks up his drink and takes a swallow.

"Should we head home?" I ask him. "If I drink any more, it's not going to be pretty."

"You're handling it better than her," Talon says, nodding toward Tia.

"She's much more petite than I am," I say, watching my best friend. "She shouldn't drink as much as I do."

"Excuse me," Tia says, holding up her hands. "*She* is fine, I'm not drunker than your average bear."

I start giggling, which I tend to do when I'm drunk. "Fuck, my best friend is so cute."

Tia stands up and holds her hand out to me. "I need to pee."

I grin and we link arms, then walk to the bathroom. Glancing at my reflection in the mirror while she does her business, I take in my flushed cheeks and glassy eyes.

Yeah, I should have stopped two cocktails ago.

My mind wanders somewhere it shouldn't—to Rake.

What was he doing right now?

Was he alone in his bed, or was someone else lying in his sheets with him?

Tia comes out of the toilet and washes her hands as she says, "Talon is fucking hot."

I grin. "He is good-looking, isn't he?"

"Delish," she says, drying her hands, then fixing her hair. "I look like I have bed hair, sex hair, but it's just messy drunk hair."

I look at her and grin. "Well, drunk looks good on you."

"Are we going home with anyone tonight?"

"No," I say quickly, giggling. "You and I are going to spoon. No men invited."

"But . . . Talon?"

"How about you make a decision about him another time?" I pause. "When you're sober," I tell her, thinking that by tomorrow she will have forgotten about him. Tia always finds men attractive but either sleeps with them and finds something wrong with them, or changes her mind about wanting them before an actual date can even happen.

"That sounds like a sober idea," she says, pulling me to the door. "Which calls for another drink."

She tries to drag me to the bar, but I take her in the direction of our table, where a woman has found Slice in our absence and is sitting on his lap.

I look to the bathroom. "How long were we in there?"

"Just a few minutes," Talon says, smirking. "He works fast."

"Hello," I say to the woman, who just gives me a dirty look in return. "Okaaaayyy then."

"Bitch," Tia mutters, then looks at Talon. "I'm hungry. Should we go and eat somewhere?"

"Diner?" Talon asks, amusement etched all over his face.

"Sounds good to me," Tia says.

"Slice, you coming or you staying?" Talon asks his friend.

Slice moves his head around the woman. "Nah, I'm heading off. You cool?"

Talon nods and stands from his seat. "Yeah, I'll get the women home safely."

Talon puts an arm around each of us as we walk outside.

"How are we getting home?" I ask, squinting my eyes. Talon's been drinking, and I have to wonder how he got here in the first place.

"We'll just get into one of those taxis," he says, nodding to the far right of the parking lot. "I can't be fucked waiting for one of my men to come and get us."

"Must be good to be king," I tease, hiccupping. "Okay, I'm getting really hungry."

"Me three," Tia adds.

We get into a taxi and head for the diner, where Talon pays the taxi driver, then opens the door for us.

"I'm paying for the food, since you paid for the taxi," I tell him.

He glances down at me with a scowl. "Don't insult me, Bails."

"See, gentlemen do exist," Tia pipes up. "And they happen to wear leather. Who'd have thought?"

Talon chuckles and slides us a menu each as we sit down. "What are we having?"

"Anything with potato," Tia says, scanning the menu. "Fries. Lots and lots of fries."

"I'm getting a burger and fries," I say, rubbing my eyes and not caring if my makeup goes everywhere. "Thanks for bringing us here, Talon."

He smiles, eyes crinkling at the corners. "It's no problem. I actually had a pretty fun night." He pauses. "First time I enjoyed women's company knowing I wouldn't be going home with them."

I roll my eyes at him. "Nice."

He grins.

"Is my makeup all over my face?" Tia asks, looking at me.

"Yup," I reply.

She looks at Talon. "Don't judge me by what I look like right now."

He rests his arms on the booth, studying us. "Yeah, you both look pretty different from how you looked at the start of the night."

I roll up a napkin and throw it at him.

We order our food, stuff our faces, and then go home.

All in all, a pretty good night.

ELEVEN

THE banging on my front door makes my head pound. I force myself to lift my face off my pillow and open my eyes. Pushing myself up on my knees, I yawn and stretch.

More banging.

I see the blond hair on the pillow next to me and smile, poking Tia in the back.

"Someone's at the door," I groan.

She lifts her head. "What's the time?"

I grab my phone off my side table and glance at the time. "Seven a.m."

"Mom said she'll bring the kids here at nine, after breakfast, so it isn't her," she says, scowling. "It better be a food delivery of some kind."

"Yeah." I roll my eyes. "Trust me, we're not that lucky."

Thump, thump, thump.

"For fuck's sake," Tia growls, getting off the bed and tightening her ice-blue robe around her. "Can't a woman sleep off her hangover in peace? I'll get it."

"You're the best," I tell her, sinking back into the mattress and kind of feeling sorry for whoever was at the door.

I close my eyes and am about to go back to sleep when I hear her call my name.

"What?" I call back, eyes still shut.

My door opens, and suddenly the air in the room gets sucked out. I slowly open my eyes and then sit up when I see who is in my bedroom.

What the hell?

"Have a good night?" Rake growls, storming inside my room and starting to pace.

"What are you doing here?" I ask, trying to tame my hair with my fingers. I probably look like utter shit right now. Do I still have makeup smudged all over my face?

Probably.

Great, just great.

"What the fuck are you thinking, hanging out with fuckin' Talon and Slice? Do you want to fuck a biker so badly? Is that it?" he yells, his face going red, hands clenching. "You turning into a biker groupie? Do you know how fucking dangerous it is?"

Tia steps into the room then, looking like a fucking ice queen, before I can even answer.

"How dare you talk to her like that? You don't even fucking know her at all, do you? And you have no say over what she does. Why don't you just get out of her house until you learn some motherfucking manners?"

Yeah, only Tia would tell off a six-foot-something biker.

I stand up and make sure my boobs aren't on show. "We went out; they were there. We had a couple of drinks, then we went home. I don't know why I have to explain that to you, but there it is."

They're his friends after all, or whatever they are.

I look to Tia and give her a small smile. "Give me a second, honey."

She nods, gives Rake the dirtiest look I've ever seen, then slams the door behind her. Rake stands in front of me, simmering in anger, but I'm not scared. He might be an ass, but I know this man's soul, and he would never hurt me.

"You realize you're overreacting, right?" I say quietly, crossing my arms over my chest.

"You have a kid, why are you out drinking with bikers?" he growls, running a hand through his blond hair in frustration. "You saw what happened at Rift. What if something like that happens again and I'm not around to make sure you're okay?"

My heart melts a little at the expression on his face.

Behind his anger is worry . . . for me.

Everything he's saying has already run through my head, so I know he's not wrong in his observation. I close the space between us and rest my hand on his arm. "We were fine. Talon made sure we were. We went out for a drink. Tia and I never get to go out together because we take turns watching the kids. So it was a rare treat, and we wanted to enjoy it. I don't really know any places other than Knox's Tavern and Rift, so we went to Knox's."

I take a deep breath and continue. "I know it probably feels weird to you because suddenly I'm connected to your world, even though you don't want me to be. And I don't mean to. It just seems like I'm suddenly always in the wrong place at the wrong time and running into people I've met because of you."

His green eyes soften but then harden a second later. "Fucking hell, Bailey. Did you fuck him? Because I've been looking for another reason to kill that bastard."

I groan and close my eyes, frustration filling me. "No. I didn't fuck him. And you know what? If I did, it's none of your business. Why don't you continue to fuck other men's women and leave me alone?"

"I didn't know that bitch belonged to that guy. She threw herself on me; sorry for assuming she was single, not an old fucking lady," he says, sitting down on the edge of my bed and pulling me down to sit next to him. "We have a huge fuckin' problem here."

"And what's that?" I ask warily, pushing my hair behind my ear.

Rake scrubs a hand down his face, then braces his elbows on his knees. Finally he looks me in the eye. "If you fuck someone I know, I'm not going to handle it very well, Bailey."

"Rake, I—"

"When did you start calling me Rake?" he asks, something flashing in his eyes that I don't like seeing there. If I didn't know better, I'd say he didn't like me calling him Rake. But that made no sense.

I shrug my shoulders. "I guess when I realized that's who you are now."

He was my Adam, but now he's not. To everyone else, he is Rake, and why should he be anything else to me?

He swallows hard, making his throat work. "Fuckin' hell, Bailey. My life was so much easier before you came back into it. I didn't think so fuckin' much; my life was stress-fuckin'-free."

He looks straight ahead and sighs. "Those were the days."

"Stop being dramatic," I chastise, rolling my eyes. "We're going to just have to deal with this, because I don't want to have to stop seeing Anna and Lana."

"Yeah," he says, dragging out the word. "That worked so fuckin' well last time."

A giggle escapes my mouth. "They're strong women; you should have expected that."

"I know," he grumbles. "Was hoping my sister would listen to me for once." He slaps his thigh. "All right. You aren't going to fuck anyone. Period. Glad we had this talk."

He stands up, leaving me confused. "Pretty sure I never said I wouldn't sleep with anyone."

"Well, you can't fuck a biker without starting shit. None of the Wind Dragons will touch you, and if you fuck Talon you'll start a war. Oh, and if you fuck a civilian, one look at us and they'll shit themselves. That doesn't leave many men for you, does it?"

The bastard looks pleased with himself. Really pleased.

"You're unbelievable, you know that? Why do you even care? It's been years. Years. We broke up on bad terms, and now this!" I say, my voice rising with each word.

Rake stands and walks to the door, keeping his back to me. As he puts his hand on the doorknob, he whispers, "Because no matter what you did, no matter what happened in the past, you will always be the love of my life."

With that, he leaves the room.

I don't go after him.

I hear the front door open and close.

I just sit there, his words running through my head on a loop.

And then, it all hits me.

And I cry.

TWELVE

J EALOUS" by Labrinth fills my car as I start the engine. On my way to pick up Cara and Rhett from the after-school care they go to twice a week, I'm about to reverse when I get the shock of my life.

Something sharp presses to the side of my neck, and a man's deep voice demands, "Don't move."

I put the car back into park, my eyes darting around frantically, but the parking lot is empty as far as I can see, everyone already gone home for the day.

"What do you want?" I ask, my trembling voice giving away just how scared I am.

My bag was on the passenger seat, in clear view. If that's what he wants, hopefully he just takes it and leaves without hurting me.

"I need you to give a message to the Wind Dragons for me," the man says, gripping my hair from the side of my head. The knife digs into my skin further, rendering me motionless. I barely breathe as his lips come close to my ear. I look up in the rearview mirror, but all I see is light hair and a mask.

How did I not see anyone in my car? What is wrong with me? I need to learn to pay more attention, to be more careful. I wait for the message, but as he bangs my head against the steering wheel, I realize that that *is* the message. The man leaves my car and I sit there, shaking. I touch my fingers to my neck, there's luckily only a streak of blood there. I lock the car doors and pull out my phone with trembling hands. First, I call Tia and ask her to pick up the kids, then I make another call. I don't have Rake's number, so I call Anna.

"Hey, beautiful, I was just thinking about you," she says cheerfully.

I stay silent, not sure what to say and still in shock.

"Bailey . . . ?"

"Can you come and get me?" I ask her quietly.

"What's wrong?" she asks, her tone turning serious. "Bailey, where are you?"

"I'm fine," I assure her. "But something kind of just happened. I'm in my school parking lot."

"Are you safe?" she asks. "I'll be there in ten. I'm getting on Arrow's bike as we speak."

I hear Rake in the background asking Anna what the hell is going on.

And as stupid as it sounds, I hope he comes with her.

I'm sitting in the Wind Dragons' clubhouse after explaining in detail to Sin, Rake, and Arrow what happened.

"Church, now," Sin suddenly demands, storming out of the room.

All the men follow him. Rake looks at me once more before walking out of the room.

I look to Anna. "They're going to pray? They're religious? What the . . ."

Her green eyes lighten. "No, they're going to have a meeting to discuss what to do with the situation."

"Ohh," I mutter, cheeks heating a little.

She wraps her arm around me and pulls me in close. "I can't believe someone targeted you. Who would do that? Who even knows you're friends with us?"

"I saw the fight at Rift," I suggest. "Maybe it has something to do with that?"

"Maybe," Anna agrees. "Can I get you something to drink? A coffee?"

I nod. "Sure, coffee sounds great."

She leads me into the kitchen and pours while I sit at the table.

Lana rushes in, a bunch of books in her hand. She puts them on the table and pushes her glasses up on the bridge of her nose. "What's going on? Tracker said I needed to get here ASAP without stopping anywhere."

Anna gives her a rundown while placing coffee in front of the two of us.

"Are you all right, Bailey?" Lana asks me, her brown eyes filled with worry.

"I'm fine," I tell her. "Tia messaged and the kids are both safe with her at her house. I'm a little freaked out, but I'm okay. I wasn't hurt."

"The men will handle it," Lana says assuredly, placing her

hand on mine. I look to the pile of books she brought with her and see a familiar one. "Hey, I've read that book. Zada Ryan's awesome. Her sex scenes are . . . hooooottt."

"I'm glad the three of you are having a good time in here," Rake says in a dry tone as he walks in, grabbing my attention, his gaze roaming over me before he stands next to Anna, wrapping her in his arms. "So, we've come to a decision."

"What?" Anna asks, looking up at her big brother.

"Until we sort this shit out, you don't go anywhere alone," he says, looking at each of us. "And, Bailey, since we don't like the idea of you being alone in your house with Cara, someone will be staying with you."

"What?" I ask, eyes widening. "That's not necessary. Who?"

He grins wolfishly. "Me."

Shit.

"You're not moving in with me," I say for what must be the tenth time.

"Yes, I am," he says patiently, as he packs his bag. I'm standing in his room in the clubhouse, trying to talk him out of it, but he's not backing down. He opens his cupboard and some black rope falls onto the floor. I pick it up and shove it back into his cupboard. He gives me an odd look I don't have time to decipher because I'm already thinking of ways I can get out of having him live with me.

"Surely you have other things you need to do," I continue. "Women to seduce. Fights to get into . . ."

"Shut up, Bailey," he growls, slamming his cupboard door closed. "I'm staying with you until everything is clear, and that's final. Imagine if something happened to you while Cara was with you—do you think I'm willing to have that shit on my conscience?"

I bite my tongue and concede, because he's right. My own stubbornness shouldn't get in the way of my daughter's safety. "Fine."

He zips his bag and glances up. "Don't need your approval because it's happening either way, but good to know you're thinking straight."

I roll my eyes. "You're unbelievable."

"Call me what you want, but I'm not letting anything happen to you or your kid," he says, our gazes connecting and holding.

"Okay," I whisper, wrapping my arms around myself. To be honest, I don't know how I'm handling this whole thing so well. Being put in danger, for just being friends with people associated with the MC isn't something I expected. I don't know how I can be friends with everyone without putting Cara in danger too. I love them, but the payoff is too high—I just can't gamble with my child's safety. If it was just me, it would be a different story, but it isn't. But at this point, I don't know what to do besides trust Rake to keep us safe.

He nods. "Let's get going then."

I follow behind him and say good-bye to everyone. We walk outside and I'm surprised when he gets into a black four-wheel drive instead of on his bike.

"No bike?"

"I don't want to make it obvious I'll be there," he explains. "Plus, I can't exactly take you and Cara on my bike."

He's planning on driving us around?

Just how long is this going to go on for?

With questions running through my head, I put on my seat

belt in silence and look out the window. Rake puts on the radio and flips the channel, the music filling the strained silence.

After about ten minutes, I turn to him, letting my eyes roam over his handsome profile. I wonder if he likes it when women gently pull on that lip ring with their teeth, or swipe their tongues over it. I wonder just how many women those firm, sensual lips have tasted. I wonder how many he's given his heart to, and how many have given theirs to his. Even though none of this matters, I can't help but be curious.

"You going to stare at me the whole ride?" he asks in a husky tone that has me shifting on my seat.

"If I want to," I reply haughtily.

"I'll make sure to return the favor when we get inside, then," he says, sounding amused.

I look back out the window.

Rake

I'm hard.

I've been hard ever since she picked up the rope, rope that I'd love to use on her. I'd tie her arms behind her back and fuck her from behind while pulling her hair. Then I'd tie her arms above her head while I took her slow and deep.

I shift in my seat.

What an inconvenience this woman is turning out to be. It's like craving something that I know is bad for me, wanting it so fuckin' badly but having to consider the consequences of giving in.

The price is too high though; I'd rather keep my sanity, my peace of mind, and my heart intact.

"I like this song," she murmurs, turning it louder.

"What is it?" I find myself asking. When I'm with her I find myself forgetting what happened between us. I don't think about anything. I just enjoy her presence. When she first came back into my life, I had to keep reminding myself so I could stay angry and not let my guard down, but now I've stopped. There's no point, and I know I've been an asshole to her, even though she deserved it. I could be the bigger person here and cut the girl a break. At least, I can try. When I don't think about it, everything is fine. It's only when the past resurfaces that everything goes to shit.

She fits in here, with the women, and even the men are starting to like her.

The thing is, at the end of the day, she's still Bailey.

And no matter what she did, she's wearing me down a little.

THIRTEEN

Bailey

CARA picks up a slice of pizza, not taking her eyes off Rake. "Are you living with us now?"

"Yes," Rake replies gently, chewing and swallowing his own bite.

"Why?" she asks curiously, not taking her brown eyes off him.

Thinking Rake would want me to answer, I'm about to open my mouth when he cuts me off.

"Because I needed a place to stay, and your mom was kind enough to offer," he says, flashing me an amused glance.

"My mom is very nice," Cara says, nodding her head. "I'm happy you're here, Adam."

I wait for him to tell her not to call him that, but he doesn't.

"Thank you, Cara," he says, eyes softening. "You hang out with that boy a lot, don't you?"

Cara's face lights up. "Rhett? Yeah, he's my best friend."

Rake nods his head, looking contemplative. What's going on in that mind of his?

"Can I get you a drink, Adam?" my daughter offers.

Rake turns his head to me then and chuckles. "I'd love that, Cara. Thank you." Cara gets up and heads into the kitchen.

"Fuckin' hell, Bailey," he mutters under his breath.

"What?" I ask, wondering what I'm missing.

He closes the pizza box and turns his body to face me. "In high school. I remember one day we went out for dinner at a diner and these kids were being little shits. You turned to me and said that when you had kids, they were going to be well-mannered and polite, not bratty, spoiled, and ungrateful."

I remember that day. I'd actually said I was going to make sure that *our* kids weren't like that, but things obviously didn't go according to plan.

"She's a good kid," I say. "Best thing to happen to me."

"She's amazing," he says sincerely, watching her pour him some soda in the kitchen. "Reminds me of Clover a little bit, without the attitude. You're a great mother, Bailey. Then again, I always knew you'd be."

I try to swallow the sudden lump in my throat. "Th-thanks."

"You never speak about her father."

My eyes widen. "There isn't much to tell. His name is Wade. When I told him I was pregnant, he wanted nothing to do with her. I haven't seen him since then, nor do I want to, but I think it's for the best. I wasn't in a good place then; I was destructive, and the men I chose at the time reflected that."

His gaze hardens as he mutters, "All you have to do is give me his full name."

And then what? He'd hurt him? I'm about to ask what exactly he'd do to him when Cara comes back to the table with two cups. She hands the first to me and the second to Rake.

"Thank you," he tells her, taking a sip.

"You're welcome," she says, grinning. "I'll go and pour mine now."

She leaves us again and Rake and I share a look.

"You handled everything well today," he murmurs, playing with his lip ring with his teeth.

"I was scared shitless," I say softly. "I'm glad it seemed like I held it all together."

"Whoever dared to touch you will pay, you know that, right?" he states, steel in his tone. "They fucked up when they decided to bring you into this."

"I'm a little worried," I decide to admit to him. "What if they come after Cara? I can't put her in any danger."

"I won't let anything happen to either of you—you can trust me on that, okay? You don't even need to worry; your daughter will always be protected."

I nod, believing his words. The thing is, things don't always turn out how you want them to and although I can hear the determination in his voice to keep us safe, he can't really promise something like that when fate could have other plans.

"Mom, can we all watch a movie after this?" Cara asks, sitting down with her own pink cup. I look away from Rake and I notice soda stains on her white T-shirt, which means she definitely spilled while pouring, but I ignore them, knowing that she likes to be independent.

"It's a school night," I remind her. "Bath time and bed for you."

She looks up at Rake then, giving him her best puppy-dog eyes.

Rake chuckles and touches her nose with his index finger. "I'm afraid your mom is the boss, Cara."

Cara pouts. "Okay. Can I have a bubble bath?"

I nod. "Yes, that's fine. Go and get undressed and I'll come fill up the tub."

She walks off as we both watch her.

"I'll clean up," Rake announces. "You sort the angel."

"Angel?" I ask, raising a brow.

He shrugs and grins. "They call Clover Princess, and I think Angel is fitting for Cara."

I shake my head and smile at him. "I think you might be right."

"Look at us," he says a little gruffly, glancing around the room before looking at me. "All getting along and shit."

"I think if we stay in the present, we'll get along fine," I admit, getting up from my seat. "It's when we bring up the past . . . I don't think either of us wants to go back there. And both for different reasons."

He looks away. "Yeah, I'll just . . . clean up. Where am I sleeping?"

"I can sleep with Cara and you can have my bed," I suggest. There are only two rooms with beds in the house—the third I'd turned into a playroom. "She has a queen bed in her room, so it's fine."

"I'm not taking your bed," Rake says, looking offended. "The couch is fine for me."

"Don't be ridiculous," I say, lifting my hand up. "Both the beds are queens; there's no reason I can't share with my daughter."

Rake stands up and pushes his chair in. "Where are your blankets? I'll set up the couch."

I throw my hands in the air. "You're not sleeping on the couch."

"Pretty sure I am," he replies instantly, completely calm.

"You're still stubborn, I see. And irritating!" I snap. "And difficult."

"And you still like to fight just for the sake of fighting. Still turns you on, does it?" he asks, gaze flickering with amusement . . . and something else. Something I'm going to pretend I didn't see.

I clear my throat. I did used to fight with him for the sake of fighting—and for the makeup sex. But also just because I thought it added a little spice to our relationship. What can I say? I was a stupid teenager. And yet, the pull to start an argument with him is still there. Yeah, the last thing I need to do is fall into old habits.

"I'm going to get Cara into her bath," I announce.

I storm to the bathroom, muttering under my breath the whole way.

Just how long is he staying here again? Having him in my space, and in my life, is just reminding me of the what-ifs.

I don't need to be thinking about those.

The next night I make pork chops.

Rake's favorite. I don't ask myself why I do this; I just do it.

When he sees what I've made, he grins and kisses me on the top of my head. "It looks fuckin' delicious," he says, rubbing his hands together. "And I know it's going to taste even better."

I tell my heart to harden, that it has no right to be jumping in my throat.

"We'll see," I say, trying to act unaffected by his close proximity.

"We will," he says, studying me. I look away and find something to do to keep myself busy so I don't have to stand there and feel the tension radiating between us.

I stir the rice.

He pushes my hair off my neck, and says, "You look beautiful today."

Then he leaves the room.

And I finally allow myself to breathe.

I walk into the kitchen half-asleep the next morning and put some water on to boil.

"Good morning," comes a deep voice behind me, making me jump.

Hand on my chest, I turn around and face him. "Holy crap! You scared me."

"Sleep well?" he asks, but I can't reply because I'm too busy taking in his bare chest.

Sweet baby Jesus.

The most defined set of abs I've ever seen in real life. A six-pack. He has a six-pack. I mean, he always was toned and muscular, but now . . .

Fuck me dead.

He's not too bulky, still lean, but so very defined. My fingers ache to trace each ripple. My tongue wants to do the same.

He's covered in tattoos, and I'd like to know the story behind each one.

Wow.

It's safe to say he's just flawless, at least on the outside.

"Bailey," I hear him say, breaking me out of the trance that is Rake's magnificent body.

"Uhhh, yeah?" I mumble, still fixated on his smooth skin.

"Bailey," he repeats, more stern this time, but when I lift my gaze to his, his eyes are filled with humor and heat.

"You've been staring at me in silence for like five minutes straight," he lets me know.

"Oh" is all I can manage to say. "That's nice."

And I'm a teacher.

I still can't manage to turn my gaze from him.

"You've . . . grown," I say, embarrassing myself further. I point to his abs. "Those are nice."

He smiles slowly. Smugly. His heavy eyes flashing with various emotions I can't decipher.

"Glad you approve," he rumbles, returning the favor by taking a slow perusal of me.

I swallow hard and turn away from a body that should be on book covers, distracting myself by grabbing two mugs and placing them on the table.

"So you work out a lot then," I blurt out, when he doesn't say anything.

I hear him chuckle behind me, but I really don't want to face him right now. I can actually feel the heat rising to my cheeks. You'd think I'd never been around a shirtless man before. I had, just none who looked like *that*. But it was more than that, because it was *him*. He could have gained twenty pounds and I'd still be attracted to him.

"Yeah, I guess you can say that," he says, then steps closer to my back. So close I can feel the heat from his chest. "You look good too, Bailey."

I think of me, one size bigger than I used to be, with stretch marks and cellulite, and have to disagree. I mean, I'm not unattractive or anything, I'm just different than what I was. I'd had a child, and I had the body of a woman who'd had one.

"Um. Thanks," I say quietly, avoiding his gaze. I ignore the thrill that fills me at him thinking so. Why did it matter if he thought I was attractive or not?

"You're a beautiful woman," he continues, and I turn around and look him right in the eye.

"Rake—"

I stop breathing as he reaches out to cup my cheek with his palm. The feel of his hand on me has me wanting to both jump in his arms and run away from him at the same time.

"I'm going to fry Cara some eggs for breakfast, would you like some?" I ask, needing to break the tension between us.

"Love some," he replies, stepping away from me, allowing me to breathe easier. "I'm going to take a shower."

"Okay," I say, clutching the edge of the table with both my hands.

I hold my breath until he leaves.

I should have known how it would be being in such a close space with him, but I didn't realize just how bad it would be.

Even after everything that happened.

The bitterness I felt toward him. The anger. Pain.

Through all that, we still have something, a connection, tethering us together.

I don't like it. No, I hate it.

How can he still turn me on so much after all these years? I thought I hated him, but I don't. He walked out on me when I needed him the most. He left me in my darkest hour.

How can you forgive someone for that?

The truth is that you can't. I might have the darkness buried for now, but it will come to light eventually. It always does.

And then, it will destroy us both once more.

FOURTEEN

HE'S leaning against his four-wheel drive, waiting for me as I walk through the school parking lot, my black pumps clicking on the asphalt with each step. I try to hide my amused grin but fail, because flanking Rake are Cara and Rhett, both craning their necks to look up at the imposing man. He doesn't look uncomfortable though—no, he looks in control. As I get closer I can hear laughter from the two children, and I try to ignore the pain in my chest at seeing what once upon a time could have been my future.

"Sorry I'm a little late," I tell them, leaning down to kiss Cara on her cheek and then doing the same to Rhett.

I look up at Rake. "Thanks for getting them from their classes."

"No problem," he says, opening the door for the kids to get in the car and then opening the passenger-side door for me.

"Umm, thanks," I mumble, sliding into the car and wondering how we went from hating the sight of each other to him opening doors for me.

"You want to stop anywhere on the way?" he asks as he pulls onto the main road.

I look into the backseat at the two eager faces staring at me with hopeful eyes. "What do you guys want?"

"Ice cream!" Cara shouts, while Rhett says, "Burgers!"

"Okay." I grin, turning around and facing Rake. "Maybe we could stop somewhere that has burgers and ice cream. That diner maybe?"

"Okay."

"So," I start. "Just how long is this going to go on for?"

"As long as it takes," he replies simply.

"You don't think this is a little . . . awkward?" I ask, checking to see if the kids are listening, but they're engrossed in Rhett's tablet.

"I don't think it's awkward at all."

"It's just weird how things have turned out, you know? At first, with what happened at Rift that first night, then . . . ? I don't know. . . ." I trail off, looking straight ahead.

"Stop overthinking everything, Bailey, and just go with it," he says, turning up the radio a little bit. "I didn't think you'd ever be back in my life, but you are, so now we deal. Whatever happens, happens."

It isn't as simple as he's making it out to be, but I don't bother pointing that out.

I guess I'll just have to "go with it."

Living with my high school sweetheart.

Who broke my heart.

Wonderful.

*   *   *

"Every time I start thinking highly of you, you keep talking," I hear Tia tell Rake in the kitchen.

Rake chuckles, opening the oven and peering inside. "I'm just honest. It's a trait that's hard to find nowadays."

"You told me that the guy I'm going on another date with isn't into me," she says, hands on her hips. "You don't even know him!"

Rake closes the oven and leans back against the countertop. "One, he didn't bother coming to the door when he picked you up, nor did he open the car door for you. I was watching. Two, you yourself say that he hardly messages you, and three, you haven't seen him in a few days, so has he even called you? You fucked him on the first night, didn't you?"

There was no judgment in his voice, just curiosity.

Tia groans and covers her face with her hands. "I didn't fuck him. I might have given him . . . a little something though."

Rake raises an eyebrow. "Head on the first date?"

"No," Tia snaps. "I kind of liked this one, so I was hoping we'd go on a few more dates before we slept together. I was trying a new approach."

Rake tries to keep his face straight, but he fails, and starts laughing, holding his stomach. "A blow job on the first date is a new approach? Fuckin' hell woman, make the guy work for it or he won't value it."

"I said I didn't give him head! We just kissed! Okay, Dr. Phil," she says, her tone more sarcastic than I've ever heard it. "You've fucked half the female population. But what do you know about keeping a woman?"

I don't miss the way Rake's eyes flash at that comment before he masks it. "I don't want to keep a woman. But they all want to keep me, so I must be doing something right."

Tia sighs and gives in. "Okay, what do I do?"

I walk into the room and sit down at the dining table. "I'd like to hear this advice too."

Rake's mouth tightens. "I'll have to tell you some other time."

"I'm just going to tell Bailey anyway," Tia mutters. "What? Afraid she'll use your advice to land a new man?"

Rake scowls at my best friend. "I take it back, no man will put up with a woman with your mouth."

Smirking, I go to the oven to check on my brownies.

"Are they ready?" Rake asks from behind me.

I nod and pull the tray out with the oven mitts on. "Yeah, they look good."

"They smell fuckin' good." He groans, the sound making me want to do the same.

"I'll go tell the kids dessert is ready," Tia says, exiting the room with haste.

"You had to pick her for your best friend, didn't you?" Rake says, sighing dramatically.

I hide my grin. "She's my neighbor. Fate chose her for me."

I take the brownies out of the tray and onto a plate. Rake stands a little too close behind me for my liking, and when he speaks, his breath is warm and sweet on my neck. "You smell nice."

I clear my throat. "Thanks, it's uhhh, a body-mist thing I use."

"Whatever it is, it's good," he rumbles into my ear. "It makes me hungry; it's delicious."

I edge away from him and take a few steps away. "Well. Brownies are ready; I'll ice them when they cool down."

"I can do it," he offers, licking his lips. My eyes zoom in on his lip ring.

"When did you get that done?" I find myself asking.

He touches it with his index finger. "I was about twenty, I think. I got my eyebrow first, then the lip."

"Why?" I ask him, our eyes connecting.

He stills, studying me, then finally shrugs. "I was looking for distractions, I guess, and I used any I could come across."

I don't ask him to explain further. "I like them."

He nods, eyes now roaming down my body. "Good, I like them too."

He is lingering on my breasts, which are bigger than the last time he saw them.

"Ummm, good," I mumble, not knowing what to say but not wanting to be intimidated by him. I don't lower my gaze, even though I can feel my cheeks start to heat as the look in his eyes does.

Finally, when I can't take any more, I lower my gaze to his lips.

His lips quirk, in a familiar way.

I puff out a breath. "Well. I have . . . stuff to do."

"Do you need any help?" he asks, flashing me an innocent look.

I purse my lips. "I didn't think you did housework. I'm pretty sure Anna said you have women picking up after you."

He shrugs, eyes dancing with amusement. "Doesn't mean I don't know how."

I open my mouth and then close it. It really irks me that he turned into such a man-whore. And he doesn't even deny it. He just accepts my digs and acts like he doesn't care in the least what I think about it. He makes no apologies. At least I was his first, and that's something that no one can change, no matter how stupid that sounds. I'd never even admit it out loud.

"It's fine," I tell him. "You can leave if you like. Tia is here and nothing will happen to us in the middle of the day."

Rake scowls, his mouth tightening. "Pretty sure that fucker approached you in the middle of the day last time."

I hate that he's right.

I look around the room. "It's just weird you . . . hanging around here."

"I said I'd help. Put my ass to work," he says simply, like he isn't a big, bad biker, dressed in all black, like he does car pools every day. I study him. He really is a handsome man. More than that, electric. Sensual. The stubble on his cheeks gives him a rugged look, while the glint in his eyes tells you that he would definitely give you a good time. He oozes sex appeal, confidence, but there's also a goofiness around him that I haven't seen much of since being back in his presence. I don't know if that's because of me or because he's changed over the years. Maybe this life has made him harder. Or maybe he's just guarded and moody around me.

"How handy are you?" I ask, already knowing the answer. Growing up without a father, Rake was born the man of the house, so he was always the one fixing shit around the house.

He tilts his head and raises an eyebrow, knowing the question doesn't even justify an answer.

I push my hair back behind my ear. "I have a list of a few things that need fixing. I was going to call a handyman in."

"Give me the list," he demands softly. "And from now on, you need anything fixed, you call me. No point wasting your money when I can do it for you."

"You don't need to—"

"Give me the list, Bailey."

I walk to the fridge and pull down a piece of paper from the top of it. I can feel my T-shirt rise and quickly pull it down, then turn to face him. "Here."

He takes the list from my hand, our fingers touching. I pretend I don't feel the shock wave from such a simple touch, and rub my fingers together as he reads over it and nods his head. "No problem. I'll have all this done by tomorrow for you."

He walks by me, then stops.

I can smell him.

His cologne is delicious, a mixture of spice and citrus that has me wanting to melt into him.

But I stand still.

He looks like he wants to say something, but then he shakes his head and leaves the room.

I release the breath I'm holding.

FIFTEEN

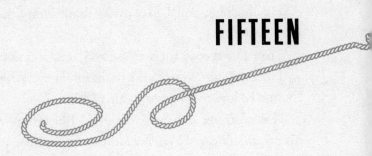

S O," I say a little awkwardly. How does one make small talk with a biker? It's easy with Rake and Tracker, but the rest of them are a little trickier. I don't really know anything about Wolf, or Vinnie, which is what all the women call him, other than the fact that he looks pretty young, has a shaved head, is handsome in a masculine way, and has dark eyes.

He glances my way but doesn't say anything. He's probably still angry I told him I wanted to drive and didn't give in to him no matter how much he tried to intimidate me with his scowl, large size, and narrowed gaze.

"I'm sorry you were stuck tagging along for my errands. I had no idea that Rake was going to make you come with me when he said he'd fix up a few things at the house," I say, nervously babbling to fill up the silence. "I don't really know anything about you."

He sighs and shakes his head. "Not much to tell. Club is my life; the men are my family. I don't mind doing whatever needs to be done. I like to be useful."

"Oh," I say, thinking of something else I could ask to break the ice a little more. "What's your favorite meal?"

He chuckles, and I find myself both liking the sound and relaxing a little.

"You gonna cook for me?" he asks, now sounding amused.

I shrug. "Sure. I mean, I'm thankful for everything you all do for me. I'd love to cook something for you."

"I don't think Rake will like that," I hear him mutter under his breath, followed by a few more deep chuckles.

"He will have to deal," I say quickly, making him laugh some more.

"My favorite meal is lasagna with breaded chicken," he finally says. "I don't like the tomato bits in the lasagna though."

I make a face. "Lasagna with breaded chicken breast? Isn't that a little weird?"

He sighs, but I see his lips twitching. "Typical woman. Ask me a question, then complain about the answer."

I smile at that.

A few minutes later, when I drive past my house and see a few of the neighbors on my front lawn, I have to wonder what the hell is going on.

"What's this about?" I ask Vinnie.

He lowers his head to look out the window. "I have no fuckin' clue, let's go and find out."

He gets out of the car but grabs my arm when I try to walk ahead of him. Rolling my eyes, I walk behind him to the right, until we stop dead.

"What the fuck?" I hear him mutter, but his voice is filled with humor.

He lets go of my arm and I peer around him. What I see has my jaw dropping open. Rake is on a ladder, shirtless, cleaning out the gutters. All he has on is a pair of dark track pants, outlining his perfect ass. I look from Rake to the women, and then back to Rake. Does he not care that he's being ogled by women double his age right now?

"Seriously?" I growl, much to Vinnie's amusement.

Rake climbs down the ladder then and turns, lifting his chin when he sees Vinnie and me. From his face, I look farther down to his smooth chest, his cut abs, and then to the V that leads into his pants.

"Fuck," I whisper as I notice I can actually see the outline of his penis in the track pants.

Even Vinnie looks away, saying grumpily, "More than I want to see of you, bro."

"Okay, show's over," I say loudly, throwing evil looks at the groupies Rake has attracted. I walk up to the man himself and poke at his chest.

"Seriously?" I hiss.

"What?" he asks. "I did everything on the list."

I point to the women who were slowly making their way off my grass. I'm sure snails move faster. "Did you not see them watching you and salivating?"

The bastard shrugs. "They're harmless. Their husbands probably have beer guts and male-pattern baldness."

My nostrils flare. "Get inside."

"Why?" he asks, smirking and running his hand down his jaw. "You don't like them seeing me?"

"Rake," I say in a deathly quiet voice. "Get inside."

"Only if you give me a kiss," he presses, licking his lips.

Is he serious right now? "How about if you don't go inside, I go inside and kiss the shit out of Vinnie?"

Green eyes narrow. "You wouldn't."

I look behind him.

The women were still there, whispering among themselves.

"Please?" I ask, using a softer approach.

He kisses the top of my head, then walks inside, pulling me behind him.

I can't help it.

I stare at his ass the whole way.

Fuck!

"Dude, you and Rake can't stop staring at each other," Tia says so only I can hear, glancing around the kitchen.

I am currently having bigger problems than the building sexual tension between Rake and me. "How fucking hard can it be to make lasagna from scratch?"

I am on my second batch. The top was burned on this one. Vinnie is going to be here in an hour or two and I want his meal ready and waiting.

"Did you do the béchamel sauce?" Tia asks, looking down at the lasagna and scrunching her nose.

I still. "The what sauce? The recipe didn't say anything about a sauce. What the hell is it?"

Tia giggles and starts opening the cupboard. "I'll make the sauce. You get everything ready for the third and final batch."

We finish the meal just in time for Vinnie, Tracker, and Lana to arrive.

"Something smells good," Tracker says, heading straight for the kitchen.

Lana rolls her eyes, then hugs me. "How have you been, honey?"

She glances at Rake and wiggles her eyebrows.

"Fine," I tell her, rolling my eyes. "Dinner is ready. Where's Anna?"

"Arrow has taken her away for a few days," she says, smiling. "Romantic getaway."

"As if Arrow knows romance." Tracker smirks, grabbing a plate and serving himself. "He'll probably just take her camping and fuck her in the dirt."

Rake slaps him on the back of the head. "My sister, asshole."

Vinnie grabs a plate, then looks at me when he sees what's on the menu, shaking his head and smiling wide. "You're so fuckin' cute right now, Bailey, you know that?"

"What . . . the fuck . . ." Rake growls, his whole body tensing, "did you just say?"

Everyone in the room stops what they're doing and looks at Rake, a tense silence taking over the easy atmosphere of a few moments ago.

Tracker stops piling food on his plate and looks between the two men. I step between them and put my hand on Rake's chest. He doesn't even acknowledge me, gaze still firmly locked on Vinnie in challenge.

"Relax, Rake," Vinnie says in a calm yet firm tone.

"I wanted to say thanks to him for going around with me while I did my errands the other day, so I made him his favorite meal."

His body relaxes a little under my palm. "Right, okay."

Everyone in the room breathes easier; I can actually feel the tension in the air clear up.

"Love the man, love the club," I hear Tracker mutter, making Rake lift his head and look at me, emotions playing on his face. I look away, not knowing how to react to the intensity coming from him.

Cara and Rhett walk into the kitchen with Tia soon after, Cara coming to sit in between me and Rake.

"Did you finish watching the movie?" I ask her, giving her round cheek a kiss.

"Yes." She grins, then turns to look at Rake. "Adam said I remind him of Belle."

I look over Cara's head at Rake. She and Rhett were watching *Beauty and the Beast*, because it was Cara's turn to choose a movie. They're slowly getting through every Disney movie ever created.

"That was nice of him," I murmur, not looking away from him.

"I think she looks like Belle too," Rhett throws in, picking up his fork.

Tia and I share a glance. Rhett is going to be the biggest ladies' man this town has ever seen with those smooth lines. I can't help but laugh when Rake bumps fists with him over the comment, obviously thinking they were on the same page.

Vinnie takes a few bites, then looks up from his plate. "It's fu—" He glances at Cara, then starts again, "It's really good, Bailey."

"Tia helped," I admit, shrugging a little sheepishly. "But I'm glad you like it."

We finish dinner, chatting easily among us. As I look around the table at everyone laughing, smiling, and teasing one another, I realize just how lucky Rake really is, how amazing his family is, and he's now sharing that with me.

I glance over at him to see him already watching me.

Something passes between us. A moment of understanding. A moment of thankfulness.

He smiles then.

And so do I.

SIXTEEN

One week later

DON'T think it's too much to ask for you to wear a shirt when you're walking around the house," I say with my hands on my hips.

Like seriously, there is only so much I can take.

"No one's even here, what's the fuckin' problem?" he asks, opening the fridge and pulling out a bottle of water.

"I'm here," I point out.

He closes the fridge and steps closer to me, cornering me against the countertop. "What's the problem, Bailey?"

I swallow. "N-nothing is the problem. You don't see me walking around half-naked. It's common courtesy!"

He opens the bottle and takes a sip. All I can do is stare at his throat, his ripped arms, and his chest as I wait for him to continue.

"It's not like I'm walking around without any pants on," he says after he swallows a mouthful and puts the lid back on.

No, he's wearing pants.

Jeans, in fact.

Jeans that should be freaking illegal.

Low on his hips, the top button undone.

"Rake, I . . ."

He lowers his head. "Bailey, what's the real problem here? Are you as turned on as I am? Because I've been walking around hard ever since I fuckin' saw you again, so if I have to suffer, then so do you."

"Wait . . . what?" I groan. "Pretty sure we had a silent rule not to bring shit like that up around each other."

Rake exhales, then moves close enough to bury his face in my hair. "Fuck, Bailey. Do you think it's easy for me to see you after everything we had and not be able to touch you? I want to fuck you, punish you, and worship you at the same time. I want to make you hurt; I want to take away your pain. I want you to feel what I felt when I lost you, and I want to save you, all at the same time."

"Do you think I wasn't hurting, too?" I breathe, looking deep into the depths of his green gaze. "You destroyed me. You broke me."

"You're the one who cheated, Bailey," he grits out, voice hoarse. "I would have stayed faithful to you until the day I died."

I shouldn't take his words; I should call him out on the truth right now, but I don't. Maybe it makes me a coward, I don't know, but I do know that when everything comes out, it's going to be worse than it is now. Rake will go from hating me to hating himself, and maybe I'm a sucker, maybe I love him more than I love myself, because I think I'd prefer that he hated me. Does that make me weak? Or strong? I don't know. He needs to know the truth, I know. There is no right time or right way to say this though, but it does need to be said. It's long overdue.

"So would have I," I say with such bitterness that he tilts his head and searches my eyes. "I thought we said we wouldn't touch the past."

His abs touch my stomach. His lips move close to mine but not touching.

His eyes still search.

I don't know what they're looking for, or whether he will find it.

He closes the space between us, his lips pressing over mine. I want him to kiss me deeply, like he used to, but he doesn't, and I know it's because he's waiting for my permission. I give it to him by sucking on his lower lip. After that, all bets are off.

He picks me up and sits me on the counter, while his tongue slips inside my mouth. He kisses me like I've *never* been kissed before, filled with such intensity and passion, but it's almost as if I can still taste that hint of regret and bitterness.

I ignore it.

Reaching up, I wrap my arms around his neck and pull him closer.

I feel him; I taste him; I *remember* him.

My right hand slides down his back, feeling the muscles there. I stop just above his ass but then let my fingers roam over that too, squeezing his tight globes. Rake starts to kiss down my jawline and then my neck. When he hits that spot, I'm ready to beg him to fuck me right here, right now. But I don't. Because I don't know how I will feel about it afterward.

"Rake," I whisper.

"Wait," he murmurs, continuing to kiss across my collarbone.

I close my eyes, feeling not thinking, and when he pulls down my bra and sucks one nipple into his mouth, then the other, I don't stop him. No, instead, I thread my fingers through his hair and bring him closer, urging him on.

He slides his hands up my thighs, lifting my dress with it, then slides a finger inside my panties.

"So wet," he groans, biting gently on my nipple before moving back.

When he leans me flat against the counter, spreads my thighs and rips my panties off in a succession of quick movements, I'm torn between pleasure and pain.

The pleasure my body wants and the pain my heart is going to have to handle afterward.

He kisses up my thighs.

"Rake," I say breathily.

He pulls back and looks at me. "Don't make me stop, Bailey. Fuck. We need to get each other out of our systems, otherwise the tension is going to drive us fuckin' insane. I'll make you feel so good, you have no idea."

His words are like a bucket of ice water being tipped on my head.

" 'Get each other out of our systems'? Like what, a one-night stand? Fuck each other and then pretend it never happened?" I ask, my jaw getting tight. I close my legs and shove my dress down, then fix my bra, covering my breasts from his view.

He looks away. "What do you expect from me, Bailey?"

"More respect than that," I snap, placing both of my hands on his chest and pushing. "Move."

"Bailey—"

"I said move," I say between clenched teeth. "Now."

He moves.

I jump down from the countertop and walk to my room.

I stop in my tracks when I hear him say, "You fuckin' broke my heart once, if you think I'll give you that power again, you're getting your hopes up."

He has no idea.

No fucking idea.

And here I am, trying to protect him from the truth.

Why?

Why am I putting him before myself?

Why am I protecting a man who has no trouble throwing what he thinks I did in my face over and over again?

I spin around and stalk back toward him. "You know what? Let's get this all out in the open."

"Let's," he says, looking down on me. "We had a fight, like we always did. You went to some fuckin' party to get back at me and fucked the first guy who looked your way, didn't you?"

At this point, I'm seeing red.

I'm fucking seething.

No, I'm *bleeding*.

Can't he see the blood practically dripping from every ounce of my being?

I'm transported back to that night seven years ago. The night that changed everything.

I shake my hips, letting the ruffles from my skirt swivel around me. Christa hands me another drink.

"This is my last one," I tell her over the music. I need to get back to Adam, because I know he's probably searching for me right now. In an act of rebellion after Adam and I had a fight, I decided to take up Christa's offer on coming to this party, but I didn't intend to stay long. I didn't like going anywhere without Adam, to be honest; no matter how needy that made me sound, it was the truth. Not only

did he make me feel safe, but he's also my best friend. How many girls are lucky enough to say the same?

"You never do anything fun." Christa pouts. "It's like you're a married woman."

My lips tighten. She doesn't know me well enough to make that evaluation, but I also didn't like this bitch judging me. We weren't good friends or anything, more like acquaintances.

"One that everyone is jealous of," I throw out there. Everyone wanted to be Adam and me; it wasn't a secret. I've seen the looks of envy from the other girls. Adam is the hottest boy in school, and he's all mine.

Christa's expression drops for a second, before it becomes a mask. I know in this moment I shouldn't have come here tonight. I was being stupid to even consider it. I throw back the rest of my drink, wiping my mouth with my hand, and pull out my phone and turn it on, about to call Adam to come and pick me up. But then, suddenly, I don't feel so well.

"Christa," I mumble. "Can you get me some water, please?"

"Sure," she says, leaving me alone on the upstairs balcony of the house. How much did I have to drink? I suddenly feel drunk, too drunk for what I'd consumed tonight. I fumble with my phone but have difficulty getting my fingers to work.

What the fuck?

"A-Adam," I whisper to myself.

Everything goes black.

When I come to, it's like I'm in a horror movie. My vision is blurred and my head is dizzy. I'm on my back on a bed. I stare at the ceiling. There are cracks on there. I don't know why I focus on those, but I do. A man is on top of me.

I try to scream, but nothing comes out.

I struggle.

I feel nauseous.

I feel weak.

Through the loud noise, the buzzing in my head, I hear his voice, and I smile.

Adam has come to save me.

He will make everything better.

Only he doesn't.

Instead, he just leaves me to my hell.

This is it. I have to tell him now. Fuck him and what he thinks he knows.

"We fought, yes. I went to a party, yes. I had about two drinks, and then I was going to call you to come pick me up. I didn't want to be there; I wanted to be with you." I take a deep breath, knowing the next part was going to be extremely hard to get out. Rake watches me expectantly, his expression giving away nothing.

"Christa gave me the drinks," I continue. "You know I didn't know her well. She seemed like a fun girl, although I did see her checking you out, but then, all the girls did." I laugh without humor. "I was fucking drugged, Adam. Roofied. I blacked out and when I came to, I was being raped. I was completely out of it. When I heard you coming into the room—I thought you were there to save me. But. You. Left. Me."

I hit his chest with my hand. "You fucking left me! You were supposed to save me! Why didn't you save me?"

Tears start to drip down my cheeks, and finally I allow them to fall. I don't hide them; I don't suppress them; I embrace them. I accept them. These tears, they are me, my pain. A symbol of my suffering. And as I let them drip, I set myself free, a weight lifted at last. I can actually feel the moment the pain shifts from me to him.

His expression crumbles, brows furrowing. His eyes fill with pain, an expression of all-consuming horror spreading over his handsome face.

He feels it.

He rubs his chest with his palm.

Yeah, he feels it.

I didn't want to tell him, I didn't, but now it's done. He knows. The thing is, no matter what, he knows one fact about me. One fact that was always true, from the day he met me, to the day I'll die.

I never lie.

"And the worst part," I say through my tears. "Is after all that. You slept with the girl who drugged me. And you flaunted it in front of me."

"Bailey," he whispers, the one word so broken, so raw, and so filled with pain that I want to hold him, but I don't.

Because this time, I need to protect myself.

I run to my room and lock the door behind me.

Then, I bury my face in my pillow and simply cry.

SEVENTEEN

Rake

I SIT on the floor in front of her locked door, my head in my hands, and listen to her cry, each whimper destroying a part of my soul.

But I listen, because I deserve to hear each sob. Each fuckin' tear on that pillow is because of me.

Every word she said replays in my head on a loop.

How did I fuck up so badly?

How did I do something like this to the one person I loved more than anyone else on this earth?

I think back to that night, trying to figure out where I went wrong.

"Hey, Adam," Elizabeth, a girl in my English class says as she slides up to me. I spare her a glance and a lift of my chin before stepping away from her and walking to the front door of Jesse's house. The loud music hits my ears as I open the unlocked door and step inside. There are people everywhere, both familiar faces and unknown ones. Jesse always throws parties; his parents go away a lot and don't give a shit about what he does as long as the place is cleaned up be-

fore they get home. Bailey and I would usually make an appearance together, spend a little time with our friends before sneaking off to be alone. The last party we were at, we left early and went swimming together at the lake instead. I smile as I remember how she'd stripped down and thrown her clothes in my face before diving into the water.

"Hey, Adam!" my friend Tristan calls as he walks down the staircase.

"Hey, Tris," I call out over the music, walking in his direction. We shake hands before I get right to the point of the reason I'm here. "Have you seen Bailey?"

Tristan shakes his head. "Haven't seen her."

My lips tighten. "Heard she's here."

"Everything all right?" he asks, brows furrowing.

I cringe. "We had an argument."

Tristan grins knowingly and slaps me on the back. "You check upstairs. I'll look out back for her."

"Thanks, man," I tell him, already starting up the stairs. Bailey has been my girlfriend since I first laid eyes on her four years ago. Aside from my baby sister, Anna, Bailey is the only woman I've truly cared for. Today we had the biggest fight we've ever had, and I won't be able to relax until I sort this shit out with her.

Her phone is off, and I need to make sure she's okay. Bailey can be a little reckless at times, and it's not unusual for me to have to save her from some situation or another. She's spirited and passionate, and I like that about her. She sure as hell was passionate about her anger during our fight today. I smile to myself as I remember her tossing her dark hair over her shoulder, full of sass, her brown eyes narrowed and filled with fire. I can't even remember what we were fighting about now. I just know that she has me twisted around her little finger, and she doesn't even know it. It's always been that way when it comes to Bailey. She's my first love, and even though we're still young, I know it's a real love. People can say what they like—it doesn't bother me. I'm not the type to claim love for the first girl I see.

But Bailey isn't just any girl.

More than eager to find her and make amends, I make my way to the second story of the house and look around for a glimpse of her. My anger sparks at the thought of her here, without me, surrounded by all these men. Our makeup sex is going to be hot tonight, that's for damn sure.

"Have you seen Bailey?" I ask Christa. She's a friend of Bailey's, or at least I've seen them chatting now and again. I didn't tell Bailey that the bitch has tried to hook up with me many times over the years, but I've shut her down every single time.

Christa nods, her eyes bright. "Yeah, I have. She's in the third room."

She points to the right. "I don't think you're going to want to go in there though," she says. Her smile has a hint of cruelty behind it.

"Why the fuck not?" I growl, losing my temper. I storm to the door, a bad feeling settling in my gut. I turn the handle, but the door is locked, so I punch the bastard down.

The sight before me breaks my fucking heart.

My soul.

It destroys me.

For a second, I don't understand what I'm seeing. Why would she do this? No, how could she do this?

I don't look at her face. I can't. All I see is red, and all I feel is broken.

I don't know if she's said anything this entire time—there's just a loud noise buzzing in my ears. My feet carry me into the room, my rage acting on my behalf. I don't feel anything, adrenaline pumping through me, my fists turned to iron.

I leave, my body shaking, my hands covered in blood.

I don't even remember how the blood got there.

So this is what betrayal feels like.

It all makes sense now. I'm a fuckup. How did I not see it?

Over the years, all the women, the way I treated sex, was because of how my world changed when I thought Bailey cheated. I cut her out of my life, didn't talk to her even when she tried to talk to me. I couldn't even look at her—it hurt too much. Little did I know, it was me who should have been at her feet, begging for her to forgive me. I didn't trust women, and although I love women, I was never *in love* with another.

I couldn't give away something that belonged to a ghost.

Now she's returned, and I find this out?

Fuck.

I squeeze my eyes shut and allow myself this moment of weakness.

This here.

I created this.

That woman there, I broke her.

If I could go back in time . . .

I should have taken her out of that room, no matter what I thought she was doing, because she was mine. I was a fuckin' coward. I was no better than the fucker who hurt her.

Why did I leave without her?

Bailey cries harder.

And for the first time since I can remember, so do I.

I don't deserve anything from her. How can she stand the sight of me? The things I've done, things she doesn't even know about. The things I've thought about her, wished on her.

I lift my head and lean it against her door, a tear dripping off my chin.

Whoever hurt her will pay.

I will destroy them, one by one.

Myself included.

Bailey

I always get a headache after I cry, and after completely breaking down, my head is pounding something fierce. Wiping my eyes, I sit up and open my bedside drawer, looking for some painkillers. When I find some, I pop out two, place them in my hand, and walk to my door, unlocking it and opening it. When I walk to the kitchen and pour some water in a glass, Rake isn't anywhere to be seen, and I, for one, am thankful. I couldn't face him right now.

I don't know if I did the right thing or not by telling him the truth about what happened, but at the same time I feel lighter. The only problem is, I feel lighter because I shared the burden with him, almost giving it to him. Now he has to carry this around with him too. I know it's not selfish of me, but I still feel that way. I put some makeup on, trying to make myself look a little better before picking up Cara from her dance class. When I walk outside and see Tracker standing there, I know Rake has sent him in his place to escort me.

I'm both relieved and disappointed.

"Hey," I say to him, forcing a smile.

"Hey," he replies, blue eyes scanning my face. "Everything okay?"

I nod and look to the side of him. "Yeah. You don't need to take me, you know. I'm just picking up Cara and coming back home."

He scratches his stubble with his thumb. "Oh, come on now, don't be like that. I'm great company."

That gets him a small smile. Out of all of the men, Tracker is the easiest to be around. I can see why Lana would fall for him.

"I'm sure you are," I say, grinning when he opens the door for me.

"Let's go pick up the angel."

"I see the nickname is catching on," I say before I slide in.

He walks around and gets into the driver's seat. "It definitely is. I also hear there's likely to be an ice-cream stop. I'm all over that shit."

"Is that how Rake got you on board for escort duty?" I ask, feeling a little amused.

Tracker chuckles and shrugs. "What can I say, the man knows his audience."

I look at him and check him out. "I really like your man bun."

He turns to me and smirks, eyes twinkling. "Find me a woman who doesn't."

I roll my eyes. "All of you are so cocky."

"Confident, more like," he replies. "Now where exactly is Angel's dance studio?"

I give him the directions. Tracker fills the car with casual conversation and playful jokes that put me at ease, forgetting about the scene with Rake.

*   *   *

"No, *you* hang up," Tracker says into the phone, as I stare at him in disgust. I pluck the phone out of his hand and press END.

"Are you kidding me?" I laugh, putting my hand behind my back so he can't grab the phone. "You're a big, scary biker. Act like it!"

"Your stereotypes hurt, you know that?" he says with mock pain in his tone, placing his palm over his heart. "We're just misunderstood."

Tia laughs, looking away from the TV to see the commotion. "I might need to get some advice from Lana. Seems that girl knows exactly what she's doing."

Tracker nods and smirks. "Yeah, she does. She does this thing with her tongue—"

I put my hand up, laughing harder. "Okay, that's enough."

"Can I ask you something?" Tia asks Tracker, leaning forward and bracing her elbows on her knees.

"Possibly."

"Is Talon single? What's his deal?" she asks, watching him and waiting for his answer.

I know Tia thinks Talon is a babe, and I mean, he is, but I don't know if she wants to take it further. I know that look on her face. She's interested, or at least intrigued.

Tracker scowls and scoots forward on the couch. "What? None of the Wind Dragons good enough for you? You know Talon's MC is full of fuckheads, right?"

I hide my smile. "Who would you suggest for her?"

Tracker purses his lips in thought. "What about Vinnie? He's a great guy. There, it's settled. Vinnie is your man. Fuck those Wild Men." He jabs a finger in Tia's direction. "Not literally."

"Did you just pimp out one of your brothers?" I deadpan. "I'm sure that has to break some sort of manly code."

"It breaks the code if the woman is ugly," he says casually. "But Tia's a MILF, so he'd be thanking me."

"What's a MILF?" Rhett asks as he comes into the room with Cara next to him.

I try not to laugh, I really do, but I can't help it.

"Yeah, Tracker. Please explain what that word means," I say, trying to keep a straight face.

"MILF," Tracker starts slowly, "isn't what I said at all. I said MILK. It stands for mother I'd like to kiss."

Rhett blinks, then looks between Tracker and his mom. "I don't think I'd like you kissing my mom."

I bite my lip and stare wide-eyed as Tracker agrees. "Just on the cheek, bud. Like friends do, yeah?"

Rhett smiles. "Yeah, that's cool."

Awkward situation averted.

Rhett heads into the kitchen, but Cara stands there, staring at Tracker curiously.

"You didn't say MILK," she announces. "But it's okay, I won't tell."

She then follows Rhett to the kitchen.

And we all burst out laughing.

It's been three days since Rake and I had our blowup, and I haven't seen him since. Tracker has been staying here, only swapping with Arrow when he goes to the clubhouse to see

Lana. Lana, Anna, Faye, and Clover have all moved back into the clubhouse until we know everything is safe.

As for Rake . . . no one has mentioned him to me, so I have no idea where he is or what he's doing. I know he calls Tracker to check up on us. I see Tracker watching me curiously after he hangs up the phone, maybe wondering what's going on between us. The truth is, I know about as much as he does, which is a big fat nothing at all.

"Any news on whoever threatened Bailey?" Tia asks Tracker in a hushed tone.

"I see everyone is keeping that a secret," he replies in a dry tone, then sighs. "The only thing I can say is that it's being handled, all right? You don't worry your pretty head."

Tia throws a pillow at him. "So how come you're here instead of Rake?"

My body stills as I wait for his reply.

"I think only Bailey here can tell us what happened," Tracker says, looking out the window. "But I'll tell you one thing, when he called me to meet him here so he could leave, I've never seen him look so . . . shattered."

I look down at my hands.

"Rake generally keeps his emotions in check—you don't really know what he's thinking until he says it," he continues. "I've never seen him like that before. His emotions were written across his face for the world to see. He'd hate that. I know he would."

"We had an argument," I say as explanation. "Some things from the past came up. Some things he didn't know before."

"He cares for you," Tracker states. "I've never seen him care about a woman besides Anna and the old ladies in the clubhouse. Other women, he enjoys them, fucks them, then bails.

No commitment whatsoever. Nothing permanent. One woman is as good as the next."

Pain slices through me hearing him being described like that.

"I'm telling you this only because I want him to be happy," he says quietly, but I don't miss the steel underlying his tone. The threat. "He's a good man. Always has everyone's backs. Good heart. He deserves to be happy. And if for whatever reason you don't have it in you to give happiness to him, I think you need to sort that out now, Bailey."

"You don't know everything though, Tracker," Tia inserts, standing up for me. "I know you have your brother's back, but I have Bailey's. She'd never intentionally hurt someone. And I know for a fact that Rake is the love of her life. I just think there's so much we don't know, which is why I'm staying out of it and letting her sort it out with him." She looks to me. "But at the same time I'm here if you want to talk about it, whenever you need me."

"I know, Tia." I can feel my smile hit my eyes. "And I'm so thankful to have you in my life."

"Awww, come here, you cutie," she says, wrapping me in a hug. When she pulls away her eyes are shining with moisture. "If Rake gets you, he's the luckiest man in the world. And don't worry about him being a man-whore, that just means you're going to benefit from his experience when you pin him down."

Tracker guffaws at that.

"I don't know what's going on," I admit. "There's so much history, some of it good, some of it . . . really bad." I glance up at Tracker. "I wouldn't hurt him, Tracker, but some of the stuff he had to hear did. But I can't protect him from the truth anymore."

He nods twice. "I like you, Bailey. And I know Lana loves you."

"I like you too, Tracker," I reply. "I'm glad Rake chose you to come here. Thank you for making me feel better."

"I've been told I'm like medicine." He grins, lightening the mood. "If someone's sad, just send me in. Instantly cured. My sheer presence makes them happy as fuck."

This time it's me who throws a pillow at him.

EIGHTEEN

A FEW more days pass before Rake walks through my front door again. Thinking it would be Tracker, I open the door without pause, smiling and saying "Good morning."

"Hey," I say when I see him, quieter and more subdued than my welcome. "How are you?"

He walks inside and looks around, then turns to face me. "Check who it is before you open the door, Bailey."

I nod as he sits down on the couch, then lifts his hand to me. Hesitantly placing my smaller hand in his, he pulls me down to him. When I'm settled sideways on his lap, he buries his face in my neck and holds me, a desperate, almost hopeless air about him.

"Where were you?" I ask him, stroking my fingers through his soft, short hair.

"I needed to clear my head," he rasps, the stubble from his cheeks rough against my neck. "Come to terms with everything." He takes a deep breath and exhales before continuing. "I'm so fuckin' sorry, Bailey, for what happened that night, and for everything afterward." His voice cracks on the last two words.

"Fuck, Bailey. I don't know what to do, or what to say. There's nothing that could make this right. How can you even fuckin' look at me? How am I supposed to look into your daughter's face now and know what I did to you, her mother?"

"It's not you who did it to me," I say gently. I wanted him to know, but I didn't want to see him like this. This isn't what I wanted. I just wanted him to know the truth so he wouldn't hate me anymore, not for him to become as broken as me. I wanted to set the pain free for both of us, not to lay it all on his shoulders.

"You didn't know, Adam. You didn't fucking know. It was a messed-up situation, but it's over now. We need to stop looking back, unless it's to remember the good times."

He mutters a curse word and lifts his head. The pain in his green gaze makes my chest hurt and my heart feel like it's been constricted. In my entire life, I've never seen him like this before. I don't know what to do, but I'm wishing I hadn't told him.

Why did I tell him?

He could have gone on hating me. I'd take that over this.

I'd take anything over this.

"How did I walk away that night?" he utters, shaking his head to himself. "How the fuck did this happen to us, Bailey? How? You were my fuckin' everything, and it wasn't supposed to be like this. I might not have fuckin' known, but it's all on me. I jumped to fucked-up conclusions. I never spoke to you after that, to give you the chance to tell me what happened. How the fuck am I meant to live with myself now?"

I once thought I'd never ever forgive him for what happened

that night, but the truth is, I already have. It will always hurt, the pain will always be there, but it wasn't intentional. Yeah, he slept with Christa straight after, which practically killed me, but he thought I'd cheated on him and reacted to that. It was a dick move, but he was young and hurt, and I guess he wanted to hurt me right back, even though he didn't know I was already broken at that point. We both made mistakes, and it's time to move on.

"I shouldn't have told you," I whimper. "I just . . . you kept . . ."

"Shhhh," he soothes, running his calloused fingers down my shoulder. "You should have told me a long time ago, Bailey. Things could have been different. I would have tried to fix everything, instead of you handling everything by yourself. You're so fuckin' strong—you know that? I should have listened to you." His breath hitches. "I should have fuckin' listened to you."

I don't feel very strong, but I stay quiet, feeling safe in his warm embrace.

In the silence, it's as if I can almost feel what he is thinking.

There is no happy ending for us.

Too much has happened, too much time has passed.

"I want to talk to you about everything, but I'm too raw right now. Do you mind if we leave it for a bit?" he asks in a husky tone. "I just . . . Yeah, I don't really know what to do, Bailey. I mean, yeah, that fucker is going to pay, but . . . I don't know how to make this right."

"Where were you these last few days?" I ask again, taking the opportunity to touch him as much as I can while I have the chance.

"Clubhouse," he says, but something in his tone makes me

think that he's lying. He lifts me off his lap and sets me down on the couch.

"I'm going to take care of everything," he says, both his voice and his eyes lifeless.

"Rake," I whisper brokenly.

I'll never forget the pain etched across his face.

But also, the resolution.

He has a plan.

And, suddenly, a bad feeling settles in my gut.

"Don't do anything," I plead with him. "Please. Just leave it be now. The truth is out there, now we can move on with our lives."

He kisses my forehead, then stands up, facing me. "You're going to find someone worthy of you, Bailey."

With that, he leaves.

This was what I wanted, wasn't it?

Then why do I feel emptier than before?

"Why are the two of you dressed all in black?" I ask as I walk into Knox's Tavern, taking in Anna's and Lana's black long-sleeve tops and black pants. Both of them are wearing big sunglasses, covering half their faces. "Is this meant to be your camouflage outfits?"

They both maintain straight faces.

I sit down and try not to laugh, but I can't help it. "If you're trying to go unnoticed, why did you choose this place? It's one of the two places everyone will think to look for you."

They both remove their glasses at the same time. "We just didn't want Rake to find us."

I blink. "Did you two just plan that sunglasses move?"

Lana looks a little sheepish, flashing me a lopsided smile, but Anna just grins. "How awesome was it?"

"Not very," I admit, laughing. "You two are so damn cute though. Maybe you should buy black catsuits for next time. So what's all this about?"

I'd received a text from Anna to report to the tavern, and to not tell anyone where I was going.

"That's actually a great idea. And you're here because we overheard the men talking," Anna says in a lowered tone. "They caught the guy who threatened you. He's a part of the Kings of Hell."

I sit up straighter. "What happened?"

"He thought you were Rake's old lady, after how he protected you the night of the fight," Lana whispers, glancing around the bar. "He's still a little butt-hurt over Rake sleeping with his woman."

"So he decided to stalk me, break into my car, wait for me to get in, and threaten me with a knife?" I ask incredulously, eyes widening. "What the fuck!"

"Lower your voice," Anna scolds me, leaning closer over the table. "They're bikers. Obviously the guy is a fucking lunatic. Anyway, we overheard Rake telling Tracker what happened. They weren't going to tell any of us anything about it, but we thought you needed to know." She pauses. "But you're going to have to pretend you don't know, or we're going to get our asses kicked."

"What did he do to the guy?" I ask, scrubbing my hands down my face. "Rake isn't going to go to jail or something, is he? I don't know how these things work!"

"He beat the shit out of him," Anna says, wrinkling her nose. "His hands were all busted up. They didn't mention whether the dude was alive or dead, but I'm assuming alive."

"Do you realize how casually you just said that?" I whisper, blinking furiously. I raise my voice. "You're all fucking . . ."

"Badass?" Lana supplies, shrugging her shoulders.

I lay my head on the table and groan, until I realize something else. "What else did you guys hear? I have no idea what's going on in Rake's mind right now, and I'd love to know. Is he sleeping with anyone?"

They both suddenly look extremely uncomfortable.

"Who?" I growl, my lips tightening to a thin line.

Anna shifts on her seat. "I love you to death, Bailey, but Rake is my brother, and I really don't want to be in the middle of this one. I think you need to ask him yourself."

"There's no way to do that without sounding like a psycho. Hey, boyfriend from high school who I'm only friends with now, who the hell are you fucking and why do I want to claw her eyes out?"

"I call total bullshit on the friends thing," Lana says, pushing her hair off her face. "There's wild sexual tension every time you two are around each other. In fact, I based one of my new sex scenes on it."

"Agreed," Anna chimes in. "Everyone can see it. You're both meant to be together, and it's just stupid that you both keep torturing each other like this."

I sigh heavily. "I need a drink."

"You need to have a proper talk with my brother," Anna says.

"He's not ready," I say, and realize that I truly believe that. "He's still hurting, and he's not ready to even consider a future with me. He won't see what's right in front of him: that I'm his. No matter what. He'll never find someone who's more right for him than I am."

Anna and Lana don't know everything that happened back then, and to be honest, I don't want to talk to them about it, which means they don't understand just how complicated the situation is. All lines between Rake and me are blurred. Our past is messed-up, and our emotions are all over the place, yet there's still something there, no matter how much we've both tried to deny it. Something, connecting us together. We can fight for it, to make it work, to strengthen the connection, or we can let it go and try to find it in someone else.

I want to fight, but I want him to fight too. There's something we share that's worth it—what we could have been if fate didn't get in the way. The happily ever after that was stolen from us. It's not going to be easy, but I think that in the end, we could get something back that we lost. Each other. The love we had. Maybe it's a lost cause, but there's a fine line between love and hate. After seeing him, seeing the sadness in his eyes, it's like the coin flipped. I don't want to hurt him. I want to heal him.

"Don't let him know there's going to be a future," Lana says, grinning wolfishly.

"What do you mean?" I ask, resting my chin on my palms, giving her all my attention.

"Sometimes men don't know what's best for them," she starts. "Why don't you just tell him you want him? Be honest. He'll get hooked, lines will get crossed, and before you know it, you're on the back of his bike and the only one in his bed."

My eyebrows rise. "That's terrible advice. You've been writing one too many romance novels."

Anna nods her head. "I think you should just be honest. Tell him how you feel."

"If he doesn't feel the same, it's going to hurt," I say quietly, looking down at my hands. "We might not get the happy ending. And I don't want to play games with him. I just wish he could see what we could be."

"Sometimes you have to play games to win. Nothing worth it comes easily, Bailey," Lana says gently. "Just ask yourself this: Is he worth the gamble? Is he worth the chance of a broken heart? He either is or he isn't. You're either going to fight or you're going to give up on the two of you ever being back together."

"Will you always be wondering 'what if' if you don't try?" Anna adds, green eyes sparkling. "You could end up having everything you were meant to have, Bailey. The love of a man who was meant for you."

Lana looks at Anna. "Fuck. That line is going in a book."

"Copyright," Anna replies swiftly, grinning at her best friend. "You use it, I'll get Faye to sue you."

Lana rolls her eyes, then turns back to me. "What do you say? You going to officially join our crazy bunch?"

Am I going to put myself out there like this? Make the first move? Convince him we're worth fighting for?

Fuck.

I am.

Fuck the past, it has no place here in the present. I don't need the typical happy ending. I just need Rake.

I swallow. "Where is he right now?"

NINETEEN

WE find him at Rift.

The place is closed, only employees walking around the club, except for Rake, who is sitting at the bar alone, pouring his own drinks.

She puts her hand on my shoulder and squeezes. "Eye on the prize."

I stare at Rake's muscular back. "Right."

Anna grimaces, then shakes her head and smiles. "Fucking awkward when the prize is my brother's penis."

"Anna," I growl.

Neither of them leave.

I sigh. "I'm calling in my favor from winning the drink competition. Please leave and don't be nosy about anything that happens here tonight."

"Fine. I'm going," she says, putting her hands up. "Good luck."

I watch her leave and then sit down on the stool next to Rake.

"No bartenders on duty?" I ask, staring at the bottle of Scotch. "Can I have some?"

I need it.

Desperately.

He turns to look at me with furrowed brows. "What are you doing here, Bailey?"

Feeling a little nervous, I take his glass and swallow a gulp. It tastes horrible and burns my throat, but I manage to swallow it.

I start to take another one until he gently takes the glass out of my hand. "Tell me what's wrong."

I notice his hands then.

Raw knuckles, swollen and looking extremely painful. He sees where I'm staring, then hides his hands under the bar.

"Bailey," he continues. "If you don't tell me what's wrong, how am I supposed to fix it?"

I look into his beautiful eyes.

"Everything is okay. I just wanted to talk to you. We haven't really spoken much since that day," I shrug, licking my lips.

I want you.

Let go of the past.

Be mine again.

"Do you ever regret the past?" he asks, not looking at me. "Do you regret dating me at all in high school?"

"No," I say instantly, the truth pouring from my lips. "I don't regret anything, not even the bad things, and especially not you."

"How can you not regret the bad things?" he asks, now scanning my face.

I exhale, thinking of the best way to explain this. "I guess if something changed, I wouldn't have Cara, would I? And she's everything to me, so I can't have any regrets, because my life led me to having an amazing daughter."

Rake nods, his eyes going soft. "She's amazing because she has an amazing mother."

"Thank you," I whisper, then clear my throat. I gather my courage, and say something the younger me would have said. "So here's the thing. I want you, Adam."

"Bailey—"

"I want you more than I've ever wanted anything in my life," I continue as if he hadn't spoken. "I don't care about what happened between us; I've let everything go, and so should you. And I'm not asking for much, just the chance to be with you again."

"Fuck," he says huskily. "Bailey—"

I put my hand on the center of his chest. "Don't even think. Do you want me? It's just you and me. No one else is here; nothing else matters. It's just your energy and mine. Do. You. Want. Me?"

There.

I put myself out there, for him to either claim or reject.

The next move is his, and if he doesn't want me, at least I can say that I tried.

He studies me for a few seconds that feel more like hours.

We look into each other's eyes, unmoving, until finally he stands, the stool falling onto the floor, the noise breaking the trance.

He steps closer to me and puts his hand around my waist. "I'll always want you. That's not the issue here."

Well thank God for that.

I reach up on my tiptoes, and I wrap my arms around him, and I kiss him like I'm starving for him.

I don't care who's watching.

I don't care about anything except that his lips are on mine again.

That his tongue is dancing with mine.

That in this moment, no matter how fleeting, he is mine.

He slants his head and delves in deeper, his hands pulling me closer into him. I can feel his hardness pressing into my stomach, which turns me on even more, fuels my desire for him.

Why did I wait so long for this?

This is a fucking great idea.

Rake lifts me up in the air, and I wrap my legs around him. He walks with me into the VIP room, the same place we first saw each other after all those years. Closing the door behind him, he lays me back on one of the black suede chaise lounges and looks down at me with a hungry expression, his eyes heavy and his mouth a little swollen from our kiss. He's about to say something when I lift myself up and kiss him again, cutting off whatever he was going to say. He makes a sound deep in his throat and pushes me back into the lounge, his hands cupping my face.

Are we going to have sex right here?

Surprisingly I'm okay with that. I just want him inside me, slow and deep, right now.

I lift up his shirt and run my hands up his smooth back, closing my eyes as he starts to kiss down my neck. My breath hitches as he undoes the top button on my white shirt and kisses the cleavage it reveals.

Another button.

And another.

Fuck.

He exposes my black bra, then pulls down the cups, revealing my small, pebbled nipples.

"Fuck, I've missed these," he grits out, before his mouth is on them, gently sucking and licking.

My back arches. I want more. I want everything.

My hands tangle in his hair and pull gently on the short ends.

"Rake," I pant. "Please."

I'm not above begging.

"What do you want, baby?" he asks softly, plumping my breasts together, licking one nipple then the other. When he finally pulls back to unzip his jeans, I'm so wet that I can actually feel how damp my panties are.

"I want you inside me." I breathe heavily, watching as he pulls out his hard cock.

Fuck.

Yeah, I didn't remember it being so big.

No one else I've been with even compares.

He pulls a condom out of his wallet, and I push away the fact that he always has one ready and waiting. Right now isn't about that; it's about us finally enjoying each other, reuniting, without letting anything else get in the way.

No thinking, only feeling.

He slides my pencil skirt up my thighs, and pulls down my panties, admiring me for a few seconds before he spreads my legs and dips his head.

"Need a taste," he murmurs to himself, tongue peeking out as he licks my center with one long, deep swipe.

Holy. Shit.

"Just as good as I remember," he says, before lowering his head again and eating my pussy. I lift up my hips, grinding myself into his face. Does he want me to come right now? Because I am going to come. I lick my dry lips and cry out as the orgasm hits, making me whimper in pleasure and slam my head back into the soft couch, my eyes squeezed shut.

"Adam," I creak, his real name falling from my lips without thought.

He moans, his fingers tightening on my thighs as he continues to worship me with his mouth. I reach my hand down, threading my fingers through his hair and lifting his head up with a tug.

"Please," I beg, looking him square in the eye. I want him inside me, now. It's been too long without him. The other men I've been with don't even count anymore because they don't compare to him in any way or form.

"Fuckin' hell, Bailey," he grits out, holding his big, hard cock in his hand, tearing the condom package open with his white teeth and rolling it down his length. He looks at me as he slowly pushes inside of me, and I look back, my heavy-lidded eyes on him the whole time.

When he's all in me, his mouth slams down on mine the same time he starts fucking me, one of his hands tugging a handful of my hair, the other softly cupping my cheek. The mixture of the rough and gentle gesture, of his perfect kisses and his cock hitting all the right spots, has me more turned on than I've ever been in my life, the intensity of the moment stealing my breath away. I moan into his mouth, my nipples rubbing against his chest, the added friction having me on the verge of coming again. He removes his hand from my cheek, lifts my legs over his shoulders, pulls me toward him, and reaches down between us to play with my clit as he continues to slide into me, now deep and slow.

"So fuckin' perfect," he says between clenched teeth, green

eyes full of lust. "So many things I want to do to you. You have *no* idea."

I sure as hell want to find out.

"You're so beautiful," he continues, sucking a nipple into his mouth, then releasing it with an audible pop. "Fuck. I remember everything about you. This freckle"—he licks the freckle under my left breast—"I fuckin' love this freckle."

I swallow at hearing the word *love* pour from his lips.

He kisses me again, deeply and passionately, and it's not long before I'm coming for the second time.

"Fuck, fuck, fuck," I moan, breathing heavily, lost in wave after wave of ecstasy.

"So fuckin' good," he mutters as I squeeze myself around his cock. I ignore the smug satisfaction in his eyes as my body goes limp.

When his rhythm instantly changes to quicker, shorter thrusts, I know he's ready to come.

I dig my nails into his back, because I remember that he always liked that.

He comes, first looking at me, then burying his face in my neck, whispering my name.

He stays there, holding me, for a few long seconds.

When he lifts his face, for once his eyes aren't guarded.

No, they're soft.

Gentle.

They're the green eyes of the man I love.

Then, his lips twitch.

"What?" I ask, having no idea what he could find amusing at a time like this.

"Looks like the old Bailey is back, huh?" He tilts his head to the side, eyes sparkling. "The Bailey who takes what she wants now, then asks questions later."

I grin at that. "There's no old or new Bailey. There's just me. I've evolved yes, but I'm still the same." I pause. "Maybe a little less reckless."

He laughs at that, chest shaking. "Just a little."

"Okay," I agree. "I'm much less reckless. But that's a good thing."

He smiles, leans forward, and kisses my mouth, a sweet, chaste kiss.

"What we just did was pretty reckless," he says against my lips. "Because now you've given me a taste of something I want badly but can't have."

"Rake—"

"Bailey," he sighs, then kisses my brow. "Come on, I'm taking you home."

He pulls out of me, and takes care of the condom while I redress and think of what I'm going to say to him. Because I've now decided one thing.

I'm all in.

Rake

I don't know what the fuck just happened, but it's like her pussy just stole away all my stress and lowered my guard along with my pants.

Being with her again, I can't even express how amazing it was. I haven't had sex with emotion since her, and after having her again, there is no way I could go back to a meaningless fuck.

What the hell am I going to do? This whole situation is a fuckin' tragedy, messed-up and confusing. I don't see a way out, a way to fix what happened with us, but at the same time, I'd give anything to be able to push forward with her.

The thing is, I don't deserve it. I don't deserve a second chance, I don't deserve redemption. How can I ever forgive myself? I don't think I can, and it's going to eat me alive.

"You're quiet," she says, studying my profile from the passenger seat.

"Just thinking," I tell her, not wanting her to think I regret what just happened. "Do you want to stop anywhere on the way? For some food or something?"

"Should you be driving? You were drinking. . . ."

"I had one drink," I assure her. "I'd only just started when you came."

"Okay," she says simply, taking me at my word. My heart pounds in my chest, because I know that this woman next to me was made for me.

But I can't have her.

No, teenage me took care of that. Fucker.

TWENTY

Bailey

"HERE'S to being able to leave the house without an escort," Tia says, clinking her glass of wine with mine. "Although I'm going to miss the man candy around the place."

I smile and nod, silently agreeing. "Someone will still come around at night to check on us though—Rake's orders."

"Oooohh," Tia coos, wiggling her eyebrows. "What's the bet that it's him who comes by tonight?"

"Why would he do that?" I ask innocently, my eyes narrowing slightly.

She stands up and does a vulgar thrusting move with her hips. "Because you so fucked him! And don't even lie! It's written all over your glowing, secretive little face!"

I burst out laughing. "Okay, okay. Guilty. Now please stop dancing like that. If Rhett walks in, you're going to scar your son for life."

One more hip thrust and then she regains her seat but not her dignity. After Rake and I had sex at Rift, he drove me home.

The car ride with Rake wasn't awkward, but there were a lot

of unsaid things hovering in the air between us. Questions that I don't think either of us have the answers for. So we sat in silence, but he did walk me to my door and kiss me softly on the mouth before leaving.

"Seriously, how old are you?" I ask in amusement, shaking my head back and forth.

She flips her blond hair over her shoulder. "Doesn't matter how old I am—how old do I look?"

I grin at that. "Twenty."

She flashes me an adoring look. "I love you."

She's only twenty-five, but she does look younger.

"Right back at you."

"How was the sex?" she probes, taking a sip of the red wine, then putting the glass back down.

I look up at the ceiling and sigh. "Fucking amazing."

Tia cheers.

And for once, I can't stop smiling.

"Told you," Tia mouths as Rake walks into my house.

"Rake," she says, nodding her head at him, which gets her a chin lift in return. "I'm off. I'll see you tomorrow, Bailey."

"Yeah, come over for breakfast," I tell her, kissing both her and Rhett on the cheek. "Good night."

"'Night, Aunt Bailey!"

They both leave, and Rake and I are now alone in the room.

"Where's Angel?" he asks, looking around the living room before sitting down on the couch and looking up at me.

"She fell asleep," I say, sitting down next to him. "I carried her to bed."

He nods and strums his fingers on his thigh. "We need to talk about what happened yesterday at Rift."

"Okay," I say slowly, taking a deep breath. "I liked— No, I loved what happened."

His head snaps to me. "So did I, Bailey, but fuck. How is this a good idea? And after everything that happened, how could you want to . . . I don't know what to do right now. My head is all fucked-up. I don't think you need to be doing this with me right now."

My lips tighten. "Don't tell me what I do or don't need, Rake. I'm the one who came and found you yesterday. I told you I wanted you. I still do." I pause. "I always have, and I probably always will. It's just how it is between us. I'm done trying to fight it."

He opens his mouth to talk, but I continue. "I'm not asking for anything. Can't we just enjoy each other without worrying about anything and everything? Don't overthink it. Life is short, just enjoy it."

With me.

When his expression remains unsure, I press, deciding to take a gamble on how he would react. "I'm a beautiful woman, Rake. I'm not perfect, but I'm worth something and I have needs. If you don't want to be with me, you need to stand aside completely and watch as someone else takes the place you were always meant to have."

"I told you what would happen if I saw you with someone," he growls, a muscle ticking in his jaw. "I'm not the same boy you remember, Bailey. I've changed over the years, and I don't know if you can accept me as I am right now, because you're going to hear some things that you don't like."

"You think I haven't already heard that you've fucked your way through the country?" I ask incredulously. "Trust me, it's the first thing people tell me about you."

He simply shrugs, not ashamed in the least. "Yeah, there's that, but other shit too. The last thing I need is to get in deeper with you only to have you run scared later down the line. Because you know what, Bailey, if you become mine, I won't fuckin' let you leave. I will keep you, no matter what the fuck I have to do."

I shiver at the promise in his tone. I don't really know what to say right now, because I went to him thinking he would only be interested in sex, like he had mentioned before. But somehow, it seems his tune has completely changed. I don't know why, but I can't deny the thrill I feel at his words.

"You're right to be wary," he continues. "I think you should think it through next time before you walk into a club with the intentions of fucking someone."

I roll my eyes. "Last time you said we should fuck each other out of our systems so we could move on. I just thought I'd finally take you up on that offer."

"You were angry with me when I said that, remember?" he says, scrubbing his hand down his face. "Jesus, fuck. What do you want from me? You should know by now there's no getting each other out of our systems. No matter what we do, or what we say, we're always in there. Vein-deep."

Vein-deep.

He's so fucking right.

He reaches his hand out and takes mine. "With what happened . . . I don't know if I can do this, Bailey."

The pain in his voice has me squeezing his hand with mine.

"Now that I have you back in my life, I don't want to lose you."

He lifts my hand to his lips, kissing each of my knuckles. "I don't know what to do, what's right. But I know that I want you again. And again."

"Can't that be enough for now?" I ask in a small, hopeful voice.

He smiles, even though his eyes don't do the same. "You know I can never say no to you."

That makes me smile, hearing something he used to always say to me all those years ago. "I was your weakness."

He barks out a laugh. "You still are."

We both go silent, studying each other, the air thickening between us. When Rake stands and leads me to my bedroom, I follow him eagerly. Locking the door behind him, he switches the light on, then turns around to face me. I kind of wish he'd kept the light off, so he can't see my every flaw, the marks on my stomach and my imperfect body, but at the same time, this is me. And he needs to want me as I am, not as I was.

"Undress," he commands.

I swallow hard. His dominance turns me on, but it also makes me want to push him.

To disobey.

To test him.

He wasn't commanding like this before, but he was just a boy then.

Now he's all man.

"And if I don't?" I ask, arching an eyebrow.

He inhales deeply, nostrils flaring. "But you will, won't you? Or you won't get what you want."

"And what is it you think I want?" I ask boldly, taking a step back toward the bed. Rake prowls forward, closing the space between us.

He slides his cut off, placing it on the end of the bed, then pulls his T-shirt up and over him in that sexy way men do, with his arms crossing each other. "You want to be fucked. You want to come. You want me."

He's right, of course. I do want all of that.

But I also know that no matter what, he will give it to me.

I check out his perfectly toned body, then look down at his jeans.

"Keep going," I demand.

Rake raises an eyebrow, his lip twitching in amusement, but he does as he's told, unbuttoning his jeans, then sliding them down his muscled thighs. He's left standing in a pair of black boxer shorts, which have me sinking my teeth into my lower lip.

He's so sexy, it's unbelievable.

No one will ever compare, no one.

"Undress, Bailey," he repeats, and this time I listen, sliding the straps off my dress and letting it fall to the floor. I take off my bra, and let it do the same. My hands automatically cover my stomach, without me even realizing it.

"Hands to your sides," he says huskily. "Do you know how beautiful you are? I don't care if you have a few marks on your body. You should wear them proudly."

I drop my hands.

Did he really mean that?

He could get any woman he wanted, but it's me he's looking at like that, like he wants to devour me.

"Baby, take those panties off," he says, licking his lips. "And get on the bed on your stomach."

I remove my black lace panties, the ones I put on just in case this happened tonight, and get on the bed, lying flat on my tummy, just as he told me.

"Good girl," he praises, climbing on the bed himself and putting his hands on my hips. "Now get up on your knees."

I lift up on the bed with my hands and my knees at the same time.

"Beautiful," he murmurs. When I suddenly feel his tongue on me from behind, my whole body jerks. He slaps my ass. "Stay still and let me eat this pretty pussy."

I stay still.

Biting the pillow and making sounds I don't think I've ever made before, I wait in one place as Rake licks my clit and my center in a rhythm that has me wanting to scream. A few seconds later, I do, my thighs shaking uncontrollably as I come all over his mouth. He holds me in place while ringing the last of the orgasm out of me, until I plead with him to stop. He lets me gently drop on my tummy, then rolls me over and smiles down at me, heat filling his eyes.

"Can't stop, Bailey." He kisses my ear, then says, "We're only just beginning."

TWENTY-ONE

A RE you sure I look okay?" I ask Anna again, squinting at myself in her mirror. The black skirt is shorter than I'd usually wear, the black top tight in all the right places. Paired with knee-high boots, I look sexy, but also like I might fit in on a street corner.

"It's a biker party," she replies, checking me out from head to toe. "We'll be wearing the most out of everyone there, trust me."

"Not very reassuring." I sigh, pulling at the skirt. "Whose idea was this again?"

"I think it was yours," Lana says, giggling. "You said to make you look so sexy Rake won't be able to take his eyes off you, so we did."

"I'm going to curl your hair and give it a little volume," Anna says, pulling out a curling wand from the top drawer. "Sex hair."

I sit on the bed and listen to "2 On" by Tinashe as she gives me the "sex hair." Lana comes out of the bathroom looking stunning in a black dress, her dark hair piled on top of her head and her lips a sexy fire-engine red. I've gone with a darker crimson, one that complements my complexion.

"Almost done," Anna says, fiddling with my hair. "Are you drinking tonight?"

"I'll have a drink or two," I tell her. "I really have no idea what to expect."

"Men from other chapters of the Wind Dragons will be here," she says, letting a curl fall around my face. "Some of their women, maybe, but usually not. There will be lots of other women here just looking for a man to fuck. Our men will be here, of course, keeping a close eye on us. But the bottom line is, it's a party. Food, music, mingling."

"But biker-style?" I ask, wide-eyed.

The women both laugh at that and repeat after me. "Biker-style."

"You two better not leave me alone all night," I grumble, looking down at my boots and second-guessing them for the millionth time.

"We won't," Anna says, leaning down and facing me, checking out my hair. "And neither will Rake, especially with you looking like this."

She straightens up and wolf whistles, making me grin.

"I'm going to go see what Tracker is up to," Lana says, smacking her lips together. "I'll be back."

Anna and I share a glance.

"She's so getting fucked," I blurt out, making Anna laugh and fall back on her bed.

"Yeah she is," she says, touching her dead-straight blond hair. "I wonder what Arrow is up to."

"Oh, hell no," I instantly say, jumping on her and pinning her to the bed. "You're so not leaving me."

"Stop cock-blocking me, Bailey!" she yells playfully. "Let me go find my man and his huge cock!"

She rolls me on my back and straddles me. I'm about to push her ass off and teach her a lesson when a throat is cleared. We both look to the door to see Arrow and Rake standing there, wearing completely different expressions. Arrow looks . . . a little turned on, while Rake looks just plain confused.

"Any other woman, Bailey," he says in exasperation, shaking his head. "Pick any other woman to do this with, please, I'm fuckin' begging you."

Arrow throws his head back and laughs, and I just watch him, because I don't think I've ever seen him laugh before. When even Rake gives him a sideways glance, I figure I'm not the only one.

"I'm not complaining," Arrow says gruffly, then looks to Anna. "Bragging to everyone about my huge cock, babe? Don't want to make all the other men feel bad, do you?"

Rake flashes Arrow a look, but then focuses his attention back to me. "Are you two done here?"

Anna slides off the bed, then I do the same, flashing everyone in the minuscule skirt I'm wearing.

Anna, being the good friend she is, laughs and says, "Sexy red panties."

I'm about to tell her to shut up when she stands closer to me and whispers, "Definitely looks like sex hair now."

I grin.

She returns it, then takes off with Arrow, leaving Rake and me alone in their room.

"I want to be inside you right now," he murmurs, giving me

a slow once-over. "Do you know how good you look? Good enough to eat. Fuck, I'm gonna be fighting with all the men tonight."

I close the space between us and rest my hand on his chest. "Thank you."

"We need to get out of my sister's room right now, because us fucking in here is downright creepy."

He wraps his arm around my shoulder and leads me outside. Glancing down at me, he says, "Welcome to my world."

The question is, will I survive it?

"Is that woman stripping just because she can?" I ask Faye with wide eyes, unable to look away from the woman's bared nipples.

Faye laughs, her wavy auburn hair flying around her face. "These women will do anything for some attention from our men. Ignore them. Although they are some pretty good boobs, right? They have to be fake." She shoves a fry in her mouth and tilts her head, still staring at the woman's breasts. "Her nipples are really perky."

Having no idea what to say to that, I blurt out the first thing that comes to my mind. "You smell like cherry blossoms."

She grins and nods. "My body lotion. It's the shit, right?"

Faye's a beautiful woman, and even though she's the most powerful woman in here, she doesn't throw that around. She's always cracking jokes and making light of situations, and although I wouldn't want to get on her bad side, she's been nothing but nice to me from the get-go.

"So you and Rake, huh?" she says absently, her eyes now on

Sin. "'Bout time that happened. You guys were eye-fucking each other every time I saw you."

I laugh at that, shifting in my seat. "Yeah, I guess it is about time. But it's more complicated than anyone knows. I mean, yeah, things are okay for now, but I don't really know what's going to happen in the long run."

"Nothing worth having is easy, Bails," she says. "Sin and I didn't have it easy. Anna and Arrow probably had it the worst. Tracker and Lana had to fight for each other. But in the end it's all worth it. And people might say Rake is the sluttiest out of the men, and between you and me, well, he is." She shrugs unapologetically. "But I think if you get his heart, he will be the most loyal, devoted man you could ask for."

I'm about to reply when she says, "Oooh, look, her pants are coming off now!"

"Do you care if Sin looks?" I ask curiously, watching the woman now dance around the garden in nothing but a G-string. No shame whatsoever.

"Sin might glance that way," Faye says, a smug look on her face. "But that's all he will do. He knows what he has, and he won't do anything to ruin that. He wouldn't survive if he lost me. And to be completely honest, I trust him. I know he won't cheat."

"The way he looks at you," I admit, looking down at my lap. "I want that. Relationship goals."

Faye touches my shoulder. "You already have that, sweetie—the look is just a little guarded and unsure right now. You just need to work it out with him. And for the record, I'm happy with his pick. All the men have picked awesome chicks, and it really makes my life easier."

We both share a smile at that.

"Now," she says. "It's your turn to deal with this shit, because we've all been there."

"Deal with what?"

She nods her head, and I look in that direction, to where a woman is talking with Rake, her hand on his chest, just like I had mine not even an hour ago.

"Who is that bitch?" I growl, rising from my seat.

Faye grabs my hand. "Don't go up there. I have a better idea."

I don't like the mischievous, scheming look on her pretty face, but she's the president's wife, surely she knows what she's talking about, right?

"What?" I ask, my blood boiling as I see the woman step closer to him, and him do nothing about it.

Nothing.

He invited me to this damn orgy party! Or whatever it's called!

"I'm going to kill him."

Faye gets in front of me, blocking my view. "Acting out right now isn't going to teach him anything, and you're both still in that unsure stage. Do you want to come off as jealous and crazy?"

"No," I grumble quietly, exhaling.

"So can you go up there and make a scene about this? I mean technically he's not yours, and he's just talking to her," she continues, giving me a look that says, *Do you see where I'm going with this?*

"What do I do?" I ask, feeling frustrated and unsure. I don't know my place here. All I know is that I don't want Rake flirting with someone else right in front of me.

"See that man over there?" she asks, discreetly pointing to a handsome dark-haired man standing in the corner alone, drink in hand.

"Yeah?"

"I saw him checking you out before. You should go and say hello," she suggests, winking at me.

"Faye, I don't think—"

"Trust me, Bails. Do it. Now."

My eyes widen at her commanding tone.

Okay, if she thinks this is what I should do, then why not? She knows this lifestyle, not me.

I hold out my hand and she slides her drink in it. I tip it back, letting the alcohol slide down my throat.

Liquid courage.

I need some of that right now.

"Go get him, tiger!" she cheers, doing a little dance in her chair. "What's your opening line going to be? Ask him if he wants to go halves on a baby!" She throws her head back and laughs. "Come on, that's some funny shit."

Where does she come up with this?

I block out Faye and walk toward the man, who is currently avoiding eye contact with anyone around him. He's dressed in a white T-shirt, worn light jeans, and heavy biker boots.

"Uhh, hello," I say, smiling sweetly.

Yeah, I'm smooth.

"Hey." He grins, making me instantly relax, his gorgeous baby-blue eyes making me melt a little.

"I'm Bailey," I say, standing next to him and leaning against the wall. "Why are you standing here alone?"

"Just people-watching" is his reply. "I don't really like crowds."

I suddenly feel really bad, because this guy is totally nice and I'm about to involve him in some party bullshit by trying to even the field with Rake. Feeling stupid, I'm about to say 'bye and walk away when Rake walks up to us.

"Demon," he says to the man, eyes hard.

Demon?

"Why is your name Demon?" I ask, ignoring Rake. "You seem like a nice guy to me."

Demon laughs, eyes dancing with amusement, but Rake on the other hand doesn't look pleased at all. He pulls me into him, my back to his front, and pushes my hair to the side. He then kisses my neck. "Let's go inside. Now."

"Not yet, I'm still—"

"Bailey, now," he growls into my ear. When I don't move, he walks in front of me, pulling me by my hand until we reach his room.

"Why the fuck are you talking to that guy?" he asks as soon as the door is shut. "I told you not to fuckin' talk to any of the men. One second you're sitting with Faye, the next you're . . ."

He trails off, then looks at me suspiciously, then his eyes widen with realization. He sits down on the bed and pulls me onto his lap. "I wasn't going to do anything with that woman. I'm not going to fuck anyone else, Bailey, not while we're . . . whatever we are."

"She had her hand on you," I say without emotion.

"Yeah, she did," he agrees, rubbing the back of my neck with his palm. "Look, here's the truth, all right? I was fuckin' her before; I'm not now. I didn't want to be a dick to her in front of everyone, but I told her that I'm with someone now and I'm not interested."

I shouldn't be surprised he was sleeping with her, but that doesn't mean it doesn't hurt. I push it aside, because there's nothing I can do about it, and there's no point in me reacting over it.

"Okay," I say, brows furrowing. "I didn't like seeing her hands on you."

"I didn't think anything of it," he admits, kissing my cheek. "But I should have. I'll take better care of you. I haven't been with anyone since you came back into my life, Bailey. Even that night at Rift, I took those two women into the VIP room, but I didn't touch them. I was watching you on the fuckin' cameras, while the two of them danced and drank in the corner. When they tried to touch me, I told them that it wasn't gonna happen."

"Really?" I ask, eyes widening.

"Yeah, really. Look, I know we're still figuring out shit, but I'm not gonna be fuckin' anyone else, okay?" He pauses. "And you sure as fuck won't be even looking at anyone else."

"So, we're exclusive?" I ask, nudging him with my elbow, lightening the mood.

He grins and nods. "Yeah. And I won't leave your side for the rest of the night, okay? Where are Anna and Lana, anyway?"

"They went for a ride with their men. Faye said she'd stay with me."

I sink into his body and wrap my arms around his neck.

"Do you want to go for a ride too?" he asks me. "I love having you on the back of my bike."

I lift my head up, beaming. "Can we? I'd love that."

I trust Rake, and I know that he'll keep me safe.

"Yeah, come on, let's go," he says, gently pushing forward. "And, Bailey," he suddenly warns.

"Yeah?" I reply in a small, innocent voice.

"Don't listen to Faye's advice again about stuff like this. I love her but she's . . . well, she's Faye."

I hide my smile in his neck.

TWENTY-TWO

SHOULD be a matchmaker," Faye tells me when I return to my seat after our ride. Rake sits down next to us and flashes Faye an unimpressed look.

"What?" she asks innocuously. She even bats her eyelashes. "Nothing wrong with some innocent casual conversation."

Rake shakes his head. "Sin deserves a medal. He's a fuckin' saint."

"Hey," Faye says, sounding offended. "He's the lucky one. I'm a catch, and everyone here knows it."

Sin walks over just as she finishes her sentence. "'Course you are," he says simply. "Now, come show your man some attention instead of planting any more terrible ideas in Bailey's head."

"You saw that, did you?" Faye grimaces, wrinkling her nose. "Who is that guy anyway? I've never seen him before and he's a total babe."

"You should see his eyes close up," I add, sighing dreamily. "The lightest blue I've ever seen. Like the oceans of some tropical paradise. Like—"

"We get it, Bailey," Rake growls, tugging on one of my curls.

Sin slaps Rake's back affectionately, as if to say *Good luck*, and then all but drags his wife inside.

I see Faye wave to Demon, who shakes his head in amusement.

"Unless you want him to get his ass kicked, I suggest you stop looking at him," Rake says in a neutral tone, but his green eyes are hard and dead serious.

I roll my eyes but don't look in his direction again. "You aren't drinking?"

He shakes his head. "Nope. Need to be sober for tonight."

"What's tonight?" I ask dubiously, not liking the glint that just entered his eyes.

"We fuckin' tonight?" he asks crudely, gently rubbing his finger along my collarbone.

"Ummm, yeah?"

Well, I sure hope so.

"Then I'm not drinking," he says, pressing a kiss to my temple. "I can't wait to be inside you. Maybe we should just leave now."

"Not yet," I find myself saying. "I haven't even eaten yet, and the barbecue smells good."

"Come on," Rake says, standing up and offering me his hand. "Let's feed you then."

We walk hand in hand up to where the prospects are at the grill along with a few of the women. Tracker, Lana, Arrow, and Anna return from their ride and join us for eating and drinking.

"Look at you," Tracker teases, eyeing my boots. "Lana, you need to get a pair of 'fuck me' boots like these."

Lana and I share an amused look, because the boots are actually hers—I'm just borrowing them for the night.

"I'll get right on that," she replies, sitting on his lap and wrapping her arms around him.

When I see Amethyst, the girl I first went to Rift with, hanging on to one of the bikers, I look away, hoping she doesn't see me. I never saw her again after that night, although she messaged a few times asking if I wanted to go out again. In one of the messages, she said she's dating a biker and wanted to know if I wanted to go to one of their parties. It must be the man she left with that night. She didn't even check to see if I made it home or was dead in a ditch somewhere, and there is no way I want to be friends with someone like that.

"Who's the guy that girl is with?" I ask Anna discreetly, nodding my head toward Amethyst.

"That's Pill," Anna replies, watching them. "He prospected here but then left to the Channon chapter. I haven't really spoken to him before but heard he's pretty shady. Why?"

"I just kind of know that girl is all. She's the one I came to Rift with that night when I first saw you. I haven't seen her since though, and I kind of don't want to," I admit, grimacing.

And Channon? What a small world, since that's where Cara's dad lives. A feeling of unease spreads through me at that thought, as her dad is the last person I'd want to see.

"I'm glad you've upgraded your friends," Anna says with a straight face.

"Me too." I laugh. "Then again, if she didn't take me out with her that night, I wouldn't be sitting here right now with you guys."

Anna holds up her drink. "To fate!"

Everyone cheers.

Irish, Vinnie, Ronan, and Trace join us at our table. When

Vinnie brings a handful of shot glasses and two bottles, one gin and one whiskey, I can tell the night is going to get a little crazy.

When those bottles are empty in just a few minutes, I *know* it's going to get crazy. Lana and I head into the kitchen to get more alcohol, and she makes me a vodka tonic.

I take a sip and tell her I like it. I've never tried tonic before, and I didn't think I would like it.

"Told you," she says, making herself a gin and tonic and putting a slice of cucumber in it.

"Cucumber?"

"Yeah," she says. "It gives it a fresh taste. I really like it."

She then shoves one of the extra slices in her mouth. "How're things with Rake? You two look really cute and couple-like."

I take a sip of my drink before I reply. "I have no idea what's going on, neither of us do, but I'm just enjoying the now. I like being with him. I'm trying to forget the past shit and move forward, you know? I don't want to keep looking back forever; it doesn't help or fix anything. Time to let it all go and move forward." I pause. "And I'm really, really enjoying the sex."

We both share a cheeky grin.

Lana eyes me, opens her mouth, then closes it.

"What?" I ask, knowing she wants to ask something.

"It's just . . . I've heard a few things about Rake in bed. Are they true?" she asks, her cheeks flushing a little.

"What have you heard?" I ask, leaning my hip against the kitchen countertop.

"Just that he has a thing for tying women up, binding their hands and stuff," she says, shrugging. "Also that he can be kind of dominant and generally has more than one—"

Vinnie walks up to us, interrupting the discussion and whatever Lana was about to say.

"How many women does it take to get the alcohol from the kitchen?" he asks, a smirk on his face.

"How many?" Lana asks, raising an eyebrow and silently daring him to continue.

"More than two, clearly," he says, grabbing a bottle in each hand. Lana eats another slice of cucumber, and Vinnie opens his mouth, silently asking for one. She pops it in his mouth, and he chews slowly. "Having a good time tonight, Bails?"

Looks like another nickname was catching on in the club.

"Yeah," I say, nodding my head. "I think because I've already spent time with so many people here, it's actually pretty cool." I make a face. "Besides the women trying to get my man."

Vinnie grins wolfishly. "Your man, hey? This shit official now?"

Warmth rushes up my neck. "Well, no, but you know . . ."

"No, I don't," he says, clearly enjoying watching me squirm. "Why don't you tell me?"

Tracker walks into the kitchen at that moment, eyeing the three of us. "Alcohol, people, we need alcohol. The crowd is getting impatient."

"How many bikers does it take to get the alcohol from the kitchen?" I ask, smirking into my drink.

When Arrow walks into the kitchen, Lana and I share an amused look. "Three so far."

My eyes widen as Arrow grabs a bottle, opens it and drinks straight from it.

No chaser, no glass, no nothing.

I glance at Tracker with wide eyes, but he just shrugs. "Told you people were getting impatient."

We all walk back to the table and reclaim our seats. A pretty redhead sits on Vinnie's lap, a blonde on Irish's. Trace's old lady, Jess, comes and chats with us for a little while, and I instantly like her. Rake continuously touches me throughout the night, even if it's just his hand resting next to mine. I like the fact that he's being attentive, asking me if I want anything, and if I'm all right. I feel a little awkward when Vinnie and his woman start making out and her top slides down, showing off her breasts. She doesn't bother fixing herself, and when Vinnie starts rubbing his hands all over them, I look away and don't look back again.

A seriously cute guy named Zach, another man from the Channon charter of the Wind Dragons, has a few drinks with us. He's extremely charismatic and has all the women charmed.

"Zach," Tracker calls out jokingly when he spots him talking to Lana. "Go back to Channon!"

Zach throws his head back and laughs. "But the women here are so beautiful. Maybe I'll transfer."

Someone throws an empty cup at him.

A fight breaks out between two men, and Rake and Arrow jump in to break it up, while Tracker stands in front of us as if to protect us in case any men go flying in our direction. I love that about the men. Each protects his own woman plus their brothers' women, as if it's instinct, no thought required. It's just who they are and who they want to be as members of this club. Even though being involved with Rake brought danger, I've also never felt so protected and safe. I know he and his brothers would do anything to keep Cara and me safe. I have complete faith in them.

"It's not a party without a fight," Tracker comments, looking completely relaxed as if this was the norm. "Lana, are you paying attention to their fighting technique?" he asks, sounding both amused and proud.

"Yeah, and the blond guy could really use some time in the ring," Lana responds, studying the men.

Tracker laughs and wraps her in his arms.

Faye returns and tells everyone she wants to take a group photo. Those men who balk at the idea take one look at Sin's face and change their minds. Rake lifts me into his arms for the photo, carrying me bride-style. The more time I spend with him, the more open and playful he gets.

"Baby, we done here?" Rake whispers into my ear when the photos are over, nibbling on the lobe. "You've spoken to everyone, can we fuck now? I need some attention too, you know."

I purse my lips together, trying not to smile.

Rake being a little needy with me? Yeah, I like that. A lot.

Too much.

"Okay, let me say 'bye to the girls," I tell him, kissing his jaw. "All right?"

I stand up and he slaps my ass. "Hurry up."

I hurry.

He throws me over his shoulder and carries me back to his room.

TWENTY-THREE

'M lying on the bed naked, watching Rake as he walks bare-chested around the room. There's an intensity about him that has me curious, almost like there's something different about tonight. I hope it's because he's going to explore his other side with me, the one all the other women have alluded to. I saw the rope in his cupboard that day, but he's yet to use it with me, and I'm left to wonder why. If he's into that, why wouldn't he want to do it with me? To be honest, the thought excites me. I trust Rake with everything I have, and he's the only one I'd ever try new things with.

He slides his jeans down and kneels on the bed. I take in his powerful body, his heavy eyes, and his piercings and compare him to who he was as my high school boyfriend. He's changed so much, but it's still him. That spark in him that ignites something deep inside me will never go away, drawing me to him from the inside out.

"Going commando are we?" I ask, checking him out from head to toe.

He strokes his cock and plays with his lip ring with his

tongue. "Any requests?" he asks, eyes roaming over my body. "I think I want to go down on you, make you come twice, then let you ride me as I watch those tits jiggle."

I sit up, then get off the bed and walk to the cupboard. I open it and stare at what's inside.

"What are you doing, Bailey?" he asks, quickly getting up and standing behind me.

"Making my request," I tell him, taking out the same length of rope I picked up the day he came to stay at my house.

"Bailey—"

"I hear all these things about what you like to do with other women . . ." I try to explain. "But why won't you do them with me?"

He spins me around to face him and lifts my chin up with his thumb and index finger. "After what happened to you, I don't think it's a good idea. You were basically stuck in your own body, why would you want to be bound?"

I nod, understanding how he'd come to that conclusion. "I don't go back there anymore, Rake. And with you, there's no way I would. You don't need to coddle me. I'm not going to break."

He takes the rope from my hands. "I'd love to tie you up and fuck you. I just don't know . . . I mean, yeah, I really want to do it to you."

"Then let's do it," I tell him. "The past has no place here. It's just me and you." I eye the rope. "So you want to bind my hands?"

I feel myself getting damp at the thought of being under his control.

He nods, eyes dark and hungry, patiently waiting for me to make my decision, even though I already have.

I hold out my hands to him, silently letting him know that I'm completely sure about this.

He takes both my wrists in one hand, then lifts them above me and ties them to the headboard. When I'm secured, he peers down at me, the heat in his green eyes making my nipples pebble.

I'm curious as to why he likes doing this, but I'm almost sure it's because of his need for control. He used to pin my arms down when he was making love to me, raising them above my head, or sometimes he would pin me down with his weight. He clearly gets turned on from being dominant.

"You say no and everything stops," he says, kissing my mouth gently, his warm hands roaming down my body.

"I'm not going to say no," I say breathily. "I love you being in control."

He kisses across my jawline. "You smell so good. Like orange. You fuckin' tortured me tonight making me wait to be alone with you."

"It was my first party," I say on a moan, as he starts paying attention to my nipples.

"And it won't be your last," he says against my skin. "Everyone loves you."

His stubble against my skin, the roughness, feels so damn good. I pull on the binds, wanting to touch him so badly, but knowing I can't turns me on even more. I squeeze my thighs together, wanting—no, needing—any type of friction. It seems Rake is going to draw out my pleasure tonight, even though I'm so wet he could slide into me without even touching me.

"Stay still," he growls playfully, biting down on my nipple.

I hiss at the pain but then groan as he soothes it with his tongue. He reaches down to expertly play with my clit as he continues to tease me with his mouth, then looks me straight in the eye and commands, "Don't come until I tell you to."

"But," I gasp, knowing the second he touched me I would be on the verge. "Rake—"

"Bailey," he growls, spreading my thighs and kissing down my stomach, over my stretch marks. I can't even move my arms to cover them, distract him, or push him away.

"Rake—"

He moves down me, nibbling the inside of my thigh. "Stay still, Bailey, or I won't give you what you need."

I suck in air, making my body stay still, giving up control to him. There's no point feeling shy, or even thinking at all. I can just feel, and trust Rake, because I know he will never do anything that I don't like.

"Hmmmm, good girl," he hums his approval when I let my body relax, giving in to him. "You smell so good, Bailey. I can't wait to have my mouth on you. But first I want to make sure that you're ready for me."

I was ready.

So ready.

And he knew it.

I decide to keep quiet, biting my bottom lip as Rake continues to kiss the inside of my thighs, his stubble rough on me, one hand gripping underneath my knee, the other still on my lower stomach. After hat feels like hours but is probably only seconds, he finally lowers his face to my pussy, so close that I can feel his breath on me, but not touching.

"Babe," I choke out. "Please."

"Hmmmm, I like you calling me that," he says, not lifting his head. "Maybe I'll reward you."

His tongue peeks out and swipes through my folds, tasting me. He makes a deep sound in the back of his throat before he grips my ass with his hands and buries his face in my pussy, exploring every inch of me.

I cry out.

He doesn't stop, but instead licks my clit in short, quick strokes, which have me whispering his name like a prayer.

"Rake, I'm going to come," I manage to say.

He stops.

I feel like crying.

"Not yet," he says huskily, moving up to lick my extremely sensitive nipples.

"I need to come," I whisper brokenly.

"Wait, Bailey," he demands. "Don't come until I tell you to."

I nod, close my eyes, and try to think of anything except what he's doing to me.

Apples.

Strawberries.

Oranges.

Fuck, I can't.

"I need to come," I plead, opening my eyes, on the verge, so damn close.

I don't know what he hears in my tone, but he looks at my face, nods, then returns to pleasuring me with his mouth.

I come the second he licks my clit, my body shaking, pleasure filling me, overriding my system.

So damn good.

Rake keeps his mouth on me, prolonging my orgasm as

much as he can, until it's too much, too sensitive, and I beg him to stop.

I gulp air greedily, panting.

Probably the best orgasm I've ever had in my life.

Fuck.

I don't think I'll ever recover from that.

"Are you on the pill?"

I nod.

"I got tested when you first came back, and I'm clean." He pauses. "I haven't been with anyone since then."

I lick my bottom lip. "Okay. I want to feel you."

He groans and straddles me.

My thighs are still trembling as he slides inside of me, making me moan some more as he fills me with his big, hard cock. I lift my hips to move in time with his deep, hard thrusts, so greedy for him, wanting him to give me everything he has and more.

I can take anything he has to offer, because I was made for him.

"Love being inside you," he rumbles, staring down at me. "You feel so fuckin' good, Bailey."

I open my mouth to reply, but no words come out, so he just grins and kisses my lips.

"I want us to come at the same time," he says, tracing his lips down my neck. "Tell me when you're ready."

He slides into me a few more times, his hips hitting just the right spot at just the right angle.

"I'm ready," I whimper. "I'm going to come."

"Come now," he says, then covers my lips with his again.

I come, and so does he.

I can't even describe how amazing it feels. Not just the amazing sex, but the emotion too. He kisses my forehead, and my lips once more before he unties me, rubs my wrists, and kisses each one in turn.

"How was that?" he asks, pulling me onto him, my breasts resting against his chest. "Did you like it? Are you sure you were okay with it?"

He rubs my back, as if comforting me.

"Amazing," I reply in all honestly. "I loved it, Rake. I was fine with it—just like I told you I'd be."

His green eyes smile down at me. "You like to play, baby?"

I lick my dry lips. "I guess I do."

"Fuck," he whispers, then says louder, "That was me breaking you in, Bailey. There's so much more I want to do with you, explore with you."

"I trust you," I whisper, staring at his lips.

He lowers his head and kisses me.

A soft, sweet, gentle kiss.

A kiss that makes me fall in love with him all over again.

When I wake up from my nap, I open my eyes and see Rake sitting on the edge of the bed, watching me.

"'Morning," I mumble, wondering how long I'd been sleeping for.

I sit up and watch as he stands, a glint in his eye that makes me want to squeeze my thighs together.

"I want you on your knees in front of me," he demands, our eyes connected.

I swallow hard at his tone, my nipples pebbling.

"Now, Bailey."

I slide off the bed and get down on my knees. I do everything he demands from me, and I love every second.

Vinnie walks into the kitchen, face scrunched in confusion.

"What's wrong?" I ask him, making Rake look up from the big bowl of pasta he's devouring.

Vinnie opens his mouth, closes it, and then mutters, "I'm having déjà vu."

"What's going on?" Rake asks, still relaxed and shoveling food into his mouth.

Vinnie licks his lips, then says, "Faye broke into my room. And cleaned it. It's spotless. The condom drawer was organized by expiration date."

Rake starts choking, so I slap at his back while still eyeing Vinnie. "So she has a little OCD, so what? At least your room is clean. I'm sure you'll be happy in the long run that none of the condoms will be out of date."

"My sock drawer is now fuckin' color coded, and they're all wrapped in these little folded balls, like what the actual fuck," he continues.

I roll my eyes. "That's what you're meant to do to them. So you don't have to search for the matching sock."

"Who actually wears matching socks?" Vinnie asks, looking pretty grumpy.

Rake starts laughing, obviously having gotten over the choking. "Fuck, does Sin know?"

Vinnie shrugs his shoulders, expression turning to amusement. "I have no idea. So it's not just me fuckin' thinking this?"

I look between the men. "What are you two on about?"

Irish storms into the kitchen at that moment. "Faye just interrupted me fucking to clean under my bed. Under my bed! Where is Sin?"

Tracker and Arrow then walk into the kitchen. Tracker looks around the room and smiles slowly. "Faye is being a psycho again. She's so knocked up!"

Ohhhh.

Faye's pregnant?

They knew that just because she was cleaning all of their rooms? Seems odd to me, but I'm new here, so what do I know.

Faye is next to walk into the kitchen, holding a broom.

"Is there a meeting in here I wasn't invited to?" she asks, wrinkling her nose. "Who are we bitching about? Is it the woman Irish was having sex with? Because I don't know how she walks with those gigantic boobs either."

Irish scowls, his intimidating look probably scaring most women but not Faye.

"Does she float or sink in water?" Faye asks him, grinning at her own joke.

"Does Sin know?" Tracker asks, crossing his arms over his chest.

"Know what?" she replies, lawyer face now on, giving away nothing.

Tracker points to her stomach. "That you're pregnant?"

Faye gasps, free hand going to her stomach. "What the hell! How did you guys all know? Did Sin tell everyone already? I only told him this morning!"

We all look at the broom in her hand.

She looks at it too, then drops it to the ground like it's on fire. "Damn it! I was going to make an announcement on the weekend in a super cute way!"

The men all walk over and hug her, even Arrow, who I almost never see touching anyone besides Anna. I find it really sweet. I get up and hug her too. "Congratulations. Is Clover excited to be a big sister?"

Faye lets go of me and smiles happily. "She is. She wants a baby brother she can boss around."

"She's probably seen the way you act in the clubhouse," Vinnie jokes, wrapping Faye from behind and kissing her on top of her head.

"Very funny," Faye returns, shaking her head in amusement. "I'm going to finish cleaning and then head home."

"No locked rooms, Faye," Arrow says, narrowing his gaze. "Or do we need another intervention?"

The men all chuckle at that.

Faye rolls her eyes and purses her lips, but the glint in her eyes gives away her amusement. "Fine, no locked rooms. Arrow, your room isn't locked right now though."

She jogs off.

Arrow stalks behind her.

Rake looks to me, then to the door Faye just vacated.

"Do you remember if I locked my door?"

TWENTY-FOUR

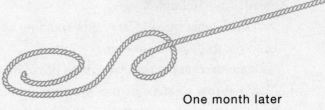

One month later

'M hungry, Adam," I hear Cara tell Rake, making me stop in the doorway to observe the two of them. They're both sitting on the couch, watching a cartoon.

"What do you want to eat, Angel?" he asks her, looking down and studying her.

"Out of anything in the world?" I hear my daughter ask. "Or from our kitchen?"

Rake chuckles at that and seems to consider. "How about, for now, from the kitchen, but tomorrow I'll get you whatever you feel like from out in the world."

Cara nods her little head and says, "Okay, deal. How about strawberries dipped in chocolate?"

I grin at her request.

"Isn't that a dessert?" Rake asks slowly, shifting in his seat.

Cara simply shrugs. "Strawberries are fruit. Fruit is healthy."

"Are there some already made up in the fridge?" Rake sounds hopeful.

"No, you gotta make it, Adam," Cara says, sighing in exasperation. "I know how, but I need an adult to supervist me or I'll get in trouble."

"Supervist? Oh, you mean supervise." Rake chuckles, body shaking in amusement. I hear him mutter *supervist* under his breath again in humor.

"That's what I said." Cara sniffs, standing up and holding her hand out to Rake. "Come on."

Rake stares at her tiny hand, then places his over it.

My throat tightens at the sweetness of the gesture. I step back into the hallway as the two of them make their way to the kitchen. Cara opens the fridge and points to the strawberries, which are just out of her reach. Rake lifts her up so she can grab them herself. She puts them on the table, then gets the chocolate out of the cupboard and hands it to him.

"We need to melt the chocolate," she says, pointing to the microwave. I decide to step in and save a confused-looking Rake, who keeps glancing at the chocolate, then the microwave. I walk into the kitchen and take the chocolate out of his hands, opening the packet and tipping it into a bowl.

"I got this, Rake," I say, grinning widely. "No need to hurt yourself."

Rake playfully grabs me by the waist from behind and pulls me back against him. "I don't usually spend much time in the kitchen," he admits.

"No, really?" I say sarcastically, shimmying out of his reach with a smile. "Do you want some too, babe?"

"I do," he says, looking down at Cara. "And if Angel loves it so much, I want to know how to make them for her."

Why did he have to be so sweet sometimes? It makes me

want to jump on him and kiss the crap out of him, but I can't do that with Cara watching.

The last month with him has been amazing. We've done a lot of talking, trying to be open and honest every time the past rears its ugly head. It's not easy, but like Lana said, nothing worth it ever is. And I'll fight for him until my last dying breath,

"Okay," I tell him, explaining the very basic steps. He puts the chocolate in a bowl then melts it in the microwave.

"That's it?" he asks, raising his eyebrows. "Anyone can do that."

"Even you?" I tease, watching as he dips a strawberry in the chocolate. He then lifts it to my mouth, and I open it, taking a bite, while his gaze stays locked on my mouth. "You have to put them in the fridge."

"The second we are alone . . ." he whispers heatedly under his breath.

I ignore him and continue to finish the strawberries, then put them in the fridge. "Cara, I'll heat up some pasta for you to eat now, the strawberries can be dessert, all right?"

"Okay, Mom!" she calls out, then races back to the living room.

Rake pushes me back against the counter.

I love the power I have over him, how I can make him want me with just the smallest actions.

That his need for me is the same as mine for him.

That we can't get enough of each other.

"You're so fuckin' . . . fuck," he says, shaking his head.

"Very eloquent," I say, trying to lighten the intensity radiating from him. "I'm so what?"

"Just," he replies, pushing my hair back behind my ear. "Everything. You're everything. It overwhelms me sometimes."

"Good everything?" I find myself asking, even though I know he meant it in that way.

"Very good," he says, resting his forehead on mine. "Never did I think, ever, in my fuckin' life, would we be here right now. Together. Winning. Beating the past. Fuck."

"We haven't won yet."

"We will," he says with confidence. "Because if there's one thing I won't lose, it's you for a second time."

"Uncle Rake, it's my birthday!" Clover yells, running up to us as we walk outside, where a big bouncy castle has been set up.

"I know, princess," Rake says, lifting her up with one arm and handing her a brightly wrapped present with the other. "Happy birthday."

Clover takes the package and beams up at Rake. "Thank you! I'll add it to the pile. Daddy said I can open them all later." She then turns to me, her big hazel eyes curious. "Are you Uncle Rake's girlfriend? Mom said he has a lot of them."

Rake playfully tickles her. "Why you always gotta make trouble for me, Clover?"

"Someone has to." She grins, her black hair blowing in the wind. This little girl is going to be an absolute heartbreaker when she's older, and with that attitude too, men better look out.

"This is Bailey," Rake says, gesturing to me. "You be nice to her, you hear me?"

"I'm always nice, Uncle Rake," she says, an amused glint in her eyes. "Nice to meet you, Bailey."

"You too, Clover," I tell her. "I've heard so much about you. And happy birthday—I hope you like the present."

"You chose my present?" she asks, staring down at the black-and-pink-wrapped gift.

"I did," I reply, wondering about why she was asking. She turns her little head to Rake. "Uncle Rake, you didn't even choose my present?"

Rake throws his head back and laughs. "Give me a break, princess. I don't know what seven-year-old girls like these days."

She grins, looking back at me. "Thank you for the gift, Aunt Bailey."

My heart instantly warms at being called that. "You're welcome, sweetie."

"Now I have some other people for you to meet," Rake says, then puts Clover down. "Clover, this is Cara and Rhett."

Clover looks down at the two children by my side, as if only just noticing them.

"More friends. Yay!" she squeals, running up to them and taking them both by the hands. "Come on, let's go play."

Cara glances back at me once but then follows Clover into the bouncy castle, Rhett, as always, by her side.

"She'll look after them," Rake says, watching me. "Come on, baby. Let's get something to eat; I'm starving."

I roll my eyes. "What's new?"

He hugs me from behind, enveloping me in his warmth. "Always hungry when I'm around you."

His lips touch my neck, and I shiver.

I'm always hungry around him too. I step forward, pulling him with me. Everyone says hello and comes over to greet us. Rake goes over to Sin, who is working the grill, with a plate in his hand, while I sit down with Anna, Lana, and Faye, who are watching the kids and chatting among themselves.

"You two look so fuckin' cute together" is the first thing Faye says to me. "I feel like taking a picture every time I see it, because I never thought I'd see this day."

Anna looks up from her phone and smirks at Faye. "That some of the men would be happily taken?"

"That Rake could be satisfied by one pussy," Faye replies casually, making me almost choke on the piece of candy I'd just popped into my mouth.

"Faye," Anna admonishes, flashing me an apologetic look that turns into a wince.

"It's okay," I tell her. "I know he was a man-whore."

Lana leans forward, resting her elbows on the table. "Yeah, but name one of them who wasn't."

"Arrow wasn't too bad," Anna says a little defensively. "At least not as bad as the rest."

"Rake was the worst," Faye says, staring Anna down. "Sorry, but you have to admit."

Anna and Lana reluctantly nod.

"Yeah, but now he's the same way he was with Bailey in high school," Anna says. "He doesn't even look at any other women. And trust me, I've been watching him."

Faye looks to me. "You're his, and he's yours. It's actually beautiful to see. Who's next? I vote Vinnie; he needs to be taken down a peg."

We all look to Vinnie, who is out on the grass, enjoying the sunlight. He pulls his T-shirt over his head and stretches out, and we all lower our gazes to his six-pack.

"Don't think it's going to be hard for him to attract someone," Lana murmurs, fanning herself dramatically.

"Where did he pull those muscles from?" Faye asks quizzically. "I don't remember them looking like that, and I've known Vinnie ever since he was a prospect."

"His getting women isn't the issue," Anna adds, tapping her finger on her chin. "His cut does that regardless. What he needs is to find a woman he wants to actually keep."

"One who loves him for him," Lana adds, always the hopeless romantic.

"Hopefully she's awesome like all of us," Faye says, squaring her shoulders. "And a total babe."

Anna rolls her eyes. "You mean hopefully she's a good woman who treats Vinnie well."

"Yeah. That." Faye grins, then looks at Clover, who is spinning around in a circle in excitement. Cara and Rhett run to her, and the three of them start laughing at something. "There's a future clique right there."

We all watch the three of them, and I have to agree. If Rake and I stay together, these people will all be a part of our lives for eternity. I find myself hoping for that to be so, for Rake to be mine, and for me to belong to this family. There is obviously a scary side to the biker life, and the thought of putting Cara in any danger has me extremely worried, but I know Rake will never let anything happen to her. My gaze finds him, still standing with Sin, who is now putting meat on his plate.

"Where's Tia today?" Lana asks softly, writing something in a notebook in front of her.

"She had to work," I tell her. "Trust me, she'd be here if she could."

Lana smiles and puts her pen down. "Maybe she could be the woman for Vinnie. She fits in perfectly with us, is beautiful, and knows how to handle men."

The four of us share a look.

"What are you all conspiring over now?" Tracker asks as he walks over, blue eyes narrowed. He takes a seat next to Lana, then pulls her seat in closer to his. "I feel fuckin' sorry for whoever it involves."

Faye smiles sweetly and blows Tracker a kiss. "All you have to know is it has nothing to do with you."

"Thank fuck," Tracker replies quickly, running his thumb over Lana's knee. "Can't believe our princess is seven years old now. I remember the day she was born."

"Really?" Faye asks, dragging the word out. "I remember you staring at my crotch with a horrified expression like she was going to drop out in front of you."

Tracker shudders as if remembering the moment. "What did you expect from me? At least I wasn't an asshole like Rake."

Faye's eyes narrow. "That's right. What did he say again?"

Tracker chuckles, then stops when he sees the look on her face. "Something like 'Say 'bye to your tight—'"

"How is that bastard even alive still?" Faye growls, eyeing Rake like she wants to punch him.

"Because he's family," Anna reminds her, unable to keep the amusement off her expression. "Oh, come on, it's a little funny."

She and Tracker laugh some more, while Lana shakes her head with a smile on her face.

"And now you're doing it again," I blurt out, making everyone laugh harder.

"Hey! It's all about the Kegels, isn't that right, Bailey?" Faye winks at me, making me laugh harder. "You gotta squeeze and release," Faye says, making a circle with her hands, closing and opening it.

"Yeah Faye, we get it," Anna says in an extremely dry yet amused tone.

Faye looks to Anna and grimaces. "Fuck, I'm being an insensitive bitch right now, aren't I?" She puts her hand on Anna's and says, "You're going to be blessed with a baby, you know that, right? It will even come out with a beard."

Anna smiles. "I know. And you're not being insensitive; I'm super happy for you. I know that my time will come."

Anna wants to have a baby? I throw her a *You better talk to me* expression and she nods once.

Rake walks over to the table, a mountain of food on his plate, and sits down next to me, offering me some. I take a chicken wing and nibble on it while Faye gives Rake a dirty look that soon turns into a smile.

"Save your bitchy looks for the prez, Faye," Rake tells her, taking a giant bite of his hot dog.

"I'm going to call the kids in to eat," Faye says, standing up, stealing Rake's second hot dog and taking a huge bite out of it.

"Hey," he grumbles, and draws his plate closer to him. "Get your own, woman!"

She grins and walks over to where the kids are getting their faces painted, then sends them to the kids' table. There're about ten children, and Arrow, Rake, and Sin carry the food over for them. Lana gets a phone call and heads inside, leaving me and

Anna alone. I see Arrow hand something to Clover, something that looks like candy. I glance at Anna, who is also watching her man.

"I'm surprised Clover still has teeth, with the amount of strawberry candy Arrow sneaks her," she comments, covering the glare of the sun with her hand. "They're little heart shapes too. Can you imagine him going into a store to buy them?"

I cover my lips with my hand, smothering the giggle that vision brings. "No, I can't."

But I can't imagine anyone confronting him about it either.

"Cara is going to be my niece," Anna muses, now watching my daughter. "I'm going to be the best aunt ever."

"Getting ahead of yourself there," I tell her, but my heart warms at the thought. "Either way, you're still like her aunt."

Anna smirks in my direction. "Yes, but it's going to be official too. Trust me, Bails. I'm always right. I'm a scientist, you know."

I roll my eyes. "Seriously? That's your answer to everything."

Anna laughs, her eyes sparkling. "What? It makes me sound smart. It's useful for winning arguments."

"Don't think you could use it against a lawyer," I tease, nodding at Faye.

"That's the truth. She always knows exactly what to say. There's so many hilarious lawyer jokes though. Every time I come across one, I forward it to her," Anna says, laughing. "Everyone hates lawyers." She pauses. "They're up there with car salesmen and real estate agents."

"You're terrible," I say, but laugh with her. "Teachers have a good reputation. I'm educating the youth of today to be the leaders of the future."

"You make them glue stuff," Anna blurts, laughing. "Your job sounds fun."

"Hey, I do more than that!" I say a little defensively. "I set them up for everything they need to know for their future years of studying! I help build the foundation for their education."

Anna nods her head sagely. "Yeah, you're right. But come on, you do a lot of gluing and painting."

I puff out a breath. "You're infuriating."

Lana sits back down and looks between us. "What did I miss?"

"A career war," Anna says, grinning. "What do you have for us, Lana?"

"Not this again," Lana grumbles, lifting her legs up on the empty chair in front of her. "If I was on a deserted island, I'd be one of the first ones they'd kill off. What could they use a romance author for?"

"I'm sure you have some other skills," I tell her, biting my lip and trying not to laugh at her random comment.

"I have no survival skills at all," she disagrees, tilting her head. "I'm book smart. Not very practical."

"Well then," I say, sounding choked. "Hopefully Tracker will be there to save your ass and stop the people on the island from voting you off."

Anna looks at Lana, squinting her eyes. "That was such a fiction writer comment by the way."

Lana shrugs, smiling. "You live in your world, and I live in mine."

"My world being reality?" Anna asks, laughing. "I'd love to see into your head. See how you come up with all these characters and plot lines. All the evil little twists you add into your books. Do you have an evil laugh you use when you kill someone off?"

Lana beams. "Actually I do. Do you want to hear it?"

We both nod.

She clears her throat and then laughs. "Mwahahahaha." She looks at us. "What do you think?"

"I think you could even go eviler," I say, considering. "Is *eviler* a word, author friend of mine?"

"Why does everyone always ask me?" She laughs. "That's what editors are for. Trust me, I make up more words than the average person."

"That's true," Anna adds, nodding her head.

"Hey at least I don't say *chipotle* like 'chipottle,'" Lana says to Anna, unable to keep a straight face. "That was some funny shit!"

"You said you wouldn't bring that up again!"

"Says the scientist," I tease, making Lana laugh even harder.

We spend the rest of the day chatting, eating, and watching the children laugh and play. Clover cuts her *Frozen* cake and we all sing "Happy Birthday" to her. This is the last place I ever thought I'd fit in, yet I can't remember the last time I was this happy.

Life definitely surprises you at every turn.

And sometimes, it's in a very good way.

TWENTY-FIVE

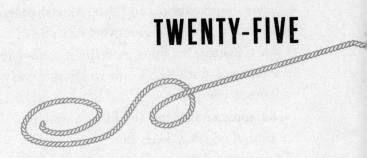

So that's the connection you have with Talon," I say, eyes flaring. "You never told me the whole story before."

"Didn't I?" Anna frowns, reaching up to tie her light hair in a ponytail. "My biological father raised him instead of Rake and me. Talon's a good guy though. It wasn't his fault our so-called father abandoned us."

"And that's why Rake doesn't like Talon," I say, coming to the realization. I cover my face with my hands. "And I kissed him!"

Anna winces at that. "Yeah, Talon is lucky to be alive after that one. Rake doesn't hurt Talon because he knows I care about him. Talon and I have a weird bond. Must have been the whole kidnapping thing."

I stare at her until she explains that one.

"He kidnapped you? Sweet baby Jesus," I groan, shaking my head in shock. "Looks like I've missed a whole lot of drama."

"You have no idea," Talon says without missing a beat, sliding into the seat next to Anna. He eyes me warily. "Rake know you're here?"

I look to Anna. "No, but to be fair, I had no idea you were going to be joining us today, Talon."

Talon simply chuckles and kisses Anna sloppily on the cheek. "Always causing trouble, aren't you, Anna Bell?"

Anna tightens her lips. "No harm is coming to her being in your presence. She's Rake's now, so I'm sure you will both keep your lips to yourselves."

Talon puckers his lips and sends a wink in my direction. "I can control myself if Bailey can."

"I'm sure I'll manage," I tell him in a dry tone, unable to keep my lips from quirking.

"Good," he says, rubbing his hands together. "I'm fuckin' starving. Can we order?"

"Already ordered for you," Anna replies, flipping the page on a magazine she was reading.

"That's fuckin' emasculating." Talon sighs, staring down at her. "What did you get?"

Anna lifts her head and smirks. "The same thing you always order, Talon. Steak, fries, and salad."

"Did you—"

"Yes," she interrupts. "I told them not to put the dressing on the salad because you don't like dressing. Which I still think is weird, but anyway."

"And did you tell them—"

"Steak medium rare, yes."

"What about—"

Anna expels a heavy sigh. "Yes, I told them you like to eat your fries with mayonnaise."

"Oh," Talon says, now grinning. "Good work, Anna."

"Just how often do you two eat here?" I ask, unable to keep the amusement from my voice.

"Now and again," Anna replies, flashing Talon a fond look. "He gets grumpy and threatens to come to the clubhouse if I don't."

Talon shrugs his broad shoulders. "I haven't been in a fight for a while, and I'm aching for one."

"Yeah. Don't do that," I say, grimacing. "Maybe you could go to a boxing gym or something like that."

Talon looks at me like he thinks I'm cute. "There's an idea, sweetheart."

I roll my eyes and look down at the deep burgundy nails I just got done with Anna as a treat to myself.

"So now that Rake's off the market, who's satisfying all the club whores?" Talon asks nonchalantly.

Anna flashes him a dirty look. "Why do I like you again?"

"What? I'm just saying: you can always send them my way."

"You need a good woman," Anna tells him, leaning forward.

"I wouldn't know what to do with a good woman," Talon tells her. "I'm not ready to settle down. Plus my life isn't exactly one that would attract the type of woman you're talking about."

"Umm hello," Anna says, pointing between me and her. "If Arrow can get me, you can get a good woman."

Talon looks in my direction. "Has her ego always been this big?"

I grin and nod. "Pretty much."

"I'm just saying. It's possible."

"That would require me trusting a woman completely, and yeah, no fuckin' thanks," he says, pouring himself some water from the jug at the table and taking a sip. "I'm good as I am."

"Fine," Anna says, shrugging her shoulders. "It will happen eventually anyway, whether you want it to or not."

"Touch wood, Anna," he says, smirking. "Don't wish that shit upon me."

Anna rolls her eyes.

"Speaking of wishes, it's my birthday next week," Talon says, running a hand through his shaggy white-blond hair. "I want you there."

Anna closes her magazine and concentrates on him. "Where are you having it?"

"At the clubhouse," he says without flinching, keeping his gaze on the woman he considers family.

"For fuck's sake, Talon," Anna snaps. "I can't walk into the Wild Men clubhouse! Arrow and Rake would murder me! And no offense, but most of the men in your MC are assholes."

"They aren't so bad," Talon fires back. "You only met most of them when you were our fuckin' hostage; of course they weren't warm and friendly to you."

"Slice is—"

"An asshole," Anna finishes. "A total asshole. And Ranger? When I punch the boxing bag with Faye, it's his face I picture as I pummel it."

"Did you even see Ranger?" Talon asks, eyes flashing with amusement.

Anna's eyes narrow in a scowl. "Not the point. I picture him being some big ogre-looking jackass with all muscles and no brain."

"Ranger has three degrees. One's in literature."

I can't help it, I start laughing at the look on Anna's face. I don't think she saw that one coming.

"The biker who kidnapped me and knocked me unconscious has a degree in literature?" Anna asks with wide green eyes. "You're pulling my leg, right?"

Talon shakes his head. "I swear. He's always reading and shit. Loves it."

"Well, fuck me," Anna mutters under her breath. "Now I'm going to picture beating him with a book."

"I want you there, Anna, and I can't move the whole thing. Where the hell would we hold it?" Talon asks. Our food arrives and we all murmur our thank-yous. When the waitress leaves, he continues, "No one will even breathe in your direction. I have the men under control. The MC isn't what it used to be, okay?"

"Can't we have our own separate celebration? I'll take you wherever you want to go," Anna tries to negotiate.

"No," Talon says simply, being stubborn. He turns to me, "You come too, Bailey."

Anna barks out a laugh at that. "You think Rake is going to let the two women most important to him walk into your MC clubhouse? What have you been smoking, Talon? Because you might want to share it so we can get in on the craziness."

My heart warms at her compliment, and I know that she's right. Rake would never let this happen, no matter how much Talon might want it and how much Anna would want him to have his birthday wish.

"Not to mention Arrow," I add, picking up my fork.

"Bring them, then," Talon says, dipping a fry into his mayonnaise. "If they can manage to keep their fists to themselves, I'll make sure my men do the same."

Anna puffs out a breath and looks down at her plate. "You're asking the impossible this time, Talon."

"Try" is all he replies. "Sneak out if you have to. Come on, Anna, you've done it before."

"And look how that ended," she replies dryly.

"Kill anyone who tries to touch you," he says so casually that it makes me feel a little uncomfortable.

Anna glances up at me. "Let's talk about this later; we're being rude to Bailey."

"Bailey is coming with you, so she can pipe up any time she likes," he says, winking at me again.

"Hey, don't bring me into this," I say. "I'm going to pretend this whole conversation never happened."

"Good idea," Anna says, strength in her voice. "We're not going, and that's final."

"I can't believe you're making me do this!" I growl at Anna a week later.

"We'll just stop by for an hour and that's it! The men will never find out; they'll just think we're having dinner and drinks," Anna says, sounding like she believes what she's saying, even though I know shit's going to happen tonight. The only reason I'm going is because otherwise she said she'll go alone, and I can't let her do that, nor can I be a snitch and tell the men of her plan. Basically, I'm damned if I do and I'm damned if I don't. At least this way I get to keep an eye on her and hope that we can pull this off and both end up home safely without starting an MC war.

"They're so going to find out," I tell her grumpily, staring out the window. "Rake's going to kill me. I just know it."

"Don't think about it," Anna says, putting the volume up on

the music. "Let's just have a good night and we'll both pull this off. Don't worry so much, Bailey."

Don't worry?

I listen to "No Love" by August Alsina and Nicki Minaj while contemplating whether Anna is crazy or not. She has to be, of course, to think we're going to get away with our plan tonight. I place my hands on my thighs and wonder, for the tenth time, if I chose the right outfit. I went with black skinny jeans and a black top that isn't revealing at all but still looks good on me. I don't want to get any attention from the Wild Men bikers, but I don't want to look like shit either. My hair's up in a high ponytail and I have a little makeup on, a natural look. Anna is dressed similarly, in jeans and a red top, with her hair down and dead straight, her makeup a little heavier. We soon pull up to the clubhouse, and Anna parks out front, a little away from everyone else.

"Easy access to get out of here, don't you think?" she asks, getting out of the car and waiting for me. I count to ten in my head, then get out, pulling at the hem of my top.

"Let's do this and leave," I grumble as she slides her arm in mine and leads me to the entrance. The man standing there eyes us warily.

"Talon's expecting us," Anna says, sounding confident.

The man nods. "Anna and Bailey?"

"Yeah," she replies. "Where is he?"

"Go straight, then turn right," the man replies. "You'll hear them, don't worry."

Anna and I share a look before we walk into forbidden territory.

"It's a lot less scary than I remember it," she says, following the noise of the men, hollering and cheering.

"It's so weird being here," I whisper, coming to a stop when I see Talon and his men. They're standing next to a pool table, playing . . . beer pong?

"I didn't expect this," Anna says, taking the words right out of my mouth.

"Anna! Bailey!" Talon cheers, throwing the Ping-Pong ball to one of his men and coming straight over to us. "You made it."

He wraps us both in his arms, pressing our faces to his chest. He smells good. Really good. He turns around, both of us still in his hold.

"Happy birthday, Talon," Anna says, handing him the small gift we got him. I wish him well too, and he kisses my cheek.

"Thank you," he says sincerely. "You didn't need to get me anything. You both being here is more than enough."

I know he really wanted Anna here, not me, but it's nice of him to include me in the equation.

"Everyone!" he shouts, making me jump. "This is Anna and Bailey. They're my guests and not to be fuckin' touched, do you hear me?"

The men nod, some call out replies, all agreeing. One man yells out, "But they're hot!" And Talon yells back for him to look but not touch, unless he wants his dick cut off.

Ouch.

"Can I get you both a drink?" he asks, kissing Anna on her temple.

"Actually," Anna says, eyeing the beer pong game going on. "Can we play?"

"What?" Talon asks, laughing. "That's the last thing I thought I'd hear you say."

Anna smiles sweetly. A little too sweet. "I've never played before, I'd like to try it. It looks fun."

Talon looks down at me. "What about you, sweetheart?"

I shrug, purposely looking unsure. "I've never played either, but it looks easy enough."

"Do you guys want to go on separate teams, since you're both newbies? We usually play two against two," he says, telling one of the men that the next game was his.

"No, I want to go with Anna," I say, grinning up at him. "Girl power, and all that."

Talon lets go of us and grins, shrugging. "Fine, but when you get your asses kicked, don't say I didn't warn you."

"We're both capable women," Anna tells him, crossing her arms over her chest. "And we have beginners' luck on our side. Who are you taking as your partner?"

"Hmmm," Talon muses, his grin turning mischievous. "I choose him."

He points at someone behind us, so we turn to look.

I instantly suck in a breath. Sweet baby Jesus.

I stare at what has to be one of the most attractive men I've ever set my eyes upon. Extremely tall and perfectly muscled, he's wearing worn jeans and a blue flannel long-sleeved shirt. Both look delicious on him. His hair is longish, dark as can be, and tied at his nape. He has a beard. Not too long and not too short, just right.

Everything about him is just right.

He walks over to us and stops next to Talon. His eyes. They're a bright hazel. And surrounded by thick, dark lashes. Mesmerizing.

"Wh-who are you?" I hear Anna ask, sounding equally as dazed.

Yeah, the man was a god.

"Anna, meet Ranger."

He's no Rake, but if I wasn't with Rake . . . well.

I'd like to have a Ranger.

TWENTY-SIX

HAT'S the guy who kidnapped you?" I whisper when we're sort of alone. "What the hell were you complaining about? He can kidnap me any time he wants!"

"I didn't see him!" she growls, grabbing my arm and pulling me farther into the corner of the room. "He knocked me out." Her eyes narrow on Ranger. "And he's going down. We can't lose this game. Do you think Talon bought the whole 'This is our first time' bullshit?"

I nod. "Totally."

She smiles evilly. "Excellent. I'm going to beat Ranger at beer pong, then I'm going to challenge him. Hand-to-hand combat. To the death."

I roll my eyes and pat her shoulder. "Let's just stick to the beer pong, honey."

"Fine," she replies, drawing the word out in a sulk. "Let's do this."

I block out Talon's instructions—Anna and I are no strangers to this game. We played it all the time in high school, and we're good. Really good. I haven't played since college, but hey, I have no doubt we're going to give them a good game.

"You going to stare at me like that all night?" I hear Ranger say to Anna.

Fuck.

His voice is deep and sexy too.

"Yes," Anna tells me, flashing him her dirtiest look. "Yes, I am. You kidnapping bastard."

"On Talon's orders," he says, tilting his head to the side. "Why are you mad at me and not him?"

"He didn't hit me and knock me out!" Anna practically yells, her fists clenching at her sides. I pull at her shirt, silently telling her to calm the fuck down.

"How else was I supposed to kidnap you?" he asks, shaking his head. "I had a job to do, and I got it done. You need to let that shit go."

I've never seen Anna's jaw so tight.

"Can we play?" I ask, trying to ease the tension, looking from face to face. "I'm thirsty."

Laughter.

"You better be thirsty," Talon calls out. "That's a lot of beer, Bails."

I stretch my neck from side to side, then pick up one of the balls. "If you're so sure of yourself, why don't we make this game a little more interesting?"

Talon studies me, seemingly intrigued. "What do you have that I want? Besides the obvious. . . ."

"How about if we win, you owe us one favor, and vice versa," I say, the only thing that comes to mind.

Talon and Ranger share a look. "Like a marker, you mean?"

I shrug. "Yeah, I guess. But only we can give it to you. Not the Wind Dragons. And nothing sexual, of course, and within reason."

"Deal," Talon says, licking his lips. "Now let's have some fun. Ladies first."

I go first.

I get the ball in the cup.

Anna cheers, jumping up and down before hugging me.

Talon grins and shakes his head

Ranger goes next and misses.

Anna cheers again, smirking at him before taking her own turn.

She gets it in.

Ranger drinks, a scowl on his too-handsome-for-his-own-good face.

Talon gets his next shot, so Anna drinks.

My turn again, I throw the ball and get it in.

Again.

The men both study us, realizing that this isn't just beginners' luck and that they've both been played.

Talon throws his head back and laughs, his body shaking with the effort. "Fuck, what did I tell you, Ranger? Never underestimate the Wind Dragon women; they're all fuckin' vipers."

Ranger scoffs, not as impressed as Talon with the situation. "We'll see about that."

We win, of course.

We end up drinking a few of the cups in the game, then more, just because.

We dance, we sing, we laugh.

The men aren't so bad, and give us a wide berth for the most part, although I do notice a few shady-looking characters. I don't know what Talon's rules are for his members using drugs, but I'd have to say that a few of the men are definitely on something. The women stay out of our way. We don't get introduced to any of them, which makes me think that there are no old ladies here.

Between all the drinking, laughing with Anna and Talon, and the people-watching, we forget one thing.

The time.

And that's when everything goes to shit.

"Where the hell have the two of you been?" Rake yells, coming out of the clubhouse. He looks a mixture of furious and relieved, but I think we'll be seeing more of the former when he hears what we've been up to tonight. I pay the taxi driver and get out. We had to leave Anna's car at the Wild Men clubhouse because neither of us was sober enough to drive. Talon tried to get us to let one of his men give us a ride, as some of them hadn't been drinking, but we knew that would only make things worse.

Yeah, we're so fucked.

"Arrow's out fuckin' looking for you, Anna, because neither of you answered your phones," he growls, pulling his own phone out of his pocket and sending a quick text message, probably telling Arrow that Anna was now here safe and sound.

"We're sorry," Anna says, stumbling a little. "We lost track of time."

Shit.

"You're drunk?" Rake seethes, eyeing both me and his sister with distaste. "Where the fuck have you been? We were worried, and the two of you were just out drinking, ignoring your fuckin' phones?"

I watch the taxi drive away, then turn to him. "My phone died," I tell him, pulling it out of my pocket and jiggling it around. "I'm sorry. We really did just lose track of what time it was. We had no idea it had gotten so late."

Rake pinches the bridge of his nose and closes his eyes momentarily, before exhaling slowly. "You weren't at the place you said you were going to be. Arrow went there."

I want to look at Anna, but I don't dare. I don't know how we're going to get out of this one without the truth coming out and Rake and Arrow both exploding at us. I feel a lot of *I told you so* coming from me and heading right in Anna's direction.

"It's my fault," Anna blurts out, making me glance at her face. "I told Bailey if she didn't come with me I was going to go alone, and I knew she wouldn't let me do that."

Rake's eyes narrow on his baby sister. "Tell me. Now."

Anna looks down at her feet, cringing. "It was Talon's birthday."

Rake's expression hardens at the mere mention of Talon's name.

"So we went to wish him a happy birthday and give him his present," she continues, shuffling her weight on each foot. "We were safe there; nothing happened to us. We just had a few drinks and forgot that we weren't supposed to be there in the first place."

A muscle ticks in Rake's jaw as he processes this information. "Please, Anna, please fuckin' tell me you didn't put yourself and my fuckin' woman in danger by taking her to the fuckin' Wild Men MC, the same fuckin' MC that broke into our clubhouse and killed Mary. The same MC that our piece-of-shit father led, you know, the father who didn't give two shits about us but raised Talon, a man you now seem to worship for some motherfuckin' reason I'll never understand. There's shit you don't even know too—just trust me when I say that his clubhouse isn't a safe place to be, not like ours. Their MC is so different from ours, and you need to remember that. Never once did I think that you'd be stupid enough to go there."

My eyes widen at all that information. Someone named Mary died? Because of the Wild Men? They broke into the Wind Dragons clubhouse? I rub my forehead, seriously not knowing what to do right now. I don't want to get involved in a sibling argument, but at the same time I can't let Anna take all the heat for this.

I step closer to Rake and put my hand on his arm. "Can we talk about this tomorrow? When everyone has calmed down?"

Rake looks down at my hand, then his gaze moves to my face. "Go and wait in my room, Bailey. I'll deal with you later."

My eyes narrow at his tone, but I know Anna and I have fucked up. We put ourselves in danger, and I know just how much Rake loves his sister.

"Arrow will handle her," I say quietly. "She doesn't need to get it from you too."

"Get inside, Anna," he tells her, just sounding tired now. "Arrow is on his way. You can tell him this fuckin' story and see how he reacts." He then looks down at me. "Are you mine?"

"Rake, I—"

"Are you fuckin' mine?" he asks, enunciating every word.

"Yes," I whisper. I was. All his. In every way.

"Then fuckin' act like it," he replies, turning and walking away.

Ouch.

I watch Rake disappear, then turn to Anna. "How's Arrow going to react?"

Anna closes the space between us, standing next to me with our arms touching. "He's going to be really angry because he'll think I put our safety in jeopardy. Here's the thing though, you were there—we weren't in danger at all, because Talon would have protected us from harm the way any of the Wind Dragons would have."

"I know," I admit, wrapping my arm around her. "We just see it as going to visit a friend. But the men see it as a betrayal, I think. You're Arrow's old lady; I'm pretty sure we crossed some kind of boundary today."

"We did," she whispers glumly. "I just didn't want to let Talon down. It was his birthday, how could I have said no? We shouldn't have gotten drunk."

"We shouldn't have done a lot of things tonight," I reply, laying my head on her shoulder. "But now we have to suck it up and feel their wrath."

"I'm sorry I made you come, Bailey."

"If I didn't I would have been worrying about you all night, so I'm not. And I saw for myself just how much Talon cares for you, like you're his sister," I say, taking her hand and pulling her toward the door. "Let's go inside before we get into more trouble."

She cracks a smile. "Maybe I should wait out here so Arrow can yell at me away from everyone."

"Nah." I giggle. "Let Rake hear it so he doesn't decide to yell at you too."

She giggles a little too, then sobers. "Thanks for being my partner in crime tonight."

"Any time, babe. Any time."

Rake

"I heard them fuckin' thanking each other for being partners in crime," I tell Sin and Arrow, running my hand through my hair in frustration.

I turn my head to look in Arrow's direction. "If Anna wasn't my sister, I'd be telling you to control your fuckin' woman right now."

Sin sighs and crosses his arms over his chest. "Arrow, control your fuckin' woman. This Wild Men shit has to fuckin' stop. I know she thinks of Talon as family, but this is crossing a line."

"Don't I fuckin' know it," Arrow says gruffly, his eyes hard as stone.

"I'll get Faye to talk to them," Sin says distractedly. "I'll handle Talon. Looks like the bastard needs to be put in his place."

Arrow steps forward. "I want Talon."

Sin studies him for a second before replying. "Fine." He then looks to me. "Handle your woman. Yeah, this was Anna's idea, but she went along with it."

I bite my tongue and just nod, agreeing with his comment. "Yes, Prez."

I walk to my bedroom, feeling tired, frustrated, but more than anything, relieved.

Bailey is okay.

My sister is okay.

The night could have gone in a completely different direction. If anything had happened to either of them, I don't know what I would have done. I'd be in prison though; that's for damn certain. I try to let Anna have her time with Talon—I know she sees him as extended family of some kind, even though I don't get it. He's not our blood, and he's not a brother, so to me, he's no one. And if he puts anyone I love in danger again, I will fuckin' end him.

Everything with Bailey has been going well; it was only a matter of time before we hit a bump in the road, and in terms of bumps, I'd take it. They both came home safely. Bailey had Anna's back, and even though their plan was stupid and selfish, they're both safe. As much as I want to wrap Bailey in my arms and hold her, I need to let her know she fucked up.

I'll just have to hold her when she's fast asleep.

After I've made her understand that she can't just do as she pleases anymore.

TWENTY-SEVEN

Bailey

'VE figured out what my problem is," Tia says, brushing her hair and looking at me through the mirror.

"You need to get laid?" I guess, sitting down on her bed and waiting for her to continue.

"Well, yeah," she says, grinning. "But that's not what I meant. I've realized that I think I'm the exception to every rule. For example, if a guy says he's only looking for sex, nothing else, I'll say I'm okay with it, and sometimes I am," she adds, putting the brush down and turning on her chair to face me. "But sometimes really I expect more and I think that they'll change their minds in the long run, when they won't. I feel like I should always be the exception to their rules. Which is stupid, isn't it? I just end up getting hurt in the end, over something that I could have easily avoided."

"You should be the exception for the man you're meant to be with," I tell her, pondering her words. "And you will be. You're amazing, you know that? Any man should be thanking his lucky stars to have someone like you."

"I know," she agrees, making me laugh. "I just need to stop

self-sabotaging myself. Going after men I know are trouble, or who don't want the things that I want."

"Do you know what you want?" I ask her, completely serious. She's always been so blasé about casual sex, acting like she wasn't ready for more, but maybe she is now.

"I think I'm only just figuring it out," she admits, flashing me a lopsided smile. "And when I do, I'm going to get it."

I shake my head at her ruefully. "I feel sorry for the poor man already."

"Me too," she agrees, coming over to the bed and sitting down next to me. "Is Rake still angry at you over last night's shenanigans?"

"Furious," I reply glumly, puffing out a breath of air. "He's madder at Anna though, and that makes me feel even worse for some reason. I never could bear to see those two fight."

Growing up they were all each other had, and whenever they fought it made my chest hurt. Apparently that still hasn't changed.

"They'll make up," Tia says with confidence. "Just let them sort it out between themselves. Some new drama will come along and this whole Wild Men escapade will be forgotten."

I groan, covering my face with my hands. "I can only imagine what drama will be next."

"At least you're getting fucked well on the regular." She pouts. "It could always be worse."

Yes, yes it could.

I walk into a war zone.

Anna is yelling, her face bright red while Rake tries to talk to her. He's being ignored.

Arrow is standing in the corner of the room, arms crossed over his chest as he studies her, his face void of emotion.

I feel like slowly backing out of the room, but then Anna sees me.

"You won't believe what he did!" she says, pointing to Arrow.

"What?" I ask hesitantly, walking to her.

"He went to the Wild Men clubhouse, called Talon out, and started a fucking fight! In front of everyone! This is why I didn't want to tell you, Arrow," she says, her bottom lip trembling.

"He should have shown some fuckin' respect then," Arrow snarls, pushing off the wall and stalking toward her. "I let you see him. I don't like it, but I don't say shit—but this is crossing a fuckin' line. A man does not invite my woman somewhere he knows she shouldn't go, then what? Sit back while we all give you hell for it? I know you think he's family, Anna, but look around you." He looks around, his arms spread wide. "Your family is right here. And look how you're treating us. I was so fuckin' worried something had happened to you; you know better than this. You know what we've all been through, what we've lost. It was a fuckin' selfish of you."

Arrow storms out while we all stand there in silence.

That's the most I've ever heard him speak.

Would this be a bad time to ask how Talon is?

"It wasn't meant to be such a big deal," Anna says, voice catching. "I just wanted to stop for an hour and wish him happy birthday. That's it. I didn't want to hurt anyone; I didn't want to start any shit. I just wanted to be able to celebrate with him. I know that I fucked up, okay? I didn't see the bigger picture; I just saw one night of a little fun, and I'm sorry I brought Bailey with me too."

I can actually see Rake's eyes soften. "Go sort this out with him. You should know better than everyone how this would make Arrow feel."

I didn't really see the bigger picture either, but now I see just how much of a mistake we made, and I definitely won't be doing something like this again.

Anna nods and heads in the direction Arrow left, leaving Rake and me staring at each other.

"Hey," I say, pushing my hair back behind my ear. "You still angry?"

He comes to me and grabs me by the hips, pulling my body up against his. "You had Anna's back. I can't exactly be mad at you over that, even though what you both did was stupid as fuck."

"Talon isn't—"

"Don't want to hear his name right now. I'm cutting you a little slack because you're new to this whole thing, but you need to understand how differently the night could have gone if anything happened. You do not fuckin' go to another MC clubhouse, I don't care what the reason is. Anna knows better, and now so do you. Now where's Angel?" he asks, tracing his lips over my earlobe.

"She's with Tia and Rhett, they—"

"I need to be inside you right now. And I'm not going to be gentle, Bailey," he whispers, making my nipples pebble. He kisses my neck, then says against my skin. "I'm going to teach you a lesson. I'm going to show you who you belong to."

"Okay." I breathe, almost in a daze, wrapping my arms around his neck. He lifts me up, gripping my ass and squeezing, and walks to his room. The door is opened, then slammed and locked behind him, and I'm put on the bed with my legs hanging off the edge. I wait quietly as Rake watches me, slowly undoing the button on his jeans, followed by the zipper, the noise loud in the silent room. His jeans are removed, followed by his boxers, his cock jutting out, hard and ready.

"Open your mouth," he commands, and I open it eagerly. He comes closer, and I take his cock in my hand, licking the head once, then sucking it into my mouth.

"Good girl," he murmurs, eyes darker than usual. "Take me in as far as you can."

I slide his length into my mouth, going as deep as I can, then bobbing my head as I suck him in and out, hollowing my cheeks.

"Fuck," he grits out as I pleasure him, taking him to the back of my throat, as far as I'm able to without my gag reflex kicking in. He gathers my hair and wraps it around his wrist, tugging my head back and looking me straight in the eye. "I want to come in your mouth."

I moan and pull back. "Do it."

"I give the commands here," he says huskily, sliding back into my mouth. I gently cup his balls in my hand and massage them, just the way I know he likes it, while sucking his huge cock. I then move my right hand to the base of him, working the bottom while my mouth takes care of the rest.

"Yes, just like that," he says gutturally. "I'm going to come, baby."

I heed his warning, sucking a little harder until he comes.

I swallow everything, then lick the head of him once more before letting go of him completely.

"Now get on the bed and spread your thighs for me."

I do as he says, excitement coursing through my veins. Still dressed, I lie back.

"Lift that pretty dress up," he says, getting on the bed himself.

I lift my dress up, showing off my red panties.

"Hmmmm. Put your hand inside them. I want you to play with yourself while I watch."

I slip my hand inside, looking at Rake and waiting for further instruction.

"Slide one finger in," he says, licking his bottom lip. "That's right, just like that. Now I want you to pull it out, and use the wetness to play with your clit."

I work my clit with my finger, my breathing getting heavier.

"Now pull your panties off completely," he suddenly says, holding on to my ankle with his right hand and spreading my thighs farther apart. I lift my hips and slide them down my thighs. When they get to my knees, Rake pulls them down the rest of the way.

I lie there in broad daylight with my legs spread wide while he stares at the most intimate part of me, yet for some reason I don't feel shy. This is Rake, and I trust him implicitly.

"What do you want me to do to you?" he asks, our gazes now locked.

"So now you're asking me?" I joke, smiling at him playfully. Feeling bold, I run my hands over my breasts through the thin cotton. "I want your mouth on my nipples, your fingers working their magic on my pussy. It feels so much better when you touch me than when I do it myself."

"Does it now?" he grins wolfishly, running his tongue over his lip ring. "That's because I've had more practice."

I flick my leg out to kick him in the thigh, making him laugh.

"Jerk."

"If I was a jerk I wouldn't make you come right now," he says, raising an eyebrow in amusement.

"You better make me come right now," I tell him, narrowing my eyes. I take my dress and my bra off, and lie back, naked and waiting. "Ready whenever you are."

Rake throws back his head and laughs, a deep and merry sound. "You think that body is enough to tempt me to do whatever you want?"

"I do," I purr, running my fingers over my nipples brazenly. "I know your weakness, Rake."

"And what is that?" he asks, eyes turning heavy-lidded as I continue to touch myself.

"Me," I whisper softly, barely spoken.

He grabs my wrists and pins them above my head, pushing them down into the mattress. His lips come down on mine, hard and heavy.

Possessive.

Demanding.

"Now, I'm going to show you who you belong to," he says against my swollen lips. "And you're going to take everything I have to give, aren't you?"

I nod.

He slides into me in one smooth thrust.

TWENTY-EIGHT

D O you ever think about what would have happened that night if I realized what was happening?" Rake says, pushing my hair off my face as we lie facing each other. After talking the Talon situation out, Rake has finally let it go. I don't think he's ever going to forgive Talon though.

"You'd probably be in jail," I say, smiling sadly. "There's no point looking back. We've come so far since everything."

"I know," he agrees, rubbing his thumb gently across my bottom lip. "I always think about it though. That night, on replay. It finds me when I'm weak, which is only when I'm asleep."

"You dream about it?"

"All the time," he admits softly, kissing my mouth. "It's my penance. To relive that moment every night and to wake up knowing that it wasn't a dream, it's a memory."

"One day you will let it go," I tell him, gaze scanning his handsome face. "The dreams won't find you because you'll realize that everything happens for a reason. I wouldn't have Cara otherwise, and I wouldn't trade her for the world."

"You could have still had Cara," he says. "But she would have been mine."

"Honey," I whisper, caressing his rough cheek with my palm. "Does it bother you that she isn't?"

"I feel like she is," he says, looking me in the eye. "Even if I know she isn't. Does that make sense?"

I nod. "I slept around a lot. After what happened. I was partying and drinking. I liked the attention I got from men. I wasn't me, not really. I was hurt and lost. When I got pregnant with Cara, I changed again, but for the better. I stopped sleeping around and partying. I became a mother. She saved me, in a way. Wade was someone I'd been sleeping with for a week or two; he didn't want anything to do with her, like I told you before. He wanted me to have an abortion, but I told him I wouldn't. I also told him I wouldn't ask him for anything, so he agreed."

"Stupid fuck," Rake growls, arms tightening around me. "How did you manage by yourself?"

"It was rough," I admit hesitantly. "I studied and worked in a bar. Tried to give Cara everything she needed, but yeah, there were some bad times. Luckily she's too young to remember them."

"Fuck, Bailey, you could have come to me. No matter what, I would have helped you."

"I couldn't come to you then, Rake. I'd left you behind, but I was still hurting over everything that happened."

He cups my face and presses his nose against mine. "We didn't have an easy road, but we're both fighters, and we're going to fuckin' get through this. My past isn't going to touch us, and neither is yours, because we aren't going to let it. Nothing is going to touch us. Nothing else matters anymore, baby. Nothing."

"Ugh, stop being so cute," I tell him, kissing his nose.

He flashes me a slow-spreading smile. "Don't think anyone has called me cute other than you."

"Probably because you haven't been cute to anyone else," I say, winking at him.

"True," he agrees, hiding his face in my neck.

I yawn. "Can we nap for a bit and then take Cara out for dinner?"

"Sounds good," he says, pulling my body closer against his, as close as it could possibly get.

"Feeling clingy are we?" I joke, kissing his jaw.

"I want to sleep with me inside you."

"Why?" I ask, brows furrowing.

"Because it's home."

"Did I tell you what happened with Talon?" Anna asks me the next day, looking sadder than I've seen her in a long time. "Arrow broke his jaw."

My eyes widen. "Can't Talon fight?"

He's the president of their club; surely he knows a thing or two.

"He didn't fight back," Anna tells me, looking down at her phone screen. "He just let Arrow punch him in the face a few times without doing anything."

"Why?" I ask, wrinkling my nose.

"I have no idea. I don't understand these men any more than you do." She sighs, tucking her phone into her pocket and looking at me. "I really don't know what to do here. Arrow and Rake both hate Talon. I don't see why everyone can't just get along. We're all tied together in some way, whether it's good or bad."

"I think the only good tie is your friendship with Talon," I say. "Everything else is kind of shit."

And I think Anna is kind of naïve about the whole situation, if I'm being honest. I can understand how she wants to fit Talon into her life, but her loyalty to Arrow and the club has to come first.

She opens her mouth to object but then closes it. "Yeah. That pretty much sums it up, actually."

"Talon will be fine," I assure her. "He's a badass MC president."

"That he is," Anna says wryly. "I need to worry about fixing shit with Arrow, not Talon right now."

"Is he still angry?"

"A little," she says, wincing. "And I understand why. He'll get over it."

"Maybe you should be good until then," I suggest.

Her lip twitches. "I think that might be for the best."

Lana walks into the kitchen, where Anna and I are sitting, a bottle of champagne in her hand. "Just published a new book! You know the routine. Time to celebrate!"

"I'll start being good tomorrow," Anna jokes, making me laugh and Lana stare at us quizzically. We both congratulate her on her new release and decide to go out to dinner to celebrate.

Actual dinner this time.

"Adam," Cara says, holding a book up to him. "Will you read this to me, please?"

Rake picks up the massive book and looks at my daughter. "The whole thing? I think we'll be here for the next day."

Cara giggles and shakes her head. "Just a little bit."

"I'm sure I can do that," he tells her gently. "Why don't you get ready for bed first and then I'll read to you until you fall asleep?"

"Okay," she agrees. "But don't leave, all right?"

My eyes widen at that.

"I'm going to be right here," Rake tells her. "I don't want to be anywhere else right now."

"Sometimes you stay at your other house," she says, shrugging. "I'll go get ready for bed."

Rake stands and stares at the empty place Cara just vacated. He turns to look at me.

"You know she looks just like you, right? I can't say no to her. Anything she wants I'll give her with just a flash of those big brown eyes."

"You probably shouldn't let her know that," I say in a dry tone. I stand up and take his hand in mine. "I can read to her if you want."

Rake looks down at me, those green eyes calculating. "You know I love her like my own, right?"

I swallow hard. "Rake, I—"

"I don't care," he says simply. "I don't care how long it's been, or that it's not my blood in her veins. It's your blood and that's more than enough for me. You're mine, and she's mine."

"Did you just tell me that you love my daughter before you've even told me that you love me?" I ask, smiling up at him, my eyes filled with delight.

"Some things don't need to be said," he says, using his hand to grip my nape and pull me closer to him. "Go by actions instead. But if you want the words, then of course I fuckin' love you, Bailey. I never stopped loving you. You always had a piece of me. Always."

"And you, me," I whisper, resting my palms on his chest. "Always."

We stare into each other's eyes, so many things passing between us in the silence.

This man, he's mine.

I know his soul.

I see it.

It recognizes my own.

It doesn't matter what happened when we were apart, or who we were. Everything is inconsequential. A love like ours was never meant to end in the first place. We're like a magnetic force: we will always be drawn back together.

Because to me, that's what true love is.

TWENTY-NINE

One month later

WHY is Faye standing there with an MC cut on and no bra?" I whisper as I walk into the clubhouse.

Lana shrugs, her eyes wide. "I have no idea, but how come she has one? Shouldn't we all have one?"

Vinnie walks in and comes to a standstill. "Faye, what the fuck?"

Faye walks toward us and grins. "I'm going to surprise Dex. It's our anniversary."

Vinnie doesn't look impressed. "Why do we all have to see it though? You know you have a private house, right?"

Faye wiggles her eyebrows. "I heard you're having a party here tonight. I want to have a little fun before I get fat and start waddling around again. Is that so much to ask, Vinnie?"

Vinnie stares at her for a moment, then pulls out his phone and walks off, presumably calling Sin.

"I want one," Lana tells Faye. "Why don't we all have these?"

Faye shrugs, looking down at the kick-ass cut. "They got it

made for me after the whole Wild Men fiasco. I think all the women should have one too. I'll talk to Sin about it."

"Is he going to care you're standing here in jeans and a cut and nothing else?" I ask, pursing my lips to stop the giggle trying to escape.

"My nipples are covered, what's the big deal?" she asks, rolling her eyes. "So Vinnie is having a huge party, and the men don't want us here. Which is why I'm here. I want to see what's going on."

"They don't want us here?" Lana asks, scowling. "Does Anna know anything?"

"I don't know. You should call her and let her know though. I went on a snack run. Chips and dip, wine, champagne, and juice for me," she says, nodding her head toward the kitchen. "I made a huge bowl of punch too."

"I had no idea it was going to be this kind of night when I arrived," I say, glancing at Lana. "Did you?"

"Nope," she says, grinning. "But let's go with the flow. Do you have a sitter for Cara?"

"You can drop her at mine if you like," Faye offers, letting go of the cut and flashing more boob than appropriate. "Clover will love the company."

"Cara's with Tia and Rhett. I'll just message and let her know I'll be home late." I pause. "And probably drunk."

Faye grabs my shoulder. "That's the spirit. I don't know what slutty festivities Vinnie wants to get up to, but I'm intrigued." She looks to Lana. "If you want to put on another show I'll look away, I swear."

Lana's face turns bright red. "I will kill you."

Faye laughs in return, and blows her a kiss. "I'll be sober. So my job will be remembering everything everyone does and talking about it in detail tomorrow morning." She pauses. "While cooking the greasiest breakfast ever."

She looks Lana and me up and down. "You might want to change into something . . . less."

Lana rolls her eyes. "I'm staying only for a little. I need to get some words down tonight. I'll call Anna now though." She walks away with her phone in her hand.

Faye grabs my wrist and leads me into the kitchen. "Can you taste this for me?"

She pours a cup of a yellow punch and hands it to me. I bring the cup to my lips and take a mouthful.

Then almost spit it out.

"This is pretty much straight vodka!" I tell her, wiping my mouth with the back of my hand. "What did you do, add yellow food coloring? There's no juice taste whatsoever."

"I added some . . . stuff to it." She sniffs. "It's from a recipe I found online."

I wrinkle my nose in distaste. "Do you want me to try to fix it?"

"It is fixed," she says, grinning. "Oh, come on, everyone will love it."

I'm not so sure, but I decide to let it be. I won't be drinking any more of it, that's for certain. "Where is Rake, anyway?"

"He and Tracker went out to buy alcohol," she says, sighing. "Apparently it was a last-minute plan." She eyes me curiously. "You're going to be okay here tonight, yeah?"

"Yeaaaah," I reply, looking to the side. "Why wouldn't I?"

"Faye," Sin growls, walking into the kitchen and eyeing his wife. "Fuck, you look sexy." He looks to me and grins. "Hey, Bailey."

"Hey, Sin," I say, smiling. "Happy anniversary."

His eyes dart to Faye's. "Fuck, so that's what this is all about."

Ooops.

"What? You forgetting our anniversary and throwing a party no one wants me or the women at? Yeah that's what this is about," Faye says, putting her hand on her hip, one of her nipples poking out.

"Fuck, I'm sorry," Sin says, holding her cut closed. He leans down and whispers something in her ear while I make a quick exit.

"Do you think Rake will fuck us both again tonight?" the girl behind me asks her friend.

"I sure hope so."

I spin around, my eye starting to twitch. I now know exactly what Faye was referring to when she asked me if I could handle tonight. It almost felt like Rake had been with every woman here, and apparently his "thing" was having more than one in bed with him.

I didn't like this.

Not one bit.

What if he got bored of being only with me?

If this is what he likes now, how does he feel going without it?

I push away my insecurities and return to the table, sitting down with a long face.

"Chin up," Faye says so only I can hear. "Don't show them any kind of weakness."

"I want to strangle them." I sigh, sitting up straight and pulling myself together. This is something I'm going to have to handle. It comes with being Rake's.

Stupid man-whore.

"But watch him," Faye says to me. "He's ignoring every woman who tries to get his attention. He's showing them without words that he's not interested."

I follow Faye's line of sight, to where a beautiful brunette girl is trying to get his attention. She puts her hand on his bicep, but he steps to the side, her arm falling down.

"Still, the fact that he's probably slept with all of them is a hard pill to swallow," I admit, expelling a heavy sigh. When I hear him laughing at something the woman says, I stand up and walk over to him, unable to just sit there and watch any longer. As soon as I approach, he grabs me and pulls me against him. "This is my woman, Bailey, who I was telling you about," he says to her, brushing my hair off my neck and placing a kiss there.

"She's beautiful," the woman says, eyeing me from head to toe. "Maybe you will let me join you sometime."

When I look at her and realize she's talking to me, I have no idea how to respond. "Ummm," I mutter, elbowing Rake as I hear him chuckle softly. "I'm sorry, but I don't think so."

She looks sad, which makes me feel bad for a moment, until I remember what exactly we're discussing here. She's sad because she won't be getting fucked by Rake tonight, or ever again.

Let the bitch be sad.

She walks away, ass jiggling.

"Bailey," he whispers, lifting my chin up to look at him. "It's the past."

"Yet it keeps getting shoved in my face."

"It doesn't mean anything," he says, green eyes boring into me.

"How would you feel if a man I slept with asked you if he could join us in a threesome?" I ask, putting my hands on his chest and pushing myself away. "You'd want to kill him. I don't really feel the anger though, just the pain and jealousy that most of the women here have had you."

I leave him standing there and return to my seat.

"You okay?" Faye asks, brow furrowing. "I know it must suck, Bailey, but if you want him, you need to learn how to handle this."

"Faye, we're going home," Sin says, bending over and lifting her up in his arms. He'd made her take off her cut and put something on underneath it, so she is wearing a black tank top that still leaves little to the imagination.

"What? Why?" she grumbles, but wraps her arms around his neck.

"Because it's late, you're pregnant, and I want to fuck you," Sin says, kissing her neck.

"Oh. Well, if you put it that way," she says, waving 'bye to everyone.

"What's so different about this party?" I ask Anna, scanning the living area. "It looks like all the other ones to me."

Anna points to Lana, who is sitting on Tracker's lap, full-on making out.

"Think of it like the clubhouse turning into a sex club for the night," she says, rolling her eyes. "People can do what they like, no judgment. It's why they preferred us not to be here. For example, Vinnie would probably feel awkward having sex in front of Faye."

"Where's Irish?" I ask, looking around but not seeing him. "I feel like I haven't seen him in ages."

"Apparently he met someone," Anna says, leaning closer to me. "No one knows anything about her but he's been going to see her heaps."

My eyes widen. "That's some juicy gossip."

"It really is." Anna grins, leaning back in her chair. "Apparently Irish is always single, so I wonder how this woman managed to get his attention."

Rake walks over to us, and even though I'm mad, I can't help notice how sexy he looks in his dark jeans and white T-shirt. "How are two of my three favorite girls?" he asks, sitting down next to me.

"Who is the third?" Anna asks, as Rake takes my hand and brings it to his mouth, kissing my knuckles. I don't look at him.

"Cara, of course."

Anna lifts her hand to her heart. "Oh my god, that was so damn cute, Rake."

"I try," he says, kissing my hand again then looking around at the people. "Not as wild as they usually are."

"Probably because you're not participating this time," I blurt out before I'm unable to help it.

Anna laughs, then stands up. "Yeah, I'm going to . . . Arrow needs me."

"I'm concerned," I admit, looking around at all the beautiful women. "Do you miss this at all? The public sex, the threesomes, the many stunning women at your disposal . . . ?"

"No, I don't. I had my fun, Bailey. I played around, fucked around. Now I just want you. I still get to have fun, just with only you, and I want that. I wouldn't have it any other way," he says sincerely, eyes pleading with me to understand. "You're enough as you are. I don't need anything else. I never did."

"I hope that that's true," I say, looking down at our hands. "If you ever want something else, would you tell me? I mean, if you're not happy."

"Nothing makes me happier than you, Bailey. I don't know what I can say to make you believe that; you'll have to realize it yourself from my actions."

He's right about that. I know being insecure isn't attractive, but this is more than that. He's literally had these women before, so it's not like I'm being paranoid. They all know him, his body, the sounds he makes . . . what he likes in bed. And it kills me that they do, but there's nothing I can do to change it.

"Stop overthinking it," he whispers, kissing my earlobe. "I only see you, Bailey. It's always been that way, and it will never change."

"When did you turn so romantic?" I ask, dragging my finger down his bicep through the thin material.

"Just now," he replies simply. "When I saw the uncertainty in your eyes. I don't want to see it there again."

I look away and consider his words. "If you say I'm enough, then I believe you."

"Good. Now come here and sit on my lap, you're too fuckin' far away."

I stand up and go to him, sitting down on his lap, my legs across his. "Better?"

"Much."

"Is that Vinnie . . ." I trail off, squinting my eyes, trying to see what he was doing.

"Yup."

"Is he . . ."

"Yup."

"Oh."

Rake laughs, nuzzling my neck. "Do you want to go to bed?"

"Do you want to?" I ask him, kissing along his jaw. "I know this is your . . . thing."

"Have you ever had a threesome?" he asks, gripping my chin with his thumb and index finger, and searching my eyes.

"No," I reply honestly. "I can't say that I have."

Although it was one of the things I had listed on a sexual bucket list I wrote a few years back.

"If there's anything you want to do, any fantasies you have, you know I'll make them reality, right? You don't need to be shy. I doubt there's anything I haven't done." He pauses. "Unless you want to fuck another guy, because that's not happening."

"Have you played out all your fantasies?" I ask, already knowing the answer. I had no doubt in my mind that he'd done everything he'd want to, like he had just admitted.

His lip twitches before he kisses my mouth.

"Softening the blow?" I tease, shaking my head.

"You're my fantasy, baby," he says, grinning cheekily.

I smile back at him. "I better be."

THIRTY

ON Monday morning, I'm walking to my classroom when I see a man standing at my door. I freeze, not knowing what to say, dread and panic filling me.

"What are you doing here?" I ask him, shuffling the books in my hands so I don't drop them.

He'd changed. Gotten older. He didn't look good—he'd lost a lot of weight, looking a little gaunt. "I want to see my daughter."

"How did you know where I worked?" I ask, looking around. I don't want any passing students to hear this conversation, but I'm also shocked and confused. What the hell was he doing here? How did he know where to find me, and why now? There's no way he actually wants to see Cara, is there? Sure, a man can change, but I get the feeling that's not the case here. He must have an ulterior motive, although I can't really think of what it might be.

He looks around before answering. "I wanted to find you, so I did. And I want to see my daughter. Set up a meet, please. . . ."

That's it? He comes back out of the blue, after not having

anything to do with Cara, not caring enough to check up on her, or do anything for that matter, and he says, *Set up a meet?* He must be out of his fucking mind.

"Bailey, I brought the printouts you wanted," Mallory, the art teacher from next door says, stopping as she sees Wade. She looks between the two of us. "Everything okay here?"

"I was just leaving," Wade says softly. He then says so quietly, I almost don't hear it, "Think about it."

He walks away, leaving Mallory and I staring after him.

"Who was that?" she asks, walking into my classroom and putting the sheets down on my desk before sitting on the corner of it. She pushes her brown hair out of her face and watches me curiously. "He seems a little shady."

I expel a deep sigh and practically drop into my chair. "Someone from my past. No idea what he wants now, but I guess I'm going to soon find out."

"Call security next time," Mallory suggests, tightening her pouty lips. "I don't like the look of him."

Neither did I.

I make a mental note to tell Rake about it as soon as I get home.

I have a bad feeling about this.

Looks like I'm about to be thrown into more danger—except this time it isn't any biker's fault. It's mine.

"The men do this for fun?" I ask, cringing as Arrow punches Rake in the stomach.

"Yeah," Anna says, flashing me a sympathetic look. "You should probably get used to it."

"But"—I make a face—"how do you stand it? Your brother and your man?"

"This isn't their first fight," she says in a dry tone. "At least this is just for fun and it's not a serious fight, unlike last time. That was the worst."

"I don't think I even want to know." I breathe, closing my eyes as Rake gets in a punch to Arrow's jaw.

"We fight sometimes too," Anna tells me, raising her eyebrows. "Faye taught me some kick-ass moves. It's a good thing to know, Bails. I can teach you some self-defense if you like."

I tilt my head and consider it. "That sounds pretty good, actually. Maybe we can teach Cara something too?"

Anna nods, her eyes widening. "Great idea. Never too young to learn how to defend yourself."

Rake and Arrow get out of the ring, and Sin and Tracker get in. Rake grabs a towel and wipes his face, luckily there's no blood that I can see. Sweat drips down his abs, and I find myself watching a rivulet.

"Can you not give my brother sex eyes while I'm sitting right next to you?" Anna says, her face scrunching in distaste. "Eww."

"Eww? Mature, Anna," I reply, laughing.

"Hey, when it comes to my brother, I'm always the bratty baby sister," she says, grinning.

"I can't help it; look at him. That body. Those eyes. Sensual lips. Huge co—"

"Oh my god! You've been around all of us too long. We've corrupted you." She stands up and covers her ears with her hands. "That's it. I'm out of here."

I start laughing while the men stare at us curiously. Rake

walks over and leans down, kissing me roughly on the mouth. "Everything okay?"

"It will be once you take me to the room and fuck me," I say so only he can hear. I bite down on my bottom lip and give him the sultriest look I can fathom. I probably look ridiculous, but Rake doesn't seem to think so.

He looks down at himself. "Let me have a quick shower first, then I'm going to fuck you so hard you'll be feeling me for the next few days."

I put my palm on his abs and rub my fingers over his sweat. "No shower. I want you just like this."

His eyes darken.

They remind me of forests.

He bends at the waist and lifts me in the air, then over his shoulder.

The men call out a few amused comments and cheers, which I ignore.

I have only one goal in my mind.

Everything else is unimportant right now.

After we enter his room and he slams the door shut, he undresses me quickly, throwing my clothes on the floor. I stand in front of him naked as he pulls down his track pants, his cock springing forth. When he brushes past me and lies back on the bed, I turn around to watch him, taking in his beauty, absorbing it.

"Climb on," he rumbles in a deep voice.

I straddle his waist and take his cock in my hands without preamble.

"I want you to sit on my face first," he demands. "Want to taste you, want you to come in my mouth, then I'll fuck you."

I move toward his face, lift my leg over and lower my pussy to his mouth.

He peeks his tongue out, diving right in, tasting everything that is me and humming his enjoyment.

"Fuck, that feels so good," I whisper, looking down at him.

I put my hands against the wall as I slowly start to ride his face, and moan as he alternates between licking my clit and my center.

Fuck.

I've never done this before.

Never felt comfortable enough to do so.

He squeezes the globes of my ass, using them to bring me closer to his mouth. He sucks on my clit, and that's when I know I'm a goner.

It feels too good for me to last any further.

I whimper his name.

I start to tremble.

Then, I shatter.

Rake lifts me off him, spins me around and moves me farther down, so I'm riding him reverse cowgirl. Pushing me forward with his hand on my lower back, he slides into me, then grips my hips while lifting his up at the same time.

"So wet," he growls, thrusting up into me faster and harder.

I grind down on him, holding on to his thighs for support.

He slaps my ass.

I groan.

He sits up and reaches around so he can play with my clit, while I take control of the rhythm. It's not long before I'm coming again, and he joins me a few seconds after.

He takes me in his arms, my back against his chest, me sitting in between his legs.

"You okay?" he asks, sliding my hair to the side and kissing my nape.

"Perfect." I breathe heavily. "You?"

"Never better. Bailey?"

"Yeah?"

"I love you."

"I love you too," I tell him gently, turning my head to the side so I can kiss his lips. "Always."

"Come have a shower with me?" he asks, scooting off the bed with me still in his arms.

As if he doesn't want to part from me.

He carries me to the shower, only putting me down to turn on the water. When it's warm, he opens the door wide for me to enter first. I let the water run down my back as he joins me, kissing me deeply and pressing my back against the cold tiles. His fingers trail down my stomach, and I part my thighs as he finds my core. One finger parts my folds and slides inside me gently, the same time his other hand softly clasps my throat.

"I want more," I tell him, so he slides another finger, and his hold on my throat tightens just a tiny bit. I make a sound of pleasure in my throat, and as he starts to play with my clit I find myself getting hungrier and greedier.

"Do you like my hand on your throat?" he asks, licking my earlobe.

I nod, my eyes boring into his, his heavy-lidded look making me want to jump on him and demand for him to fuck me hard.

I did like his hand there; in fact, I found myself wanting him to squeeze tighter.

"Yes," I whisper.

He kisses me lazily, then in a quick movement lifts me in his arms. I wrap my legs around his waist. He slides into me, and I moan into his neck. So good. He pulls my head back with his hand in my hair, so he can kiss me again. He thrusts into me, over and over again until I'm screaming his name. Then, worn out, we dry off and get into bed. I fall asleep wrapped in his arms.

Now this is living.

THIRTY-ONE

"Y OU and Rake need a room," Anna states, pursing her lips together. "You're so . . ." She looks to Lana. "What's the word for what they are, author?"

"In love?" Lana supplies, with a raised brow. "You know, the honeymoon stage. The can't-keep-our-hands-off-each-other, life-is-wonderful, how-did-I-get-so-lucky, all-I-need-to-breathe-is-you stage?"

"That," Anna says wryly, pointing at me. "That and more. I think a ladies' night is in order."

"Are you allowed out again after the Talon shenanigans?" I ask, trying to hide my amusement.

"No man controls me," Anna says, puffing out her chest. "But yeah, I've been forgiven for the ordeal. I had lunch with Talon yesterday actually. He kept saying he was sorry and he shouldn't have persuaded us to enter his domain."

"Is that why he took Arrow's hits without retaliating?" I ask, trying to figure out the man's motives.

"I think so," Anna says, drinking from her bottled water.

"Who knows what runs through his mind though. You know, besides everything that happened afterward, it was a pretty fun night."

"It was. Did you tell Lana about Ranger?"

"You mean the sexiest villain to ever exist?" Lana says, laughing. "Yeah, I heard. Is it true his eyes are like hazel depths of heaven?"

"I so didn't say that," Anna says, nudging Lana with her shoulder. "More like hazel depths of sin."

"He's a beautiful man," I agree, sighing at the memory. "Like, wow. It's unfair for a man to be that good-looking."

"And that evil," Anna adds, scowling. "At least we beat him at beer pong. That will teach him."

"I'm sure he's crying in his bed over it as we speak," Lana says, sarcasm filling her tone.

"Hey, he definitely didn't like losing," I agree, looking at Lana. "He was pissed. He's a sore loser. Maybe he's one of those competitive guys." I pause. "Who also reads Shakespeare and shit."

Lana puts down her phone. "What's that all about?"

"Apparently he's all into literature and books, and he's smart as hell," I say, shrugging my shoulders. "According to Talon anyway. Looks and brains."

"But his personality and the fact he likes to kidnap women in his spare time make him a total douche, I don't care how much he looks like he belongs on the cover of one of Lana's books," Anna says passionately, her eyes narrowed to slits. "He needs to be taken down a notch."

"So you like Slice more than Ranger then?" I joke, sharing an amused glance with Lana.

"Slice is my best friend compared to Ranger. The bastard," she says, slamming her fist into her palm.

"Really? Should we invite him to ladies' night?" I tease, dodging the pillow she throws at me.

"There aren't that many good-looking men in the Wild Men MC," Anna points out. "Don't you think? There's a couple. Talon, Ranger, of course, Slice, and there's that red-haired guy. He's pretty hot."

"Our men are better," I say, smiling widely, flashing teeth.

Anna and Lana wholeheartedly agree with me.

"Bailey!" I hear Rake yell, and something in his voice has me standing on my feet. Anna and Lana do the same, worried expressions on their faces. The door opens and Rake stands there, angry tension radiating from him. "Come here."

I quickly step to him and he holds me in his arms, his chest rising against my cheek.

"We have a fuckin' problem, baby," he says, running his fingers through my hair.

"What?" I ask, dread settling in the pit of my stomach. "What happened?"

"Rake?" Anna asks, coming closer to stand next to her brother. "What's going on?"

"Cara's father is here," he grits out, the word *father* leaving his lips like a curse word.

I lift my head. "Wh-what?"

Oh shit. He's here? Does he have a death wish? How did he even know to come here? I'm definitely missing something here, because nothing makes sense.

And to make matters worse, I forgot to tell Rake that he

showed up at the school that day. If I'd told him, all of this probably could have been avoided.

"Shit," I whisper, flashing Rake an apologetic look.

"What is it?"

"He showed up at my school asking to see Cara, but then I didn't hear from him again. I completely forgot to tell you about it."

"Seriously? That's kind of important information, Bailey," Rake growls at me, scowling. "She's mine too, and if this bastard thinks he's taking her, he has another thing coming."

"What am I going to do?" I ask hesitantly.

"Let's hear him out, then tell him to fuck off," Rake says, scrubbing a hand down his face.

"I want my daughter," I tell him, needing to have her near me. "I want to go to her, now."

"She's with Faye and Sin at their house," he says, running his hand down my back soothingly. "Trust me, no one is safer than her right now. We just need to deal with this asshole."

"So he's actually here right now? At the clubhouse?" I ask, my eyes wide.

I still don't get it. He walked into a biker clubhouse demanding to see my Cara and me?

Rake nods, rubbing the back of his neck. "Yeah, yeah he is. He wants to see you. I'll take you there because he won't negotiate otherwise, but you will not leave my side, do you understand?"

I nod, swallowing hard. "He's not taking Cara."

"No, he sure as fuck isn't. I'll explain everything to you later."

Fuck.

Why does this shit happen to me?

Rake turns to his sister and Lana and says sternly, "Both of you stay here."

"Rake—"

"Just listen this time, Anna," he says, pushing me forward until I'm out the door, then closing it behind him.

"Whatever happens," he says, staring down at me intently. "I will make sure it's okay. All right? You have nothing to worry about. He wants to start shit; I'll handle him."

I nod, not sure what to say.

I didn't really understand what was happening right now.

We keep walking until we reach the living area, where Arrow is standing, arms crossed, looking imposing as hell. Next to him is Wade. It's hard to believe he's Cara's biological father, because she looks nothing like him. It's unfair that he gets to be called that, since the only thing he did was not wear a condom, but apparently that qualifies for the title.

"Bailey," he says, standing and facing me.

"Wade," I say, forcing myself to keep my expression neutral. "What the hell do you think you're doing here?"

"Like I said before, I want to see my daughter," he says, putting his hands in his pockets. "Just want to see my little girl."

I tighten my lips. "How did you know where I was?"

First the school, now the clubhouse? This is getting a little scary.

He licks his lips and looks away. "I have my ways."

Another bullshit answer.

Arrow steps closer to the man. "Answer the lady. Or I'll ask her to leave and I'll ask you the same question in a much less nicer way."

Wade smirks, but I don't miss the flash of fear in his eyes. "My brother is on his way here. You can't touch me."

His brother?

"Who's your brother?" I ask him, looking to Arrow and Rake, who don't give me an answer.

I don't like the smugness on Wade's face right now.

Not one bit.

"He's a Wind Dragon," Wade tells me, satisfaction etched all over his expression.

His brother is a Wind Dragon?

So Wade thinks he's untouchable.

I look to Rake.

Was he untouchable?

Rake gives me nothing, his expression never changing.

Was there a rule about this? Could Rake do nothing to Wade because he was family to one of his club brothers? Did Wade truly just want to see Cara? Why now, after all this time? There is more to this, I just know it. Wade wants something, but it isn't just to see the daughter he never once gave a shit about.

When Pill storms into the clubhouse, wearing black leather pants, a long-sleeved T-shirt, and his MC cut, I don't take my eyes away from him.

So this was Wade's brother.

No wonder Faye didn't like the man.

If he's anything like his brother . . .

Bad blood.

The air fills with tension so thick I find it hard to breathe.

"My bro just wants to see his kid, Rake," Pill says, putting his hand on Wade's shoulder. "Not asking too much, I don't think."

"So you told him I was here then," I say to Pill. "What, you were gossiping about Rake's woman to your brother and he pieced together that it was me?" I look to Wade. "Stop with all the bullshit. What do you really want? You don't care about my daughter. Do you even know her name!?"

"Looks like someone doesn't know her place," Pill snaps, looking as if he wants to come at me.

"Even look in my woman's direction and I will fuckin' end you," Rake says to Pill, in a deceptively calm tone. "Trust me, you don't want to fuck with me."

"Club comes first," Pill says, but takes a step back. "You want to start shit with the Channon chapter? What, a civil war? Over this bullshit?"

Rake smirks, his eyes narrowed in anger. "You prospected here Pill, but you have no fuckin' clue about me or my brothers. Bailey is my old lady, and your brother has shit to do with the MC. No one will take your side in this. No one. I will fuckin' call Zach right now, see what he thinks. No one is going near Angel. She's mine. I claim her. Don't even think of her as your blood, because she has nothing of you in her. She's all ours."

"Zach doesn't speak for all the men," Pill says, lifting up his chin.

Arrow looks at Rake. "Your call, brother."

Rake looks down at me, then back up at Wade. "Leave, go back to Channon. You're not seeing my daughter. This is the last time I will warn you about this. Let it go, or no one will be able to save you. I don't give a fuck who your brother is."

"I'll get a lawyer then," Wade says, fists clenching. "You can't beat the justice system with your threats. Say what you will, but I am her father, something a simple DNA test will prove."

"Why now?" I ask him, steel lacing my tone. "You didn't give a shit about her for the past six years, so why now?"

"I don't need to explain anything," he says arrogantly. "She's my blood, end of story."

Such a dickhead.

How did I ever sleep with this man?

"Can't get a lawyer if you're fuckin' dead," Arrow says casually, nodding his head like he thinks it's a good idea.

Jesus.

"What do you want?" Rake asks him, looking him straight in the eye. "Cut to the fuckin' chase."

Wade looks down then up again. "I want a hundred thousand."

So that's why he's here? For money? I didn't think my opinion of him could get any lower, but he's proved me wrong. Wow. So he's threatening to try to take Cara if we don't give him a hundred thousand dollars? I shake my head, unable to believe the audacity of the worthless man standing in front of me.

"And how do we know you won't be back again? You're clearly a shit cunt, so your word won't mean shit," Arrow snarls, shifting on his feet, as if trying to stop himself from losing control.

"He won't ask for anything else," Pill says.

He obviously knew his brother wanted money.

And is supporting it.

Fuck.

Yeah, Faye was right about that one.

THIRTY-TWO

THE men all have a meeting.

The women and the kids are sitting outside; Rake said he wanted everyone together until they knew how they were going to handle this situation. I don't know what to think. Giving Wade money was only going to solve the problem for now, and a hundred grand was a huge amount. According to Anna, the MC had a shitload of money, but that wasn't the point. I couldn't ask Rake to pay that no matter how much money he had.

"Don't stress, honey," Faye says to me, placing her hand on the inside of my arm. "They'll handle it."

"I don't want to start shit," I tell Faye, puffing out a breath. "But I don't want Wade to win either. So I don't know how to make both of those things happen."

I watch Cara and Clover playing on the grass with some Superman and Batman toys. Cara laughs, the sound settling in my soul.

I'd do anything to protect her.

Anything.

In a way I feel guilty, because it was my bad judgment that gave her such a father.

She's going to have to pay for my decision for the rest of her life.

"It's not that big of an issue," Faye says, tapping her burgundy fingers on her chin. "I don't think so. The biggest problem is Pill, not Wade. Wade is easy. Pill however . . . I think Rake should head up to Channon and talk to the men there, sort shit out before Pill twists things and starts something."

"Do you think that's what he'll do?" I ask, not really liking the idea of Rake leaving. "He will take some of the men with him, right? I don't want him to go up there alone."

"I'm sure he'll take someone. Zach's up there, and he's a good man. It will all be good in the end," Faye says, pushing my hair back behind my ear. "We'll probably never hear from Wade again."

I don't even want to touch that comment.

"Why did he make everyone come to the clubhouse then?" I ask, scrubbing my hands down my face. "And he's not even going to tell me the plan, is he? I'm going to be kept in the dark about everything because I have a vagina."

Faye spits out her water at my comment. "Fuck." She laughs, wiping her mouth. "Oh, come on, that was funny! Look, we're all here so no one has to worry. Everyone is safe. We always come here when shit's going down, just in case. We all like to keep each other safe. It's a precaution; it doesn't necessarily mean we're dodging bullets."

I exhale deeply and sink down in my chair. "I didn't even know Wade had a brother."

"Is Wade as ugly as Pill?" Faye asks, cringing.

I shake my head. "No. Why is Pill even having his back for this? Surely Pill has money if Wade is that desperate for some."

Faye glances around, then leans closer to me, her auburn hair falling around her like a curtain. "I heard Sin saying that he heard rumors about Pill taking drugs. Ice. That shit isn't cheap. Maybe Wade's taking drugs with him, and the two of them need cash. Good thing is, if we can prove this, maybe Pill will lose his cut."

I sit up straight and think that over. "Interesting."

"See, us vaginas do find out some information," she teases, nudging me playfully.

"Good to know." I grin. "Even if we have to resort to eavesdropping."

She shrugs, completely unashamed. "Girl's gotta do what a girl's gotta do. As the club lawyer I end up finding everything out anyway. But I have to keep most of that shit to myself, unfortunately. I can help with the legal side of things for you though: we can file for sole custody. The courts won't give him Cara. If anything, they'll make him back pay a shit load of child support."

I smile and thank Faye for her legal help. I don't want any money from him though. I don't want anything from him.

Anna lifts her legs up on my lap. "We should put a pool in here. There's plenty of room."

I roll my eyes. "That's what you're thinking about right now?"

She just smiles. "The perks of being with a controlling alpha male. I have no doubt in my mind that everything will be taken care of. Rake isn't going to let anything happen to you or Cara. He won't let that man even breathe in her direction."

Irish walks out at that moment and flashes us a smile. "Ladies."

"Dude, where have you been?" Faye asks, standing up and pulling him in a hug. "Who is she? Where is she? Is she here?"

Irish lets go of her, but Faye still holds on to him, dangling there. "Bros over hos, man. We've missed you around here."

"I haven't been gone that much," he replies gruffly, gently extracting Faye from his person. "I've had a few things I needed to take care of, darlin'."

Faye finally lets him go and plops back down in her seat. Irish sits next to her and stretches his arms above his head, showing off his biceps.

"If you're out here, why are they still in there?" she asks, looking back toward the door.

"They're coming," he says, just as Sin, Arrow, Tracker, Rake, Trace, Ronan, and Vinnie walk out one by one. Rake offers me his hand, and I take it. He then calls Cara, who runs over to us, and takes her hand in his other one.

"We leave tomorrow then?" Rake asks Sin, who nods his head once, his blue eyes homing in on me.

"Rake is going away for a few days; Irish and Vinnie are going to take turns staying with you until he's back, all right?" Sin says.

I nod.

Rake's hand tightens on mine.

We say our 'byes, and Rake takes us home.

Rake tells me he's moving in permanently as soon as he returns. Faye was right; he's heading to Channon to sort shit out and will be back in three days. The lack of information annoys the hell out of me, but feeling tired after a stressful day, I fall asleep wrapped in his arms.

And even after everything, I still feel safe there.

* * *

The next day, I'm watching Rhett and Cara ride their bicycles in the front yard, and sipping on some fresh orange juice, Anna, Lana, and Vinnie next to me. The sun is shining and we all decided to enjoy it. Vinnie and Anna put some gin in their OJ, while Lana and I are going alcohol-free and silently judging them for drinking at one in the afternoon.

"Did you hear about that guy, Dom someone from school? I think he was in your grade," Anna says casually, her eyes covered by her big black sunglasses.

"Dom who?" I ask, my eyes darting between her and the kids.

I try to keep myself calm.

She didn't know what happened.

Only Rake did.

And Christa.

And . . . him.

Dom Rogers.

"Dom Rogers, I think," she says, taking a sip from her straw. "I saw in the paper that he died. A car crash, I think. They mentioned he went to our high school."

"Yeah, I remember him," I say in an empty voice.

I'll never forget him.

I'll see flashes of his face for the rest of my life.

But now he was dead.

And I felt . . . not happy, not sad.

I felt . . . peaceful.

It was years ago, I know. But time doesn't always heal wounds. Not a wound like that.

Nothing would heal it.

I look down at my hands, my clean hands, and somehow I just know that Rake's aren't as clean.

No, they're bloody.

They are dripping.

They were dirty before I was reunited with him, and they're even bloodier now. Feeling a little numb, as if I'm looking at my life from the outside in, I think over everything that's happened.

Dom is dead. I can't explain the liberating feeling that comes with knowing that. It might make me evil or whatever, but I don't feel any guilt that he's dead. I don't feel any remorse. I feel like it's finally over.

And now Rake's taking care of Wade, the man who gave me Cara but tried to take her back for his own selfish reasons. A man who doesn't give one fuck about my daughter, only what he could get out of her.

It's twisted, I know.

But I smile.

Because Rake is my guardian angel.

Or maybe my personal grim reaper.

THIRTY-THREE

"So . . ." I say, wringing my hands. "How's things with you, Irish?"

He flashes me a sardonic smile. "No need to make small talk, Bails. Silence is perfectly fine."

I roll my eyes at him. "I'd hate to make the night easy on you, then."

He laughs and changes the channel on the TV. "Things are fine. Is this your way of prying? I hear the women have been speculating about me."

I shrug my shoulder and risk a glance at him. His dark eyes are already on me. "We thought maybe you had someone special in your . . ."

"Bed?"

"I was going to say life, but bed works," I say in a dry tone, crossing my legs on the couch. "You're not going to tell me anything, are you?"

"Nope."

"Fine," I give in, staring at the screen. "Rake hasn't called today."

"Probably busy," Irish says, looking at his phone distractedly. "Sorting shit out. Possibly trying to kill Pill."

My head snaps to him. "They want to kill Pill?"

He looks up from his phone and starts laughing. "Kill Pill."

"Irish." I sigh, giving up on him and watching the movie.

"So how come Vinnie got his favorite meal made but I didn't get shit?" he asks after a few moments.

"What's your favorite meal?" I ask him.

"Well that's the thing. I have two. Are you going to make me both?"

This guy.

"No. Choose one," I tell him, my mouth twitching.

"I can't. It's too hard."

"That's what she said," I mutter under my breath, but he hears it and starts laughing at me.

"Fuck. And you're a teacher. Wish I had a teacher like you when I was in school," he says, rubbing the scar on his neck absently.

"You're being awfully chatty for someone who claims to like silence," I point out.

He grins. "You're cute." He pauses. "And you cook well. And you make my brother happy. And you have a nice—"

"Fine, I'll make you your two meals. Just stop," I interrupt, holding up my hand. "You think I'm great, I get it."

"Fuck if I knew all I had to do was compliment a woman to get fed, I'd have been doing it for a long time." He looks down at his stomach. "I'm kind of hungry right now, you know."

I scoff. "I'm not cooking now, it's ten p.m. and I'll need to do a grocery run anyway."

My phone beeps with a message from Rake.

I miss you so fucking much.

I smile to myself and type back.

Already, huh?

He replies instantly.

Always.

I smile wider and send:

As much as the sky is blue?

Irish groans and shakes his head. "If you start fuckin' giggling like a schoolgirl next, I'm out."

Rake replies.

More.

I grin and type back.

It doesn't get much bluer than the sky.

Next, he sends me a picture of his hard cock, with the caption

It doesn't get much harder than my dick. For you.

ruining the romantic moment but making me giggle.

Irish throws the remote, stands up, and leaves.

Which only makes me giggle harder.

"I can't stop thinking about Talon," Tia blurts out as she walks into my living room.

I look around for Irish.

"Don't worry about him, he's sitting out front smoking," she says, sitting down next to me. "I know it's stupid, but what do I do? Should I just fuck him out of my system? Yes, that's exactly what I should do."

"You know I kissed him, right?" I say, cringing. "I wouldn't have, if I knew you'd end up liking him."

She waves her hand in the air. "It was just a kiss, who cares. Not like you let him bend you over."

I expel a deep sigh.

My friend.

"From what he says he's not the settling-down type," I tell her, thinking it over. "Are you going to think you're the exception to the rule?"

She nods.

"Jesus, Tia. Think this over before you dive in," I tell her. "I don't know how this is going to go. If you just want sex, then it's easy, but if you want any more . . . Yeah, I don't know."

"I don't know either," she admits, sinking back into my couch. "I should have gone with you to his birthday thing and tried to figure out why I'm so infatuated with the man. Knowing me, I'll just want to sleep with him, then I'll get over it."

"Talon owes me a favor, you know," I say, thinking back to the beer pong incident. "I could call it in for you."

Tia smiles slowly and a little evilly. "You'd do that for me?"

"Of course," I reply. "I don't think Rake will be too happy knowing about it anyway, so I will happily use it for you."

Tia taps her finger to her lips in thought.

Scheming.

Forever scheming.

"Okay, how about this?"

*   *   *

I wake to the sound of something smashing, followed by a sound I've never heard before in real life.

The sound of a gun being cocked. I try to remain still as the person holding the gun doesn't make any further movements. I didn't think they were going to shoot me, or they probably would have already. No, they obviously wanted to threaten me, or to use me against the club.

Who was in the house?

Wade?

Pill?

Fuck, when did I get so many enemies?

When my eyes focus, I'm truly surprised to see just who is pointing the gun to me.

What the actual fuck?

I hear noises in the other room. A slamming noise, like someone getting pushed up against the wall, and I hear Irish yell, his accent more pronounced than ever. *Cara.*

My heart in my throat, my mind races. Is she okay? Did someone have a gun pointed at her too? They wouldn't hurt her, would they? What am I going to do? What if they try to kidnap her?

Panicking isn't going to help.

I need to keep calm and think.

Cara.

"Get up," she demands quietly.

All I can think about is my daughter.

Is she safe?

Does Irish have her protected? Is he okay? How many men does he have up against him? What if he needs my help right now? Shit. Not that I can do much, but I can do something.

"What are you doing, Amethyst?" I ask, sliding out of my bed slowly, not wanting her to react to any sudden movements. I need to get to my daughter, and no crack whore is going to get in my way. "What do you want?"

It's clear she's doing Pill's bidding. She must be a weak woman indeed for him to be able to put her up to this.

All this for money? Or was this for revenge?

Her fingers tremble, making the gun shake.

Yeah, she doesn't know what she's doing, and it makes me feel a little more confident.

I remind myself that she's just a stupid girl. I can take her, gun or not.

All I need is the right moment.

I hear some glass shatter. We both look to the door as we hear a commotion, a scuffle of some kind, and I use the distraction to kick her once, right in the stomach.

Hard.

One of the moves Anna showed me just last week.

She bends at the waist, holding her stomach, and drops the gun. It falls to the ground, luckily not going off.

I pick it up, awkwardly, and point it at her.

My hands are even shakier than hers were.

"Cara!" I yell at the top of my lungs. "Irish."

Amethyst takes a step toward me.

"Stay back!" I yell at her, taking a step backward. If she came at me would I shoot her? If I had to, yes, I would. I've never used a gun before, but if this idiot can figure it out, then so can I.

"Do you even know how to use that thing?" she sneers, the moonlight shining on her face. "Just give him the money, and we'll leave you all alone."

I hear my daughter scream, and it breaks me out of my trance.

There is no option other than her being safe, nothing I wouldn't do.

I'm about to rush through the door when it slams open, and Irish stands there, Cara in his arms.

I exhale.

Thank God.

All I feel is relief until I see blood on his stomach, some of it on Cara's leg. He's hurt.

"We have a huge fuckin' problem," he says to me, turning the light on and staring at Amethyst. "Of course they sent some drugged-up bitch to do the dirty work for them. Give me the gun, Bails. You take Angel."

Cara lifts her head and looks at me, and her brown eyes look terrified. I hand Irish the gun, then carry her into my arms, running my hand down her back. "Everything will be okay."

Irish grabs Amethyst by the arm and looks at me. "Stay here."

Cara whimpers into my neck.

A few minutes pass before I hear a car pull into my driveway.

When I hear Tracker's and Vinnie's voices, I relax.

My door opens, and it's Tracker.

He sits on the bed and pulls Cara into his arms.

"What happened?" I whisper.

He looks at Cara before replying. "Wade thought he could use the two of you as leverage. He knew Rake was in Channon. He's clearly not thinking right, his mind is just on drugs; he's lost his shit."

"Where is he now?" I ask, looking up at him.

Tracker doesn't reply to that, all he does is look away and say, "Pack a bag, you're going to stay at the clubhouse."

I nod.

"And, Bails," he says, standing and passing me my daughter back. "When you walk out of this room, don't look."

I pack a bag and open my room door. *Don't look?* Don't look where? I walk toward the front door with my eyes straight ahead.

I look at my daughter's angelic face. She's now asleep, feeling safe in my arms. Safe from the world. Safe from the sight before me.

But then, I look. How can I not? I see what they don't want me to. I stand still, frozen in my spot and stare.

I'm glad Cara would never see what I was currently seeing.

Her "father" dead. In our living room. Blood dripping from his chest, onto our cream carpet.

No, she didn't need to see that at all.

I wish I hadn't.

"What did you do with Amethyst?" I ask Vinnie, when Cara was asleep in Rake's bed in the clubhouse.

His mouth tightens, and he runs a hand over his bald head. "Don't worry about her; you won't see her again."

I slam my hand down on the table. "Tell me."

His eyes narrow at my outburst. "She's with Talon for now, until we figure out what we're going to do with her."

My eyes widen. "You asked for help from the Wild Men?"

Vinnie scowls, a muscle ticking in his jaw. "Don't fuckin' remind me. Our hands were full with Wade's dead fuckin' body. I owe that fuck a marker now, and I don't like owing people shit." He looks at me, his eyes softening. "Your house is being cleaned.

Wade is being taken care of. Amethyst will be dealt with. You have nothing to worry about."

"What did Cara see?" I ask, looking around the kitchen. "And where is Irish? He had blood on him, is he okay?"

"He's being stitched up," Vinnie replies casually. "Wade got him with a knife. He's fine," he says when I'm about to panic. "Wade got one jab in. Not too deep. I don't think Cara saw anything. Wade attacked Irish while Amethyst went after you. I think the bitch was meant to get you and Cara in one room while Wade took care of Irish. Then he'd probably call Rake up and tell him what he wanted. But he underestimated Irish." He looks me in the eye. "And you too."

"I didn't do anything," I say, puffing out a breath. "I was just worried about Cara. If something happened to her . . ."

Vinnie put his hand on my cheek. "She's fine. You're fine. Why don't you try to get some rest? No doubt Rake will be here the second he finds out what happened. Tracker is about to call him."

"I guess there's no more need for negotiations," I say wryly, standing up off the stool. I look at Vinnie until he's looking back at me. "Talon owes me a marker, maybe I could use it so you don't have to owe him one?"

Vinnie shakes his head. "No, sweetheart. No one pays my debts but me." He pauses. "But thank you. Do I even want to know why the Wild Men president owes you a marker?"

I shake my head.

"I thought so," he says, lifting his Scotch to his lips and taking a mouthful. "Bed, Bails."

I step toward him and give him a kiss on his cheek.

Then I go to bed.

But I don't sleep.

How can I?

I spend the long night just watching Cara's angelic face.

Rake arrives in the morning, alone. He rode all night. Me in his arms, he whispers "Sorry" into my hair.

Sorry he wasn't here. Sorry this happened.

"It wasn't your fault, Rake," I tell him, over and over. "We're fine. Irish was there, and nothing happened to us."

"I should have been there," he says so softly I have to strain to hear him. "If anything happened to you and Cara . . . Who would have thought they'd be so fuckin' stupid? Even if we gave them money and got you two back safely, we would have found them after. Same outcome, the bastard would be fuckin' dead."

Having enough of the whole thing, I look him dead in the eye. "Rake."

"Yes, baby?"

"Just hold me," I whisper, my body starting to shake.

"Anything you need," he replies. "Anything. Do you want to talk about it?"

I shake my head. "Not right now. I'm just so thankful Cara wasn't hurt. It could have gone in a completely different direction."

How could Wade do something so stupid and reckless? At the end of the day, Cara is still his daughter. She could have gotten shot with that stupid woman waving her gun around. I can't believe the lengths some people will go to. Amethyst reeked of desperation, and I have to wonder just what was going on between her, Wade, and Pill. I have a feeling there's more to it than meets the eye.

"Don't even think about it, Bailey," Rake rumbles.

I've heard the other women's stories, on how being involved with the MC brought them into dangerous situations. However, with me it was Wade who decided to bring trouble upon me. When Cara's older and asks about her biological father, I'll have to tell her that he died. She doesn't need to know the truth behind the story.

Nothing touches my daughter, nothing.

And she will have Rake as her father, and she will be loved and protected.

I close my eyes and bury my face in Rake's neck, smelling him.

In his presence, I allow myself to be vulnerable.

I show him weakness, as I cry in his arms.

He comforts me.

He holds me.

He loves me.

And I know everything will be all right.

When I wake up I hear Rake mutter something into his phone about dealing with the Kings MC "shit" later. I close my eyes and pretend I don't hear it. Maybe they weren't letting the whole Rake-sleeping-with-that-woman thing go. I don't want to think about that; I'm not ready to deal with more drama yet. "Okay, yeah, Vinnie," he says into the line. "'Bye.'"

"Everything okay?" I ask, rolling over and snuggling into him.

"It will be," he says, kissing the top of my head. "Go to sleep."

I go back to sleep.

THIRTY-FOUR

One month later

RISH comes inside and grins when he sees me. "Rake told me you wanted to see me."

I nod and point toward the kitchen. "I wanted to thank you, for everything," I say, shifting on my feet. "So I cooked your two favorite meals for you, just like you wanted."

Irish grins and steps to me, wrapping me in a one-armed hug. "You didn't need to do that, Bails. Any of the men would have done the same. It's who we are, who we decide to be when we join the club. Family is everything, and you're family."

I wrap my arms around his torso and squeeze. "I know, but still. Thank you." I let go, only just remembering his injury. "Your wound?"

"It's fine," he says, taking a step toward the kitchen. "It was nothing but a scratch. You women all need to quit fussing over me."

I follow him into the kitchen and watch his eyes widen at the huge spread. "Fuck me."

"Hope you're hungry." I grin, grabbing a plate for him and gesturing for him to sit.

"How did you know?" he asks, watching me. "I never told you."

"I asked Faye and Rake. And Tracker. And Arrow."

Irish throws his head back and laughs. "Fuckin' hate that I'm that predictable."

"More like easy," I say, pointing to the pepperoni and jalapeño pizza. "Pizza? Super easy. And ribs? Also easy."

"I'm a simple man," he replies, taking a giant slice of pizza and studying it.

"All homemade," I tell him, taking a seat and grabbing a slice. "I didn't cheat, although it would have been easy to."

He shakes his head, then says in his slightly accented voice, "That's not it. I wouldn't have cared if you bought it; the thought alone is fuckin' nice enough."

"Then what?"

"Just," he says, shrugging sheepishly. "It's really nice you did this. For me and me alone. I don't know, I guess I wanted to savor the moment."

He's so cute right now, but I don't think he'd appreciate it if I point that out, so I just smile at him and go and grab a beer for him out of the fridge.

"It's so damn good," he says, practically inhaling the first slice and going onto the next.

"Thanks," I tell him, happy that he likes it.

"Where's Rake and Angel?" he asks after chewing and swallowing.

"Rake took her to the movies. They should be back soon," I tell him, reclaiming my seat and sliding him his beer.

"Thanks, Bails. You know what?"

"What?" I ask.

"You're one hundred percent old-lady material."

I smile warmly. "I'm glad you think so."

He looks at the food when he says, "I did meet someone."

So, for once, the gossip was right. I feel special that he decided to share this with me, of all people.

My eyes widen at his admission. "What's her name?"

"Valentina."

"That's a pretty name," I tell him truthfully. "When are you going to bring her to meet everyone?"

"Very soon," he says, lip twitching.

"Is she old-lady material too?" I find myself asking.

"Fuck yeah."

We both share a smile.

When Arrow gets down on one knee and proposes to Anna, in front of all his brothers and the women, I can't help it when tears of happiness stream down my face.

"Yes!" Anna squeals, letting him slide the huge diamond on her finger, then practically jumping on him.

"About time he made an honest woman out of her," Rake says into my ear, his smile wider than I've ever seen it. He wipes the tears from my cheeks and shakes his head. "Fuckin' soft-hearted you are, baby."

"It's Anna" is all I say.

"Yeah," he agrees, kissing the last tear away. "She deserves to be happy. She deserves the best. Never thought she'd find it in someone like Arrow, but I guess weirder things have happened."

I elbow him playfully in the chest. "Stop it."

He laughs and kisses my lips, then joins in with the cheers

and shouts for Anna and Arrow. The couple comes up to us, and Anna and I hug tightly. "Congrats."

"Thank you," she replies, kissing my cheek.

"Brother," Arrow says to Rake, slapping his shoulder.

Rake nods his head, the look in his eyes saying more than any words could. "You're already my brother. I guess this just makes it official, huh?"

Arrow's lip twitches. "Guess so."

"Just hug already," Anna says, bouncing on her toes. "And hurry because I want to hug my big brother."

Arrow and Rake share the quickest hug I've ever seen, and then Anna is in his arms, and he's hugging her like she's his world.

"Will you walk me down the aisle?" I hear her ask.

"Fuck," Rake replies, eloquent as ever. "Of course I will, Anna. I'd be proud to."

I blink quickly, trying not to cry for a second time in the span of ten minutes.

Arrow leans down to me and kisses me on top of my head. My eyes widen at his rare show of affection. "You're a good woman, Bails."

"Th-thank you," I stutter, smiling shyly at him. "I like you too, Arrow."

He grins and ducks his head, going back to his woman and tugging her out of Rake's arms.

"Time to celebrate privately," he says to her, making her giggle. Rake's expression turns from pure joy to wishing someone would shoot him in the head.

"Okay, enough of that," he says dryly, taking my hand in his. "Bailey?"

"Yes, Rake," I say, giving him my full attention.

"I love you."

"I love you too," I tell him, resting my cheek against his chest. And I'd never get tired of hearing that from him.

"I want to talk to you about something," he says, sounding slightly nervous, which is very unlike Rake.

"What is it?"

"I want to officially adopt Angel," he says, running his hand through my hair. "Would you be okay with that?"

I lift my head. "Really?"

He wants to adopt Cara? Officially? Just when I thought I couldn't get any happier, he manages to surprise me. I'd love nothing more than for him to adopt Cara, and the fact that he wants it, that he thought of it, means the world to me and shows the level of dedication he has to our family.

"Yeah, really," he says, lifting my chin in his hands. "I'll talk with her about it, but I'd really love that."

"Okay." I breathe, my heart melting. I try not to cry, but instead I end up sniffling a little.

"Baby," he says, and I can hear the smile in his voice.

"Yeah?"

"Stop being cute," he says softly. "Open your eyes."

I open them.

"I love your beautiful, big, brown eyes."

"Okay," I mumble.

His lip twitches. "Happy tears. I hope they're all I see from now on."

"Rake?"

"Yeah?"

"Stop being cute," I tell him.

He laughs. I close my eyes again, and just feel him.

His warmth. His essence. It surrounds me.

Fuck.

Everything I've been through in life has led me to this moment.

And it's all been worth it.

"Who got rid of Wade's body?" Lana whispers, pushing her glasses up on her nose and glancing around. "I mean seriously, we never hear about who does all the real dirty criminal stuff like that." She pauses. "I don't think it's Tracker."

I shrug my shoulders. "Maybe they pay people to do it, or use their connections or something. Someone cleaned all the blood from the carpet too. It was like nothing ever happened. Maybe you should ask Faye, as she probably does know."

"Staying out of this," Faye says cheerfully, shoving popcorn into her mouth.

"Intriguing," Lana says, leaning back on the couch. "Irish killed someone and he's acting totally normal. Which isn't normal, don't you think?"

Faye makes a sound of amusement. "I once asked Irish how he got his scar. He said it was in a knife fight, so I joked that I'd hate to see the other guy. Do you know what he said?"

"What?" I dare to ask.

"He laughed and said, 'Me either. Skeletons freak me out.'"

"Jesus," I whisper, not knowing what else to say.

Lana giggles. "Oh, come on, it's pretty funny."

I scrub my hand down my face. "This club turns even the most innocent, sweet women into bloodthirsty monsters."

"Hey, I'm still sweet," Lana objects.

"You write porn," Faye throws in. "How sweet can you possibly be?"

"Romance," Lana corrects, lifting up her chin. "It's romance, not porn."

"Hey, whatever it is, I like it," Faye tells her, grinning. "I like to read out scenes to Tracker and ask him if he did that to you or if it was someone else from your past."

Lana's jaw drops open. "You don't!"

"I do."

I laugh, unable to hold it in. "Is that what the president's old lady does in her spare time? Harasses the men?"

"You know it," Faye beams, putting the bag of popcorn next to her. "I love them. I just like to annoy them now and again. Did you hear Pill's no longer a Wind Dragon? They took his cut and everything. He was doing all kinds of shit to get his hands on drugs and money, and didn't give a fuck about the club."

"Really? Do you think he'll want revenge over Wade?" I ask, brows drawing together. "I mean he doesn't know what happened, but surely he'll piece something together. And then there's Amethyst—we don't even know what happened to her."

"If he tries anything, he will die," Faye states simply.

"Jesus," I mutter again.

"You had something to do with Dom's death, didn't you?" I ask Rake that night, as we're both getting into bed. We moved houses, not wanting to be in the house that Wade died in. I was sad to move away from Tia, but we are only a few minutes farther from her and we promised we'd still see each other every day.

Rake stills, his body going tense. "Why do you ask?"

"I have a feeling," I say, pulling the blanket down for him to slide in bed.

He gets under the blanket and stares ahead before answering. "I don't want to lie to you, but I don't want to scare you off either."

"I won't run," I tell him. "I already know, Rake, whether you confirm it or not."

"And yet you're still here," he says, turning to his side, his gaze searching my eyes.

"Yes," I tell him. "I am. And as long as you keep loving Cara and me as you do, I'll always be here."

"If you really want me to tell you what happened, I will, but to be honest, I don't want to. I want you away from all the shit. I don't want you to think about it, or feel bad. And I know you, you will feel bad even though you had nothing to do with it; it's all on me. My choices, not yours."

"It's all over now though, right? I don't want anything else to happen." I pause. "To anyone."

"See, you're already worrying."

He rolls on top of me, and I love the feeling of his weight on me. "There's nothing I wouldn't do for either of you."

"I know," I whisper. "I can see that already, Rake."

"No one will love you like I do," he says, and I nod, because I know that too.

"My soul recognizes yours," I say softly, bringing his head down so my lips can reach his. "I see you, Rake. I was born to be yours, and you will always be mine."

"Vein-deep," he whispers.

"Vein-deep," I repeat.

"Fuck, Bailey," he says huskily, kissing me gently. "What did I do to deserve you?"

"I think the same thing every day."

"Need to be inside you right now," he says, kissing me harder, his hands starting to roam.

I smile against his mouth.

I feel so happy.

So full.

Like my heart is going to burst.

This feeling.

I'd do anything to keep it.

I get lost in him, and him in me.

The way we'll always be.

EPILOGUE

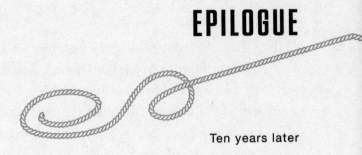

Ten years later

"M OM! Tell Dad to step away from the door, please!" Cara begs, her brown eyes pleading with mine. "Matt is going to take one look at him and run scared."

"Well, then he doesn't deserve to be with you anyway," Rhett comments, scowling at Cara. "He's eighteen, tell him to man up already. Or find a girl his age, not two years younger like you are."

"Rhett," Cara growls, tugging on her black dress. "Don't you start, please. This is my first official date, and you and Dad are making it a complete nightmare!"

"Calm down, Angel," Rake calls out from the front door. "I put my gun away and everything."

Cara puts her pink-tipped nails on my arm. "Mom, please. Imagine if this was your first date."

I cringe and sigh, looking down at my ring finger, where *Adam* is written in cursive print. Yeah, it was definitely my job to rein my husband in right now.

I get up and head to the front door, where, no joke, Rake is sitting at the bottom of the staircase, sharpening a knife.

A knife.

Jesus.

He's definitely taking this to a whole new level. Then again, this is the first time one of our girls is going on a date. I actually feel sorry for Cara, and her date for tonight.

"Rake, you're stressing the poor girl out," I tell him softly. "Can you at least put the knife away? Seriously, the boy is going to call the cops on us."

"No," he replies sternly. "Do you know what teenagers are up to these days? It's a whole new fuckin' generation of assholes. No little punk is going to try anything with my angel."

I place my hand on his shoulder. "We need to trust our daughter, instead of worrying about the boys. She can take care of herself; we've made sure of that."

Cara is a black belt and can probably kick any boy's ass. Clover and Rhett are black belts too. Rhett is now even fighting in mixed martial arts.

"Maybe Rhett and I should follow them," he muses, obviously not listening to me at all.

I squeeze his shoulder. "Rake, you're not doing that. She will be so upset with you."

"Not here to make best friends with my kids," he comments. "Here to look after them and make sure they don't get taken advantage of by horny little eighteen-year-olds." His green eyes finally look up into mine. "I'm not overreacting, Bails; this is our little girl we're talking about here."

I open my mouth, then close it. Obviously there's no arguing with the man, because he isn't going to see reason. All we can do is hope he doesn't scare off her date and ruin the experience for her.

"Remember when you took me on our first date?" I ask him quietly. "Imagine if someone ruined that for us."

"I wouldn't have run scared," he replies, scowling. "I would have done anything to get that time with you." He pauses, eyes narrowing. "And you let me kiss you and touch your tits that night. Fuck this shit—she's not going anywhere. Her ass can stay at home."

I puff out a breath and scowl. "This is her first date, Rake, and she's going. We said sixteen and we can't take it back now, can we?"

"She turned sixteen only last week, eager much?" he growls, going back to focusing on his knife.

Natalie, our second child, walks into the room. At just eight years old, with her dad's green eyes and my dark hair, she is as beautiful as she is mischievous. "Are you sharpening your knife at the front door, Dad?" She looks to me. "This family is nuts, Mom."

I have to agree.

I grab Rake by the arm and bring him into the living room, where Rhett and Cara are having a quiet argument. I don't get why the two of them don't date, but I know they'll figure it out for themselves eventually. Rhett's grown into a handsome man, and I know Cara isn't blind. Tia tells me girls are coming after him by the hundreds.

A knock at the door has Rake on his feet, but this time he comes back in with Arrow, out of all people.

"Uncle Arrow?" Cara groans, standing up. "I love you, I do. But right now is not the time for you to be here."

"Why not, Angel?" Arrow asks, lazily scratching his beard. "I thought I'd tell your date about the time I spent in jail." He pauses. "You know. For killing someone."

Cara covers her face with her hands. "I'm going to be a virgin for the rest of my life."

"I sure hope so," Rake calls out cheerfully, looking pleased. He looks to Arrow. "I'm sure Matt would love to hear that story, Arrow. Good man."

Rhett makes a comment I don't hear, but Cara sends him a cutting look.

Natalie walks up to Arrow and hugs him. "Uncle Arrow, why didn't you bring Nate and Tory with you?"

"They were doing their homework with their mom," Arrow tells Natalie. "I'll bring them tomorrow if you want to see them."

"Awesome," Natalie replies, then looks at her big sister, who is on the verge of having a breakdown. "Relax, Cara. If he isn't willing to jump through hurdles for you, then he isn't worth it."

"Agreed," Rhett mutters, still looking extremely unhappy.

"Wise girl, Natalie," Arrow praises, then grins at Cara. "You look pretty, Angel. But maybe you should put on a jacket or something."

"I said the same thing," Rhett grumbled, staring at Cara's cleavage.

Another knock at the door, softer.

This time, everyone gets up together and descends to the door.